MILLIE'S Angel

A PARANORMAL ROMANCE

I0592625

KIM PETERSEN

This is a Whispering Ink book
brought to you by Whispering Ink Press an imprint of
Whispering Ink Press.

KIM
Petersen

Cataloguing-in-Publication entry is available from the National Library of Australia:

http://catalogue.nla.gov.au/
Title: Millie's Angel
Author:Petersen, Kim (1973 -)
Paperback: 978-0-6481595-3-7
ePub: 978-0-6481595-4-4
Mobi/Kindle: 978-0-6481595-5-1

Edited by Paul Vander Loos
paulvanderloos.wixsite.com/editor

Cover & Formatting by Patti Roberts - Paradox Book Design

Visit http://www.kimpetersen.com.au/ and sign up
to receive a free ebook!

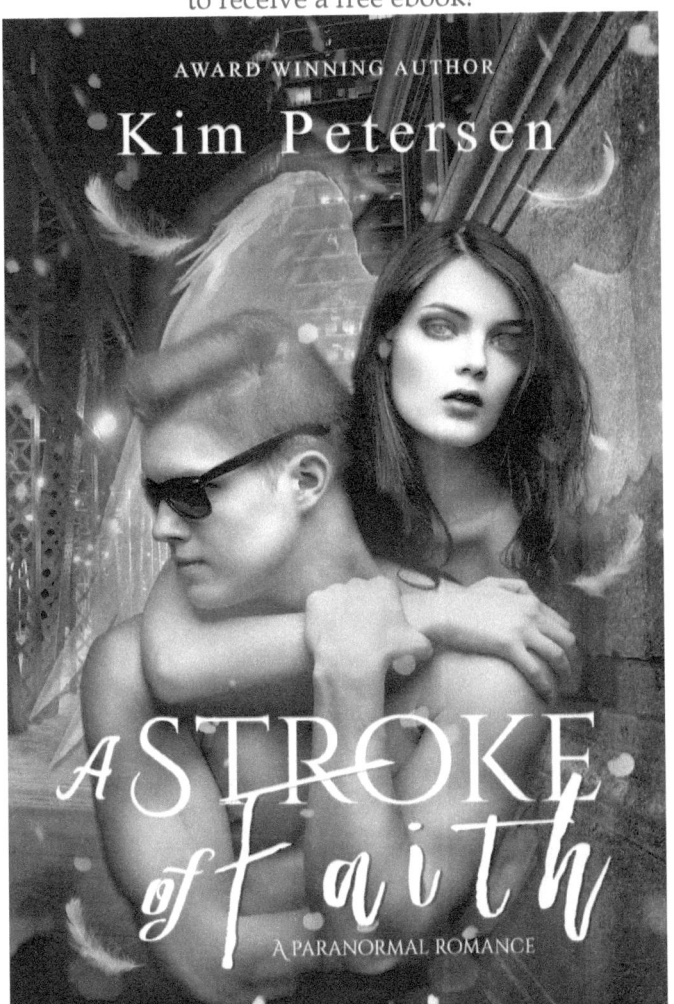

AWARD WINNING AUTHOR

Kim Petersen

A STROKE
of Faith

A PARANORMAL ROMANCE

*For the path that reveals the golden threads
of light ahead of me,
and the family that steps upon it beside me
– With all my heart, thank you.*

"Actually, you are destined to reach the point
where you realise
that through your own desire you can
consciously create your successive
destinies."
"Make believe – great wonders are
possible."

Neville Goddard

PROLOGUE

October 11, 1987

Dear Journal,
Today was a good day! My 14th birthday! I got some really cool stuff. The coolest bubble-gum jeans ever! Mum and Dad took me out for dinner; oh, and of course my little brother Ace had to come … I suppose he had nowhere else to be! Anyway, we went to the Black Stump, my second favourite restaurant (second only to the Spaghetti Factory). I really only like the Black Stump for the fire engine drinks (Don't tell anyone), but yum!

Mum gave me this journal tonight. She told me it was to keep track of my dreams; she said I should write about my aspirations. Especially when I have an inspired thought, she said. And I should always be true to myself and listen to the whisper within me. Whatever that means. She looked sad when she said it. I wonder why. Sometimes, I catch her crying in the kitchen over the dishes. She pretends she's not and most of the time I pretend I don't see her cry because I don't know what to say to her. I wonder if it's me or Ace, or even my father because I hear her bicker at him some nights when he comes home later than usual. Other than that, I don't really hear them talk about much at all really. I wonder if that is normal. Well, silences are normal in this house. Sometimes I want to scream as loud as my lungs will allow me just to break an awkward silence. Sometimes, I don't know how I will endure another and another … but I do. Ace and I have learned to live with it, I guess.

Dad just came in to say goodnight. I know Mum said I should use this journal to write my dreams, but I'm thinking I'll write whatever I am feeling or thinking about as well as those dreams. Lately I've noticed my dad looks at me different to the way he used to. His green eyes seem new to me, even though I've looked at those eyes a million times. I don't know, it's almost like a look of surprise – the kind of look you get when you see a ghost or something. Maybe it's just me; maybe I'm losing my mind already at fourteen … maybe not.

As for those dreams; I have an overwhelming feeling that something is missing. It's like an empty pit in my tummy and I have no idea why. I guess I need to figure it out before I can hear the whisper within me.

Millie xo

CHAPTER ONE

T he afternoon sun offered no escape from the heat as Amelia Anderson made her way home from the bus stop. She pushed back a dark lock of hair that clung to her forehead and paused in the scant shade offered by an old paling fence that ran bent and crooked along the front yard of a dilapidated old house.

She thought she might collect Ace and head down to the bay where she planned on spending the rest of her afternoon daydreaming about the cutest boy in school, Damon Richards. *Oh my, if only he might notice me,* she thought. All the girls in her year at school had a crush on Damon.

His hair was a rich dark brown, and from her viewpoint behind him in science class, she sometimes thought it might even be black. Shiny dark strands tumbled over eyes that were like a crystal blue lagoon, and accentuated his square masculine jaw. Millie had lost herself in those dreamy depths too many times to count. And with his tall athletic build, she had also lost herself within his imaginary embrace. Only he was unaware of her daydreams about him.

Those eyes and his confident swagger betrayed his almost arrogant nature. However, she didn't care.

To Millie he was perfection, and despite the attention of all the other girls, she would make him notice her one way or another – eventually.

She skipped up her pace, engrossed with thoughts of Damon and eager to get to the bay where she could be alone with the deliciousness of her contemplations while her brother played by the water's edge. Millie threw the white front door open with a little more force than she had intended. She ignored the little flakes of old paint that drifted to the floor as she burst into the house.

"Ace," she called through the stale heat of the hallway, "Let's go to the bay!"

Her voice echoed back but there was no reply. Usually she could find her brother in the lounge room eating his after-school fill and watching TV when she arrived home in the afternoons.

"Ace!"

There was still no answer. *Strange*, she thought, as she dumped her bag in the hall outside her bedroom door and made her way across creaking floorboards. There was no-one in the kitchen. She paused at the fridge to grab a can of Coke. "Score!" she muttered to herself. It was rare to find a can of Coke ready to be plucked from the fridge. The fridge's noisy old motor kicked in as she shut the door, temporarily disguising the silence in the house.

She drew closer to the back door and peered out into an unruly backyard. She stepped out and made her way down the three cobblestone steps that led off the porch into an unkempt garden filled with overgrown flower beds dotted with ferns of various sizes. Their leaves were hidden among weeds and vines that hid the gardens that had once flourished. Grass the depth of her calves teased her legs as she caught a glimpse of her brother's sandy blond hair in the far corner of the yard.

"Ace!" she called to him.

Picking up her pace, she ran over to where he sat in silence staring into the flattened bed of lawn he had made for himself.

"Hey, what's wrong?" she asked breathlessly.

Red-rimmed eyes gazed up at his sister. He shielded his eyes from the bright sunlight and the bottom of his lips trembled. "It's Mum" he said softly. "Have you seen her? She's in her room."

"No, why? Is she home already?" She slid down to her knees. "What's wrong with Mum?"

Ace flung himself at his sister in a clumsy attempt to hug her. "She's hurt." His voice was full of panic, then he cried out louder. "She's hurt!"

Millie sprang to her feet and ran towards the house with Ace hot on her heels. She slammed through the fossil that passed for a screen door and opened the door to her mother's bedroom with a jolt, unprepared for the horror that would confront her.

"Mum?" Millie whispered.

Her mother lay still on top of a spread of lilac sheets on her bed, looking as stiff and unmoving as a body without a breath of life within it. She was still in the nightdress she had been wearing the evening before, only now the gown had been torn in places.

Millie could see dried blood stains around the shredded neckline of her gown. Smears and droplets littered what had been an elegant white lace nightdress. Leaving her mother now adorned in a night dress that resembled something out of a bad horror movie.

She was hardly recognisable. Her long golden mane of hair was a tangled stringy mess, and the strands that curled around her bruised and swollen face were now burned a deep crimson-pink, as if someone had dipped the ends of her hair into a pot of paint. Some of those strands had dried up against the side of her cheeks, giving her a ghoulish appearance against the pale of her skin now tarred with the crust of rusty-coloured blood.

Her normally blue eyes were bruised thunder-grey and puffed up to the size of large strawberries. Each corner seeped with a continuous flow of pink fluid. The skin around her left eye had been torn into a savage gash. The ridge of her delicate nose was now bent and so swollen that it dwarfed all her other features.

Millie called out as she rushed to her mother's side and perched herself carefully on the bed beside where her mother lay motionless. "Oh my god!" she anguished.

"Ace, call for an ambulance – *now*!" Millie screamed over a shoulder to her brother who was still lumbering by the bedroom door.

Her mother reached out to touch her with her lips parting as she attempted to say something to her daughter. A grimace of pain crossed over her face and a weak groan escaped her bruised lips.

Millie gently moved in closer. "Oh Mum," she cried, tears now cascading freely down her face, "Who did this to you?"

"No ambulance, Millie," she whispered. "Please." Her mother lifted a bruised arm and tried to reach out for her daughter, but it fell short. Her head lolled sideways before falling into the soft folds of the pillow, unconscious.

Millie sat beside her unconscious mother while they waited for help to arrive. She rested her hand protectively over her mother's, unable to move while her mind whirled in a painful twist. *Is she going to die? Who could have attacked our beautiful mother so brutally?* Millie thought.

Ace cowered like a broken shadow in the corner of the bedroom, the stumps of his fingers stringing together in a muddle. "M … Millie?" Straining to control the teary anguish that threatened to bubble over. "Is Mum going to be okay?"

The sound of his voice startled her as she looked over to his confused figure hovering in the corner. Her eyes bore the red-blotched evidence of her own tears. She knew that her eight-year-old brother was as lost, confused and shocked as she was. And she knew that she needed to be strong for him.

"She's going to be just fine, Ace." Her voice

tremored. Then firmer, "Just fine."

She beckoned him over to her and circled the crook of an arm around him when he sat on the floor beside the bed. The two of them were silent beside their mother until the ambulance arrived to rush her to the hospital.

Millie's head felt as if it might explode after the ambulance left. They had little answers to all the questions they were asked – *"Who did this to her? What happened? Where is your father?"*

Millie could only assure the paramedics that they would soon follow suit to the hospital upon their father's arrival home. Holding her face in her hands, she crouched in the hallway against the peel of the old wall paint. Her mind swirled with questions and hurt for her mother.

She needed to call her father but she was hesitant to call him at his work. She knew he would not run to Lilly's bedside in hospital. His recent coldness towards her mother was testament to this. Her stomach was so knotted up with grief that she felt nauseous. She leaped up clasping her mouth, and ran down to the bathroom. Her body convulsed violently while she heaved up the contents of her stomach into the toilet.

Afterward she lay, her body curled up against the cool bathroom tiles. She tried to take deep breaths and steady her mind. "Help me, help me, please!" she murmured to herself. As she lay trembling on the gritty tiled floor, the chirping of birds slowly infiltrated her awareness, their sweet strains penetrating the walls of the bathroom from the trees outside. Quieting her mind, she listened to their soothing tones.

Their song became boisterous, and she felt as if they were directing their music to her, even though there was no way they could know she lay on the bathroom floor beyond the walls that separated them. She began to feel them, and the rhythm of their sweet melody vibrated through her being. She felt an odd tingling sensation crawl up her spine, settling around the back of her slender neck, and she began to perceive a powerful awareness that she was not alone.

Millie opened her eyes, welcoming the peculiar sensation. The late afternoon sun played through the small panels of the stained-glass window, shooting a vivid rainbow of green, blue and red hues against the tiled walls. And as she gazed around the room, her body came alive with a great sense of wellbeing and love. She felt calm.

The knot in her stomach loosened and the whirlwind in her mind settled, replaced by a peculiar euphoria that she had never experienced before. As the shaded hues of the glass traced their way around the walls, Millie gasped as a pattern of wings began to form in front of her. The coloured wings grew larger until she could only gaze in awe at the divine creation taking place before her. She sat in wonderment in what seemed forever as she beheld what appeared to be the feathers of the heavenly angels that had come to her.

Eventually the beauty of the wings faded away

with the dissolve of the sun on the horizon, leaving a cast of dreary shadows in their wake. Then, with a deep calm resonating through her, she prepared to make the phone call to her father.

CHAPTER TWO

November 3, 1987

Dear Journal,
Today was the worst day of my life but strangely it was kind of one of the best at the same time. It wasn't the best because someone beat up my poor mother. Ace and I found her almost destroyed and I didn't know what to do; I felt helpless and lost. The part that made it the best I can't yet really begin to put into words. I felt all control out of my reach when I discovered my mother today, and yet I realise now that I never really lost it to begin with. How can we really lose control of ourselves when all we have in this world is our very own human being, the only sure thing which we can control?

Maybe, I just heard that whisper within me because I heard and saw something so real to me, I shall never forget it. I'm not sure if it was a part of me or something completely separate, but I know in the deepest part of me, the part that always seems to feel empty and lost, is now feeling a little bit less than empty.

Mum will be ok, Dad told us. He didn't seem to be too upset by it all. He seemed more concerned with me and Ace than our mother. Just as I feared. It makes me feel sad. Why does it have to be like this? Why do people behave in ways that offer less than love? I ask this not only because I don't understand but because I just experienced such a pure sensation of love that I don't know how there can be any other way. And the thing is, I kinda already knew it was always there. I know I sound crazy. I will probably read this back some day and think I had gone completely insane. Maybe not. But for the rest of my life I am going to try my very hardest to live through the pure love I experienced today!

When I was little I would often awake with bad dreams through the night. My Dad would come to my bedside and wrap me up in his big arms and tell me, "Everything is ok my little Millie-pie". His smell was of Palmolive soap and a slight scent of mint shaving cream; I loved his daddy smell. He made me feel so safe and secure I would drift back into an easy sleep while he stroked my hair.

I'm going to bed now. Feeling lost and found all at the same time, and somehow tonight I am missing the warmth and the comforting smell of my Daddy all those years ago, for those words I cannot yet find. I know I shall find them some day!

Sending love to my Mum in her hospital bed tonight.

Millie xo

Glen Anderson mopped the sweat off his brow with

the back of a large dirty hand. He was finishing up a routine service on an old bottle-top machine at the milk factory where he worked. *Damn machine!* he thought. *They should get rid of them and spring for new ones; bunch of old scrooges up there.* He had worked there for twelve years yet there was little pay left after all the bills were paid.

He had a solid build. His thick voluminous hair fell short of his shoulders and curled against the blue collar of his work shirt. Healthy locks framed a big head. His eyes were green with a smattering of golden flecks around the irises, lending to a distinct green lantern impression. A broad nose complemented thick voluptuous lips above a square chin marked with a deep cleft.

His floor manager, Barry, called out to him, interrupting the grumbling momentum of his thoughts. "Glen, there are people here to see you."

Glen glanced up towards the office – the brain centre of Pure Dairy that towered over the factory floor like a wooden fort. It was quiet this evening due to routine maintenance but by day it was always buzzing producing full cream milk the old-fashioned way. The milk was delivered with a generous layer of cream in glass bottles for the public. Glen saw two uniformed policemen at the top of the stairs peering down at him with serious eyes. He sighed quietly to himself. He was not surprised at their presence, and had not looked forward to their visit. He picked up a shaggy worn rag that lay nearby, and deliberately took his time as he attempted to wipe off the layered grease that swathed his hands like sprayed on tar, then made his way towards the two men that awaited him.

"Glen Anderson?" The smaller of the two men asked.

Large booted feet climbed their way up the stairs slowly towards them, each heavy step echoing with a hint of trepidation. Glen noticed the tall officer was younger than the shorter man, and the one inverted thin blue line on his uniform signified that he was a constable. The officer was looking down at him with a smug expression. His hands rested on his hips, with his right hand lingering over the leather case strapped around his gun. *Ahh,* Glen thought, *this one thinks he's invincible.* The shorter man was somewhat older than his counterpart, the softer fading of his light brown eyes betraying his look of resignation. He stood a little hunched over and had an air of defeat about him borne of investigating too many depressing cases over the years. He was of higher rank than the constable, as shown in the two blue lines on his uniform.

Glen offered a hand to the young policeman. The young man reached out to shake Glen's hand, but fell short when he glimpsed the grimy offering. Amused, Glen flashed his biggest pearly-white smile.

"How can I help you guys?" he said.

The officers introduced themselves then got straight to business. "Your wife is in hospital, Mr Anderson," the older officer said. "She has been violently assaulted. She's in a critical condition."

Glen knew he was being scrutinised, and his response was vital. He clutched at his sandy blond hair. "What? Oh my God! Is she okay?" he shouted, twisting his hair in clumps. "Who could have done this? I must go to my wife!" His eyes began to moisten.

"Well, that is why we are here, Mr Anderson, to investigate your wife's assault. Would you like us to take you to the hospital?"

"No, I need to clean up first and check on my kids." He started to turn away from the men. "I got to go, thank you; will you excuse me?" His voice was a mere shake of a quiver now.

"Of course, but we will have to ask you some questions after you've seen your wife, Mr Anderson, do you understand?"

Glen followed the senior policeman's stare as it settled on the grazed swell of his greasy knuckles, and watched him write something in the little notepad he carried.

"Yes, of course." Glen wiped away a tear, leaving a black smear across his cheek before stuffing his hands deep into his pockets. He started down towards the factory floor.

The policemen left, leaving Glen alone again on the deserted factory floor. He packed away his tools in his toolbox and headed out to the only hospital in Rockton. Nestled on the shores of Botany Bay, Rockton was the only town Glen knew all his life. Despite its bayside location and neighbouring middle to upper class suburbs, Rockton remained a working class southern suburb in the outskirts of Sydney. It was a melting pot of differing cultures with a strong community spirit. Its main road was littered with rundown store fronts and unkempt streets. Rockton memorial hospital was one of the few buildings in town to recently receive a cosmetic overhaul along with some new state-of-the-art surgical equipment.

The hospital was alive with the bustle of doctors, nurses, patients and visitors when Glen arrived about twenty minutes later. He found his wife's room with the help of a busty middle-aged woman who sat behind a huge bench desk below a sign that read "Administration". She welcomed Glen with her sweetest smile but there was a hint of disappointment when she became aware he was searching for his wife. And with one last hopeful push of the only assets she still possessed, a pudgy short finger pointed him in the direction he desired.

Pleased to leave the scampering noise of the lower floor behind him, Glen took the stairs to the upper level of the hospital and scoured the quiet corridor until he found the number he wanted. He grasped the knob tightly, and twisted it slowly to open the door so as not to cause much disturbance. Lilly lay still under the crisp white sheets of the bed. Glen saw the shallow heave of her breath beneath the stiff linen. The dim room would have been silent if not for the constant beeping of the heart monitoring machine that now appeared to be an extension of his wife. Her delicately boned face was mostly hidden beneath bandages. He could see her bruised right eye, but an eye patch covered her left eye. Glen moved closer and peered at her broken body, wondering how close he might have been to finishing the job. *Was it a job?* No, he really hadn't wanted to hurt his wife. Still, the thought circled his mind while he stood and watched her like a tiger contemplating its wounded prey. She began to stir under his lantern stare, as if she sensed his mammoth threatening presence so near to her. His tongue licked grinning lips as the breath beneath his own ribcage raced faster.

"Hello my sweet," he said, his voice dense with irony.

Her body stiffened. Lilly exposed the slit of her right eye to reveal the towering image bent over her bed. He was so close that she could feel his stifling warm breath near her. She impulsively drew in a sharp breath, then moaned as a flash of pain seared through her bruised lungs within a broken ribcage. She felt as helpless and depleted as she appeared, but the will within her would not allow him to see that weakness. Her good sky blue eye stabbed back at him with all the frostiness she could muster.

Some minutes passed as their eyes met in a silent war of wills before finally the flame of Glen's stare simmered as the set of his lips softened in a smile.

"Who did this to you, Lilly?" he asked in a quiet voice.

"You know who did this to me, Glen." She looked away as tears welled up from the frustration of being too exhausted to maintain her rage.

He sighed. "It really wasn't me, Lilly; *you* do know that, right?" His gaze fell as he began to stroke her arm. "I mean, I have never hurt you. I would never, I ... I just couldn't."

Lilly's bloodshot eye rose to meet with his again.

"You should never have spoken of her to me, don't you see, my darling Lilly? She belongs in the past, not in the now, we cannot speak of her. I cannot hear her name or speak of her." The flash of his stare drove his conviction, as tears cursed freely across the bridge of his cheeks. He leaned closer and whispered, "I cannot be held responsible for what happens when I hear that woman's name. You should've known that, Lilly."

She turned away from him, trying hard to control her trembling rage. "You are a monster, Glen," she said, shuddering. "Get away from me!"

"Darling. Please, you have to realise it was that other part of me." He reached for her once more. "The darkest part," he whispered.

"You know, all I ever wanted was for you to love me the way you loved her." Her voice trembled as she met his pleading gaze. "But none of that matters anymore. You are a just monster to me now, and I don't want your love."

"You don't mean that, Lilly. I know you wouldn't do anything stupid; it's just the painkillers talking. What have they given you?"

"Go away Glen," she murmured, fatigue creeping in on her. "Just leave me alone now."

Glen gave a long deep sigh as he turned to leave the room in silence. He paused in the corridor outside Lilly's hospital room, and hunched over, shaking. He clutched against the wooden railing that ran along the walls of the hospital corridors, and wept. The big man was like a broken child lost to the grace of nurture, feeling the tremendous guilt and disgust for himself creeping through his body and settling in the centre of his gut. *I am a monster! I have hurt someone I love again! I am a monster!* Horrible thoughts gripped him like an unrelenting vice and he felt frozen to the wall.

"I am so, so sorry, dear Lilly." Glen felt as though a large palm came up to grip his heart, feeling the kind of despair he had experienced only once before fourteen years earlier. *And here I am writing it all over again*, he thought. He knew the chilling grip of the *black snake*, and he feared the strike of its hateful venom.

He glimpsed two nurses turning into the corridor and struggled to pull the weight of his body up from the floor beneath him. The banter of their laughter echoed down to him as he quickly recovered his dignity. He wiped away fresh tears, and hung his head so they would not see his face. He stumbled towards the exit stairs and went home to his children and a six pack of beer.

CHAPTER THREE

November 15, 1987

Dear Journal,
I have fallen in love! And no, it's not Damon Richards – yet. I have fallen in love with the most gorgeous of men, Michael Hutchence. He is wonderful (sigh); when he sings, his voice is like a warm chocolate ribbon of silk that wraps itself all around and through me … Mmmmm, I can almost taste it sliding down my throat and making its way through my entire body like a delicious hot chocolate! And I listen to INXS often these days … it soaks up the silence of this old crappy house.

Mum is coming home from the hospital today; I am glad she will be home again … maybe things will feel a little better around here. Ace and I are making her a special dinner tonight. We are cooking her favourite – lasagne with a green salad and a passionfruit tart for dessert. I hope we can pull that tart off okay, because she makes it sooooo good.

Dad hasn't said too much lately, but hey, what's new, right? He just looks at me weird and I just can't wait to get away from him honestly … it creeps me out. He used to talk to me, and look at me with those kind eyes. Now, pretty much nothing, just a strange uncomfortableness growing between us and I have no idea why. He's still the same with Ace. They watch TV and eat popcorn together and when I try and join in, Dad throws me a sideways glance, clearly annoyed by my presence. So, I stopped trying to join in on their "boy time".

Can't wait to have Mum home again. I have missed her hugs and our little private giggles about boys and school at bedtime. Mum tells me I shouldn't go out of my way to get any boy to notice me. She says I am special and if Damon Richards doesn't notice that all on his own, then he shan't have the pleasure of my company. It always makes me laugh, but then she tells me to believe in myself ... and I'm not always so sure how to do that. I guess that's what most mothers say to their daughters.

When I was a little girl, sometimes when I would look in the mirror, a part of me would wonder what I was doing in the body that reflected back at me. Because the girl with the emerald eyes that I saw felt foreign to me. It almost felt as if I were an imposter! Strange ... I hadn't thought of that in years ... until recently. Something has started to stir within me and I'm very confused right now, but somehow, I know it has to do with that whisper my Mum told me about.

Well, got to go and make passionfruit tart now.
Millie xo

The heat of the oven pushed the already soaring

temperature of the kitchen up through the roof. Millie could feel her brow beading with tiny droplets of sweat while she finished up cleaning the dishes that they had used to make the passionfruit tart. Between the clank of wet dishes, she heard the grumbling noise of a truck out front and a flurry of voices calling out to one another.

"What's going on out there?" she asked her brother.

Ace was standing by the kitchen bench with his head nearly buried in the bowl they had used for the passionfruit mixture.

"Huh? I dunno," he said, barely pausing for breath before continuing his own kind of dish clean-up, which evidently involved the tip of an eager tongue.

Curious, Millie dropped the dish brush in the suds-filled sink of warm water and grabbed an old clean tea towel to dry the wrinkles of her wet hands. Pausing before the big stand-up fan her father had recently bought, she lifted her arms up and briefly enjoyed the breeze. She bent over slightly to position her face directly in front of the bristling blades. "Ahhhh … niceee; thisss isss niceee, Aceee!" Her voice came out distorted and robotic with the swift spin of the air circulating close to the fan.

Ace looked across and laughed at her before joining her in front of the fan. "Sillllyyyy Millllieee," his vibrating voice said as they both broke out into a fit of giggles.

Still clutching the tea towel, Millie made her way

down the creaking hallway towards the front of the house. On the way, she played her usual old game of trying to step in the right places without setting off the old groan of the tired floorboards. The quieter steps were becoming more challenging to find. When she stepped out into the morning flood of sunlight that hit their front porch, she saw a big removal truck in front of the house next door with four men busy scurrying to-and-fro unloading furniture. Three of the men were juggling a huge dark brown three-seater lounge setting, while the fourth directed the whole awkward journey through the gate and into the house. Leaning against the warm bricks of the house, Millie watched in interest, curious to catch a glimpse of her new neighbours. The emeralds of her almond eyes glinted with a spark of interest when she first caught sight of her.

Jumping two steps at a time down to the paved path of the front of her new home was a girl that looked to Millie to be around the same age as herself. She had a mane of long blonde hair flowing in a golden sheen behind her and wore a pale yellow dress which cinched in around the small of her waist with a wide black cummerbund, skirting out in flurry of layered frills to her knees. Both her wrists were bejewelled with chunks of thin gold and black bangles, and her feet were bare. Millie watched her curiously as the girl frolicked her way out to the truck on the street and peered through the back doors, checking on the progress of their move. The girl turned about on thin willowy legs, taking in her new neighbourhood until her eyes found and rested on the watching figure of Millie still leaning against the wall of her porch. Millie smiled before looking away, feeling slightly embarrassed that she had been caught out staring. Turning to go back inside and continue her special menu for her mother's return that afternoon, Millie stopped short when she heard the girl call out, nearer to her now.

"Hi there," she said, smiling with a wave of her bejewelled arm. "I'm Emily."

Millie pivoted on the balls of her own bare feet to face her new neighbour. Now that she was closer, Millie could see that Emily might be a little older than she had first figured. Millie thought she was very pretty, as she eyed her over inquisitively. Glimmering hair framed bright blue eyes that perched above the smallest of noses Millie had ever seen. Beneath that button nose, a rosebud mouth parted, petite with a smile upon the heart-shape of a china-doll face.

"Hi, I'm Millie. I live here." She gestured towards the old house behind her.

Emily laughed. "Well, I live next door to you now!" Blue china-dolls sparkled.

"Em!" An overweight woman called out from the neighbouring porch. "Em! I need your help please!"

"Yeah Ma," Emily called back, grinning at Millie with a glint of mischief in her rolling eyes. "I get the feeling, Miss Millie that this …" She gestured a small hand between herself and Millie, "Is going to be fun!" She gave Millie a playful wink, turned on her heels and ran back over to her mother, disappearing into her new home.

Millie lingered for a few moments longer while pondering her brief interaction with Emily; and feeling a small rush of excitement surging through her, she grinned, somewhat baffled at her own reaction. Somehow, she knew Emily was about to play a starring role in her life.

A few hours later Millie was doing a final check over the house while her father and Ace went to fetch her mother from Rockton Memorial. She wanted to make sure the house was as pristine as could be for her mother's arrival. She even picked a handful of the wild yellow and orange flowers from their "jungle garden" as she liked to refer to it. She had lovingly pruned and clipped the stems as well as she could and placed them in her mother's favourite vase in the middle of their dining table, complete with the best table cloth she could find. She stood back to survey her work with a critical eye. *Hmmm... It looks nice*, she thought, quite pleased with her effort. Work done, she decided to spend the rest of her time waiting for her family to return, and dancing around the house to the tune of INXS. *Original Sin* filled the oppressive warm air of the house while she was lost in the voice of lead singer Michael Hutchence. She drifted and twirled around the lounge room, so caught up with her own melody-filled world that she almost missed the boisterous pounding at the front door. She lowered the volume and cocked her head to one side until there was an even louder boom at the door.

"Alright, alright, I'm coming!" She stomped

towards the door and yanked it open with annoyance.

Irritation gave way to surprise when she saw Emily standing there sporting an amused grin.

"Hey, heard the music," Emily beamed. "I'm a fan too."

"Yeah, they're great," Millie mumbled self-consciously and opened the screen door for Emily to enter.

"Wanted to see if you'd like to hang out a bit." Emily strutted in and sniffed at the aroma wafting from the kitchen. "Mmmm, smells good in here." She casually threw over the lemon sleeve of her shoulder.

"Oh, thanks; I'd love to, but my mum is due home from the hospital any minute," Millie said as she followed Emily down the hallway.

Emily paused on bare feet to taunt Millie with her blue-eyed stare. "Sure you can't spare *just* five minutes?" She reached into a pocket hidden among the frilled layers of her skirt, and pulled out a gold packet of cigarettes and a box of matches.

Noticing the alarmed look that crossed Millie's face, the sheen of her golden hair fell lower down her back as she laughed. "You're not a nerd are you, Miss Millie?"

"Of course not!" Millie scowled, impulsively grappling for a handful of the long dark hair cascading around her shoulders and beginning to twist the strands between nervous fingers.

Smoking was not something she had ever thought of trying and she knew her father would kill her if he ever found out she would do such a thing.

However, she really liked Emily and didn't want her to think she was lame. "So, let's go out back then." She flashed a smile she hoped would conceal the unease rippling through her.

"Cool."

They sat together on the cobblestone stairs overlooking Millie's backyard, watching the late afternoon sun stream through the lush green of the avocado tree that stood gallantly to the right side of the yard. Sunlight bounced bright among the ferns and the wild bushes in the garden, shooting striking reflections in all directions. The fading warmth of the rays seemed to bring a fresh shimmer of life that Millie found quite magnificent.

"So, I guess your folks don't like to garden huh?" Emily said, taking a cigarette out and lighting it.

They both giggled and Millie watched Emily closely as she dragged on the cigarette before passing it over to her. She took the cigarette awkwardly between shaky fingers and slowly brought it towards her lips.

"Nah, not lately. They used to keep the garden real nice," she said, deliberately trying to bide her time on that first drag of smoke. "A lot of things have gone downhill around here lately," she mumbled, almost to herself.

Here goes nothing! Millie thought, as she began to draw on the lit cigarette. First instinct was to cough in disgust, but recovering quickly she relaxed and allowed the thick smoke to flow easily into her waiting lungs, before slowly exhaling as if she had performed the action a hundred times before.

Emily eyed her with approval. "Well, I think, Miss Millie, that we should change that."

The girls sat on the rough surface of Millie's back steps sharing the cigarette between them a few minutes longer. Emily told her that her family had moved to Rockton from interstate so her mother could be closer to her grandmother because she was unwell. Millie also learned that Emily was fifteen and that her sixteenth birthday was not too far off – a fact she was looking forward to. She also discovered that her new friend had two older brothers who belonged to her stepfather from a previous marriage, and that her real father had died when she was seven years old. "He was awesome and fun," she'd told Millie wistfully, "but his taste for women and whiskey was beyond his control."

After her father's death, her mother had turned back to being a devout born-again Christian. "Our life revolves around the church – literally," Emily said. There was a clear distaste in Emily's words when she had remarked on her mother. "I mean, she's a complete fanatic, Millie. I have to go into deep battle to be able to express myself the way I want! Free will, right? Pfft! I cannot wait to grow old enough to move away from them."

Millie had shared a few things of her own with Emily. She revealed the depth of her terror when she and Ace had found their mother two weeks ago all beat up and bleeding in the bedroom. She confided how disturbing it was that nobody was saying who was responsible for her mother's brutal attack. The intensity of the mood lifted when she mentioned coyly how she had a major crush on Damon Richards – the most gorgeous boy in school – but feared he would never know the depth of her feelings. Millie found Emily so easy to talk to; she had never been so open with a friend before and she barely knew Emily, which both surprised and fascinated her. The little time they shared that Sunday afternoon, sharing a smoke and profound conversation, left both girls feeling the beginnings of the strong bond that had already invisibly paved its way between them.

After Emily had left, Millie lingered upon the cobblestones for a while longer, soaking in the quiet beauty that nature displayed before her with a swell of appreciation dancing in her heart. She watched two butterflies with big black and blue wings flutter by before pausing in front of her and showing off their radiance as if trying to communicate the secret of their fluttery language. She voiced a "hello" to them as they hovered before her for a moment before fluttering about her head in quiet enchantment for a few minutes.

They finally took a moment to rest on a leaf in the garden near where she sat. The charm she found among her surroundings heightened the wellbeing she experienced. She felt in tune with the butterflies and the trees in the garden, and when she heard the trees rustle in the breeze and the gentle chirping of birds, a great feeling of happiness washed over her.

Millie found the special moment interrupted when she heard the front door open and the heavy fall of footsteps across the floor inside the house.

"Goodbye beautiful butterflies," she whispered, as her gaze scanned the unruly garden. "Goodbye garden." She sprang to her feet and ran through the back-porch screen door, eager to greet her mother.

CHAPTER FOUR

November 22, 1987

Dear Journal,

Mum has been home from hospital for a week now; it's good to have her back but she seems different. She is very quiet. The silences have grown longer within the crummy walls of this house... even when Dad's not around. We haven't yet had any of our usual night-time talks together either. It's like she's here – but not. She is somewhere else. Perhaps she is still stuck in that horrible hospital bed, but I hope this will pass soon, because I miss her still.

On a higher note, I am loving having a new friend who lives so close to me. Emily and I are spending most afternoons together now, talking and going for walks to the bay and... smoking! I have discovered I actually like to smoke now; I must be growing up. Nobody around here has noticed anything different about me though. But I feel different. I am different. I feel like a happier person when I'm with Em. She is great company. What would I have done if she hadn't shown up? Maybe her new presence in my life has something to do with the angel wings I saw in the bathroom that day, because I have always wished for a close friend like Emily. And now I have just that!

I used to watch my parents closely as a child and wonder who they actually were, not the flesh and blood readily exposed to me, but as the beings beyond the physical that were visible to me. Who they were on the inside. I would often wonder who was behind the person I saw... I mean, it's a valid question, right? Who are we really? I have a great knowing that I, Amelia Anderson, am not my name nor my body nor my failures or accomplishments for that matter. I am more than that. And so are my parents.

Where is this coming from?

Going to sleep now.

Millie xx

Lilly grimaced as she attempted to tie her hair back from her face. *Ouch! Damn ribs,* she thought, squeezing her eyes. *Damn Glen.* It had been three weeks since he had attacked her that Tuesday morning, not long after the kids had left for school. It all still lingered fresh in her mind, and in her body. She was shocked that her husband could turn on her in a rampage so savage; it was inhuman. She could do nothing to defend herself against his brute strength. He had thrown her about the house much like a child throwing a ragdoll in a fit of attention. Then, when his rage was finally quelled, she had watched his shadow through the slits of her swollen eyes as he walked away and left for work like any other day. He had left her broken body limp with relief and her heart torn with a feeling of powerlessness unlike anything she had experienced before.

Since the assault, she could not help but relive the incident over and over in her mind, like the spinning reel of a badly shot horror film. They had been arguing. Their relationship had grown cold and distant and Lilly wanted something from him, anything from him other than a nod and a grunt here and there. She missed the closeness they had once shared despite Glen's growing hostility, so she asked him whether there was somebody else and what had she done to make him so cold towards her. He met her questions with a steely glare and accusations suggesting she could not be doing her job as a wife to throw such "preposterous" questions at him. Then she said *her* name and said, "Well, I guess in your eyes I will never be good enough for you." She had started to turn away to get ready to go to her pharmacy job, but threw in one last jibe – "… because I am not Samantha". It was at that moment that he leaped to his feet and caught her unexpectedly in the attack.

She peered back at her reflection in the mirror, carefully inspecting her effort at concealing the now light discolouration of her bruised skin. Satisfied, she applied a touch of natural pink coloured lipstick to the slight swell of her lips. *This will do, nobody will know the difference,* she thought flatly, then prepared to leave the house for her first day back at work since the assault. Lilly had worked at the local pharmacy since Ace had started school about four years ago. She liked working there with the other women, and her boss Harry

Cornell was easy to work for. He understood that his employees had families and other commitments and he tried to accommodate these circumstances when the need arose for the people that worked for him. He knew Lilly had been in hospital but Harry and her colleagues were under the impression she had been involved in an accident. Lilly was unsure what to tell them when the questions would inevitably come, but she decided she would tell them nothing of the truth nonetheless. *I told the police nothing; I can do that again,* she mused as she strolled along her street towards the town's main road. She had particularly liked the older of the two policemen who questioned her at the hospital. He had been very compassionate and his tired eyes showed her a kindness that was a rarity in her life. The policemen knew who had assaulted her and she knew they could not press charges without her. The senior officer had given Lilly his card and told her to call on him anytime she needed him. She had thought of his empathy as she tucked the card safely away in her purse.

Lilly had no interest in pressing charges against her husband, as she knew if that were to happen, her time left would be short. Besides, she knew too much about his sordid past, about Samantha, for Glen to allow her to lock him away. She was also aware he would not allow her to divorce him. No, this situation had to be handled in the correct manner or next time she could end up just as *she* did. All those hours laying in that hospital bed gave her enough time to consider her next move and she intended to follow it through;

her only regret would be for her children. She hesitated before reaching the pharmacy doors. She smoothed down the crisp white pharmacy uniform dress over her slim curves, removed her sunglasses and practised a meekly placed smile, then walked inside to start her work day with the breath of apprehension deep within her aching lungs.

Her day would have been like any other work day had it not been for a beautiful arrangement of pale pink and white lilies delivered to her while she was serving a customer. She immediately knew they were from her husband. In their earlier years together, they were the only flowers he would ever buy her – "A beautiful lily for an even more beautiful Lilly," he would say to her with that doe-eyed look that would send her heart fluttering with joy. Oh, how she had loved him! An all-consuming, intoxicating love. She would have done anything to please him, and she did, to an unthinkable extent no less. She believed every word that came out of his mouth, even when the whisper she heard within her told her otherwise. But now she was over believing his lies; she would no longer be his personal puppet waiting for the tips of his fleshy fingers to vivify her.

The ladies around her gushed at the sight of the bouquet. "My husband!" Lilly said, displaying her best sweet smile while resisting the urge to throw the flowers in the garbage. Instead, she arranged them in a glass vase and placed them to the side of the front counter for everyone to enjoy the sweet scent that emanated from them. The appearance of the flowers had prompted one of the other pharmacy assistants, Jenny, to ask what had happened.

"So, are you okay, Lilly?" she asked, pushing her glasses up the ridge of her narrow nose. "I heard you were attacked; was it Glen, honey?"

Lilly shot her a sharp glance. "Thanks Jenny; I'm good now," she said, continuing to unpack a small box of medications that had just been delivered. "And no, I wasn't attacked. It was a car accident, honey," she said, her voice quivering with annoyance.

"Oh dear!" Jenny stumbled. "That is quite horrible, Lilly. I'm sorry to have assumed differently; it's just the girls … well, you know how girls can talk."

"That's the problem with all those little tongues wagging, Jenny," Lilly snapped. "Tales appear to grow as long as the tails on the dogs that entertain them."

Much to her relief, nobody dared mention the incident to her again.

After she finished work for the day, Lilly strolled back along the main road. The street was filled with the noise of school children alighting from buses, chatting and laughing and in high spirits. There were the crowds pressing through the November heat, and going about their afternoon errands. Heavy traffic blanketed the warm air in a thick hazy cloud of exhaust fumes, adding to the discomfort felt by the ordinary wending their way through the street and oblivious to anything else going on. Lilly felt anything but ordinary. She had decided that ordinary was now behind her. A new focus encompassed her future. *No longer will I live an ordinary existence*, she thought, as she jostled past some teenagers gathered about in front of a milk bar. *I will live with purpose and I shall live.*

Lilly had grown up on Queensland's Gold Coast. Her parents still lived in the family home on the canals in Broadbeach. How she longed for the comfort of her mother's warm embrace and the words that fell in support from her tender lips. Lilly did not share her marital problems with them nor the recent attack her husband had just bestowed upon her, as they had warned her against Glen in those early years. Their pleas for their only daughter fell on deaf ears and a blind heart. *That will be my first stop.* Lilly reached the big glass doors of the Rockton Bank – *But not my final destination* – as she knew that would be the first place Glen would go looking for her. But she had to see her parents; it had been years. She slid her sunglasses over her head. She took a deep breath. *Here goes nothing!*

She breezed in through the bank's entrance. Silently, she asked God to assist her with the task before her of applying for a personal loan, because she had never done so before and the thought unnerved her. Glen had always taken control of the money coming into the household, including her earnings from her job at the pharmacy. Lilly could keep very little to herself that went unnoticed by her husband, so she had no choice but to apply for a bank loan if her plan was to succeed. Her future depended on the right outcome today, because for her plan to work, she would need some money of her own.

When she arrived home later that afternoon, Lilly was feeling rather confident that her loan application had gone well. The bank manager had told her it would be a week before an outcome would be reached after going through her details and references. She felt good about taking a step towards her plans. She was relieved to see Millie was not home as she knew her daughter was vying for some time with her, and she couldn't bring herself to give her that time yet, not with her leaving so soon. Thinking of her children suddenly made her feel guilty. She couldn't take them with her, as much as she wanted to. He would track them down relentlessly. She knew Glen's dark side only too well, and it was a side to her husband she would never underestimate again. He still loved his children and she would not dare put it to the test. For now, it was her intention to go on as normal while she planned the details of her escape from a life and a town she was eager to leave behind. And she knew, with a bittersweet tinge, that she would never come back to either of them.

Lilly changed into a black singlet top and a pair of denim shorts, loosened her hair and crouched down to the bottom of her wardrobe to pull out an old locked wooden box buried deep under several other boxes that contained shoes. Settling herself on the floor, she unlocked the box with a key that dangled on a chain of gold that she had hidden under her bedside drawers.

She hadn't looked into the box for at least fourteen years. Her eyes fell upon photographs of a young vibrant woman with tumbling waves of dark hair complementing the delicate features of her face. She gasped at the smile she saw in the photo. *It's Millie!* After so many years choosing to escape the past, the similarity took her by surprise. Among the few moments frozen on old square photographic paper was a birth certificate and a band of white gold with a script painstakingly engraved on the inner circle of the ring. There was also a letter written on pale pink recycled paper from a mother to her newborn daughter. She held them in the warmth of her grasp for a few moments before wrapping them in some tissue paper and placing it all in a plastic bag and securing it tightly with tape. She returned the wrapped items to the box, gazing sadly at the faded chipped paintwork of the white and gold shells that had been a grand decoration at one time – *Another time,* Lilly thought, as she placed the box back in its original position – *Another life.*

After she hid the key to the box, she sat on the edge of her bed engrossed in her thoughts and enjoying the privacy of her brief moments alone before she had to face her family and play a hard game of pretend. She felt numb inside. It was as if her mind had already become detached and her physical body just had to catch up. Lilly knew the disconnection was inevitable, but it was as if she had little control over the speed at which her feelings overtook her. This surprised her because she loved her children and she had never envisioned a future without them – until now. Her freedom loomed in front of her in an enticing vision of little responsibility and no more walking on eggshells around an unpredictable, dangerous husband.

Ace broke the train of her thoughts when he appeared like an awkward shadow in the doorway to her bedroom.

"Hi buddy." Her smile didn't reach her eyes.

"Hi Mum." The muddle in his eyes portrayed his uncertainty.

She went up to him and encircled her slim arms around him. She pulled him close and embraced him with a sudden rush of affection. He squirmed a little in her grip and looked up at her as her eyes brimmed with tears.

"I love you Ace," she said, still holding him close. "Don't you forget that, okay?"

"Okay Mum." His voice was sullen as he slowly extricated himself from her embrace.

He studied her with a quizzical expression for a moment then grinned. "So, what's for dinner?" he said, taking her hand and leading her to the kitchen.

Lilly chuckled. "How does fried rice and honey soy chicken sound?"

"With vege chips?" Ace asked with a hopeful arch of his brows.

"But of course!"

"Sounds good then." Ace answered. "I'll help you."

She went to the fridge to fetch the ingredients.

"That would be lovely," she said while gathering the food. "Where is Millie?"

"With Emily," Ace said as he cracked an egg for the omelette. "She's always with Emily. She never takes me down to the bay now."

"Hmmm," she breezed in response.

Pausing between eggs, Ace focused on her. "Can you take me to the bay, Mum? We haven't gone there together in ages."

"Huh? Oh, yeah. Sure." She looked away from him. "One day soon, okay."

Lilly was glad her daughter had found a new friend in Emily. Their friendship seemed to be blossoming, and for Lilly this recent development between the two girls could not have come at a better time. She knew now that Millie would have a good friend to support her when she left her family. Right now, she grasped at anything to keep her from feeling guilty when it came to her children.

CHAPTER FIVE

December 6, 1987

D ear Journal,
Never thought I'd say this but I cannot wait to go to school tomorrow! I have two words: DAMON RICHARDS!! Oh my god! He has really started to notice me. Thanks to Emily. She taught me how to apply black eyeliner and mascara, and she helped me to sew the hem up on my school uniform skirt – add a push-up bra and voila! Stand to attention honey! Ha ha! So, he's asked me out on a date next Saturday night. I've asked Mum and she didn't even want information about him, or where we'd be going. Easy peasy. Actually, I haven't ever had this much freedom and I am loving it. Why question it right? Right?

She's been home for three weeks now and she hardly talks to me, so that makes the two of them now. I am done trying to figure it all out with my parents. She still cries though, more it seems. I've tried to offer her comfort but she doesn't want it from me. I see her cuddling Ace though. I guess because he's the baby. I've always known she had a softer place for him in her heart; maybe it's that. Maybe it's just me.

Lately I've been having dreams of coloured angel

wings, lots of them hovering and floating about, and a face … at first a blurred vision but I can always feel her before the vision of her comes to me. The feeling is so nice; all I can think to describe it is love. She comes closer and closer. She is saying something but I cannot hear her. And finally, when she comes into clear sight, she is me! Then I awaken.

I don't know what the dreams mean – if anything at all, but I have started to sketch and colour my angel wings and my visions of her. I have found that I really enjoy drawing, and I'm not too bad at it. A new talent I have discovered, and I am becoming quite passionate about it. It calms me, makes me feel good to create with my hands. So, I have decided to develop this newfound passion of mine and see where it goes.

For now, most of which consumes my mind is Damon, and I can't wait to spend some time alone with him next Saturday night. I wonder where he will take me. I am so excited!

Keep you updated journal, chow for now!

Millie xo

P.S I didn't even know push-up bras existed!

Millie was in a deep sleep when she began to feel the slightest of finger tips pattering over her face, and then drift over the fine hairs of her arm. She threw an arm up over her face and turned over, letting out a grumpy moan and trying to fight the feathery strokes that were intent on rousing her out of a cosy slumber.

"Wake up sleepy head," Ace said softly, tapping the hand that shielded her face. "Mum said to wake up, Millie."

He decided to give up on the gentle option and take it up a notch.

"Wakey, wakey Millie-pie!" he yelled, leaping on top of her.

"Ace! Get off me!" She ripped a pillow from beneath her head and swung hard, hitting her target on the side of his head and sending her brother throttling to the floor. She smirked down at him with an air of triumph. "Little shit."

"At least I'm not a big one like you Millie Stinky-Poo," he retorted.

They both broke out into a fit of giggles.

"You okay?" she asked, stretching.

"Yeah," he said while getting up from the floor. "Hey, did you know that cows have best friends within their herds?" He raised his eyebrows.

"Err … no, Ace." She was out of the bed now. "I didn't know that. I guess even cows need best friends," she said, smiling and ruffling his hair. "Now, let me get ready for school, okay."

Ace left her room, and the smile on her face became one of intimate excitement. Secret little butterflies danced about in her stomach while she thought about the day that lay before her. She savoured the intoxicating pleasure that arose from the flutters in her tummy while she made her bed then eagerly dressed and ready for a school day that held the guarantee of exquisite moments with Damon ahead of her.

Forty minutes later she bounced through the old front door, stopping short on her porch to look for Emily. She didn't have to look far.

"Whoa! Hey Miss Millie, look at you!" Emily was perched on the low brick fence bordering Millie's front yard. Her hair was swept back in a tight ponytail. She made her school uniform appear quite trendy by adding dozens of thin coloured plastic bangles to her wrists. A red tie was loosely wrapped around her neck, and long black feathers dangled from small lobes. She looked like a delicate punked-up porcelain doll, but when she spoke, her voice betrayed an innocence. "Sexy spunky girly. You'll have all the boys hot and bothered today!" she laughed.

Millie blushed as she skipped down the stairs. "Too much eyeliner?" she asked with a worried frown.

Emily laughed as Millie paused before her. "No silly; you look gorgeous." She flung an arm around Millie's shoulders. "Let's go to school. I know a certain someone that will appreciate how sexy you are looking today," she teased.

"Emily, stop!" Millie retorted, although secretly satisfied with her friend's reaction to her appearance.

She had certainly made a special effort. She had meticulously applied charcoal eyeliner to accentuate the strike of her green cat-like eyes, and finished them off with a thick layer of black mascara. Nude pink gloss was smeared over her lips, enhancing the high contours of her face. Millie hoped Damon would appreciate her efforts today, as it was all for him. *And so far, it was working like magic*, she thought with relish. *I just about have him where I want him.* Despite this, she felt a sense of uneasiness in the pit of her stomach. *No!* she reassured herself. *It's all okay.* She pushed aside the doubt and focused on pleasing thoughts of him. Circling an arm around Emily, the two girls started off towards the bus stop.

"You realise you'll get in trouble at school for the earrings and the bangles," Millie said, admiring her friend's individuality.

"Meh!" Emily chuckled. "Who cares? I like this look." She gave Millie a mischievous wink. "Besides, did you know that if a boy breaks one of these rubber bangles off my wrist, it means he wants to get with me?"

Millie stopped dead in her tracks and gaped at Emily. "No … really?" Her brows knitted into a frown.

"Ahhhh Miss Millie." Emily threw her head back and laughed. "You don't really know much, do you? … Hey, do you want one to wear?"

"No thanks," Millie snapped. "Hurry up Em, the bus is about to come".

Millie ignored the stares from other girls as she walked to her first class of the day – science. She knew she wasn't the most popular girl among her peers of late but this did not concern her. She had never been "Miss Popularity". Fitting in with the crowd was not a priority for her. She would rather express who she was and feel the freedom that comes with it, than conform to the ideas of others on how she should be. The only trouble was, she was still figuring out her self-identity and had a long way to go yet.

Millie kept looking straight ahead and held her head up high as she made her way down the second-floor corridor to class. Hushed conversations followed her – "Look at all the make-up", said one. "Who does she think she is?" another sneered, accompanied by giggles. As she reached the heavy brown doors of the science lab, Millie turned and faced her adversaries, giving them the biggest smile she could muster. And with a quick wink of an eye, she tossed up her long loose curls and disappeared into the classroom. *Jealous bitches!* she scowled to herself. But dark thoughts vanished as her stomach did a hasty flip when she caught sight of Damon beckoning her to sit beside him.

Millie felt his eyes on her as she made her way towards the seat he had saved for her. As she came nearer, she could sense the hunger lingering within those ocean-blue eyes. The passion dwelling there sent the butterflies inside her fluttering madly. She was suddenly conscious of her every move. Her hands and her whole body felt clammy while her heart thundered under her breasts. He was handsome. Dark hair fell casually around the collar of his white school shirt and wisped about his face, highlighting the set of his eyes and enhancing the strong projection of his jaw. Perfectly etched lips widened in a brilliant smile as she sat down next to him.

"Hello beautiful," he crooned.

"Hi." Millie smiled briefly, then shyly looked away. She gazed about the clatter of the classroom while trying to calm the maelstrom inside her.

"You look lovely today, Millie." He smiled as he lifted his hand to sweep the dark wavy locks from her face.

"Thanks Damon," she muttered, and blushed. "You look good too."

Millie felt a wash of relief when the class fell quiet as their teacher arrived to commence the lesson. This would give her a chance to compose herself. *Silly girl, he is only a boy!* He slid his chair closer to her, and she thought her heart might just pop right out of her chest when he rested his hand on her thigh and caressed her. She caught the glare of a few girls who were scrutinising them and obviously wondering how this new liaison had occurred under their watch. They were clearly not thrilled at their apparent new rival who had seemingly swept in from nowhere to dominate Damon's attention – the boy every girl wanted to call her boyfriend. Millie avoided their gaze and began to relax. She rested her own hand on top of his and wrapped his hand in her long slender fingers.

He kept glancing at her during the session as the teacher muttered about creating pure water from saltwater through an evaporative process. With each stolen peek, her smile grew wider with courage until eventually she couldn't help but laugh.

"What are you laughing at?" he teased.

She bit down on her bottom lip to subdue another giggle. "You," she whispered before the teacher insisted for their attention.

As Damon turned to face the teacher, she caught the grin that smattered across his face.

As the other students left at the end of the lesson, Damon pulled her aside and whispered in her ear. "I can't wait for Saturday night, Millie."

Millie smiled back at him. "Me too," she replied, delighting in the way her name sounded on his lips.

He brought a hand up under her chin and his face came down to hers. Millie could feel his warm breath tickling the tip of her nose. She gazed up into those limpid blue orbs and found herself lost in them as his lips came down to meet hers. She parted her lips in response and closed her eyes, feeling silly to be watching him in the most intimate moment they had shared so far. His lips closed over hers lightly, and it felt every bit as sweet as she had imagined them to feel in all her past delicious dreams starring him as her romantic charming main character. She felt the wonderment of her heart's desire manifesting in her experience – A thought that exhilarated her and knew it worth further pondering later. When Damon pulled away from her with a smile playing at the corners of his lips, she caught the affection in his eyes, in contrast to the cockiness that she usually saw there.

"See you later," he said softly.

"Bye Damon," she said, her voice mirroring the rush of tenderness he displayed towards her.

Damon turned on sneakered feet and left the classroom in a hurry to arrive at his next subject on time. Watching until he was out of sight, Millie took her time as she picked up her backpack that was littered with her favourite brooches and band names. She walked out in a dream, still revelling in the feelings that her first kiss had provoked in her. She picked up her pace and skipped down the hallway. It was all she could do to contain herself from the sweet emotions pulsating through her that made her want to dance and jump for joy. And she couldn't wait to tell Emily.

Millie arrived home that afternoon in high spirits. She walked into her bedroom and paused when she saw a new white dress laying on her bed with a shoebox sitting next to it. *What's this?* she thought, a little confused. She couldn't remember when she had received such a gift apart from birthdays and Christmas. *What a beautiful gift!* She picked up the dress and held it out before her. She ran a hand over the soft fabric. The frock had small short cap-sleeves that would just reach to cover her shoulders, with a cinching bodice that would hug her curves in all the right places. Her most favourite feature was where the cinched-in waist gave way to delicate layered ruffles of white laced material that would finish just above her knees. *Oh, it's lovely! This day is getting better and better!* She held the dress to her nose and breathed in its crisp new smell.

"Are you going to try it on?" Her mother's voice startled her. She was standing in the doorway quietly watching Millie inspect the white dress.

"Oh, Mum, you scared me!" Millie laughed. "Did you do this?"

"For your date on Saturday night."

Millie saw the compassion in her mother's eyes, then she noticed something peculiar. Her mother seemed to be enveloped in a cloudy mist. It was a pale lemon-yellow, blushed with a dark pink that seemed to float and hover about her, following her movements like a shadow. She gazed at the phenomenon with a mix of curiosity and puzzlement etched on her face. *Am I going crazy?* she thought. But as she looked up at her mother's gentle smile, all thoughts of the coloured haze faded from her mind. That expression of love that she had so missed in her mother's expression was back.

Relief washed over her. She ran up to her mother and flung her arms around her just like she had when she was a little girl. Her eyes became moist with tears. "Thank you so much, Mum," she cried, her voice muffled against her mother's shoulder. "I love it!"

Tears burst and overflowed down her cheeks. She started to sob as she cherished the warmth that she had missed more than she realised. She tightened her embrace, not wanting to ever let her go. The confusion and stress of the past few weeks poured out in waves like a burst dam. She cried for every close moment lost between them. Every secret they hadn't shared. Every cuddle and every smile shared and known only to them. But most of all, she cried for the image of her mother when she had found her bloody and broken on her bed that day. She knew that horrible day had changed her mother forever, as she was all too aware that her mother was incapable of being the person she was before that brutal attack. And with a heart that weighed heavy with a deep ache, she understood.

"Oh baby girl," Lilly soothed, holding her daughter's trembling body close to her. "It's okay. It's okay." She rocked Millie gently and stroked the back of her hair for as long as her daughter needed her comfort.

Finally, Millie pulled away. It crossed her mind to make the most of this rare moment with her mother a little longer, as something gnawed deep inside her, telling her that she might not have the opportunity again for a long time.

"I'm sorry, Mum," she said, wiping away her tears. "I've just missed you so much lately."

Lilly's eyes clouded over as she quickly pulled away. She looked over at the bed where the shoebox sat unopened, and cleared her throat. "I see you have not looked at your new shoes yet."

Her mother's response to her did not go unnoticed. Millie fought hard to control the well of tears that threatened to engulf her again. All the elation she felt earlier eluded her now, and with her heart weighed down, she turned towards the shoebox and opened it. They were white lace covered pointed slippers with tiny delicate heels that matched her dress. Millie looked at them for a long time before mustering up a deliberate smile. "They are beautiful, Mum." She turned and peered up at her. "Thank you," she said, her voice a muted muffle.

"You're welcome, sweetheart." Her laugh was forced and stilted. "After all, it is your first date."

Lilly turned to walk away and paused, turning to look at her daughter. The expression on her face was resolute. "Remember what I told you, Millie. Trust the whisper within you... always."

Millie looked at her, solemn. "And what if I don't like what the whisper inside me is telling me?" she said softly.

"Then I guess we listen anyway," she said as she made her exit.

CHAPTER SIX

December 6, 1987

Dear Journal,

DATE NIGHT!! Oh, and am I just a tad excited! Em has loaned me her thin golden bangles. She said it will set off my new dress. Which, by the way, she loves. She is coming over later to help me get ready for the big night. She is the bestest friend in the world. Thank God for Emily!

My Dad actually said more than two words to me this morning – can you believe that? He asked about my date tonight. I told him we were going to the movies, and when he questioned me further, my Mum told him that she had it covered, then glared towards him really sternly! Probably the most I've heard her say to him lately … but he didn't say a word back to her – surprisingly. I have also noticed Dad spending more time cleaning the house these days – another strange happening around here.

After Mum gave me the dress that day, she's barely said much to me at all … nothing of importance anyway. No more "I love you's". No more hugs. No more anything really. And I still miss her more than ever. I have so many questions to ask her about boys and this first date. I would love to bounce some ideas off her too. About how something I had placed in my imagination for so long is now something I am actually experiencing, and how I wonder if this works for other things we want in our lives. And, of course, I would love to discuss my dreams with her. But I know she is not open to any questions; I have tried.

At least I have Emily. Thank God for Emily! She knows lots more about boys than me; she's been on heaps of dates. She knows what they like and how to behave around them ... she gives me loads of tips. I can handle this.

I think.

My dreams continue... Wings of vibrant beautiful shades and butterflies of violet. Deep violet. The background is illuminated white – like a light, a radiating light. Magnificent whales have appeared breaching enormously out of this radiating light only to disappear beneath it again. These dreams are no ordinary dreams. I know this because of the way they make me feel and I can almost hear what she says to me now ... but not quite. I know I'll hear when I'm ready. I just know.

My visions and dreams are fuel for my art and I am sketching like crazy ... love it! Keeps me occupied through the strange hours at home.

I have decided to experiment with this imagination thing I've been pondering. I am going to envision every day that I am a successful, well-known artist in my future. For that is fast becoming my dream. And the whisper within me feels pretty good about it too.

DATE NIGHT! Gotta go!

Lilly hummed a sweet little tune to herself while she prepared her famous passionfruit tart. It was Saturday morning and *Oh what a morning!* she thought to herself, feeling as light and as fluffy as the eggs she had just finished whisking for the tart. The sun's radiance awakened the magic in all creatures in the garden outside. Birds of striking reds and blues flew about chattering to one another, and dropping seedlings along their way to the rich foliage below, assisting in the birth of new life for the lumbering presence of the red cedar, gum and avocado trees that surrounded the house. Bees and butterflies buzzed and fluttered through the trees and the garden bed, coming to rest now and then to drink from the sweet nectar offered to them from flowers eager for pollination. The trees seemed to sigh with pleasure while they stretched mighty branches littered with lush green leaves towards the nurturing rays of the sun, while enjoying the hive of activity as the life around them basked and bristled in the freshness of a new day.

Lilly watched the beauty before her through the window of the kitchen. She smiled to herself, pleased this Saturday morning held such promise. She felt excited because tonight when Glen was at the milk factory working, Ace in his bed sleeping and Millie out on her date, she would be leaving this house behind forever. She continued to hum to herself as she busied herself in the kitchen with the tart. *This is a special tart*, she thought. This was her parting gift to the family she was about to leave behind.

Glen stamped into the kitchen behind her. "Good morning, honey," he said.

He reached above her for a mug for his morning fix of instant coffee, and hovered over her longer than necessary. "Cooking up a storm already?" he said, pleased at his wife's renewed interest in cooking.

She hid a grimace at his closeness as she looked up at him and flashed a smile. She could smell the fresh apple scent of his shampoo combined with the faint mint of his aftershave. Her stomach churned. "I am making a tart," she said, withdrawing from him.

He sat down heavily at the dining table in the kitchen, smoothing his hair in place and preparing for his morning ritual of two cups of coffee over the newspaper.

He looked at Lilly and grinned. "A tart!... yum! You must be feeling better. I could hear you humming from the bathroom before." He raised his eyebrows. "Haven't heard that in a while."

Lilly wasn't quite sure if he was expecting her to answer. She looked askance at him as he sat absorbed in the newspaper. She decided he wasn't really interested in her reply, but decided to deliver one anyway.

"I am feeling better, Glen. It's a beautiful day out there," she said, pausing while she replaced a tea towel to its hook, "And the world is my oyster."

Glen looked up from the article he was reading,

and looked at her with a puzzled frown. Before he could respond, she flashed him a brilliant smile and said, "I'm going to hang out some washing." Then she left the kitchen, leaving him to contemplate her annotation.

Outside in the backyard, Lilly was enjoying the slight salty breeze drifting in from the bay and the warmth of the sun against her skin while she pegged wet garments on the clothesline. She was feeling giddy with the anticipation for that evening's escape, and a secret smile played on her lips. She was so engrossed with her daydreams that she failed to hear Glen follow her outside.

"I think it's time I cut the grass out here," he chuckled.

He grabbed her arm as she grappled for a peg and pulled her close to him, engulfing her slim body against the solid mass of his own. "I've been thinking about what you said at the hospital. I want you to know that I do love you, Lilly" Glen murmured in her ear.

Immediately, she tensed at his touch. Her reverie turned sour as the strength of his arms around her provoked a feeling of powerlessness. The fear she had felt when he had attacked her swept through her in a flood like a river thundering over a waterfall. She struggled to control the anxious feelings threatening to overwhelm her, not daring to give away her true feelings towards him. *Not now! Not when I'm so close!* Lilly told herself. It was his trust and assurance in her that she needed for her plans to come to fruition, because she was certain he would not let her out of his sight if he suspected her plans were to leave him. Lilly knew he would never allow her to leave. She circled her arms around him and gave him a quick squeeze, and forced a laugh.

"Love you too. Now help me with the washing while you're here." She pulled away gently and threw a wet towel towards him.

Glen chuckled and reached for some pegs. He was feeling good, especially when Lilly had just repeated those three little words back to him. He watched her as she bent over the basket and picked up a pair of jeans to hang. He stared at her longingly and licked his upper lip as he gazed upon the swell of her buttocks hidden beneath an old pair of denim shorts. Aroused at the sight of his wife clad in her shorts and a flimsy white singlet, he gave her a playful slap on her buttocks when she leaned over to pick up another garment.

She jumped away. "Glen!" Lilly recognised the look in his eyes and relaxed a little. *I can handle this …* "Not now!" she said sternly.

Her demeanour had awakened his desire, and he was suddenly looking forward to some long overdue intimacy sessions with his wife. He decided that after his double late shift that night he would bring his wife home her favourite flowers. *A beautiful lily for an even more beautiful Lilly*, he savoured. The loathing that shadowed her eyes when she looked back at him, went completely unnoticed by him.

Ace, having just finished his daily routine of keeping check of new presents appearing under their Christmas tree, pressed his face against the flyscreen of the old porch back door. He poked his tongue out against the mesh then watched in fascination as the tiny squares filled with his saliva and eventually popped. When he tasted the saliva patterns, he crinkled his nose at the unsavoury flavour of the dusty old fly screen. "Yuck!" he cried, before continuing his saliva creations. A glimpse of his parents in the yard together interrupted his creative moment. Curious, he walked silently through the door and sat down on the cobblestones to enjoy the sight of his parents actually talking and spending some time together. His hopes peaked when he saw them embrace for the first time since he could remember. His heart soared when he overheard them declare their affection for one another, and heard their laughter. And as he watched quietly, he knew then that everything was going to be just fine.

His father was the first to see him sitting there as they came towards the house. "Hi little man," he said, grinning.

Ace smiled up at him when Glen tousled his hair as he walked up the cobblestones to pass him. "Hi Dad … Hi Mum," he said. His eyes followed them. "Mum, Dad?"

They both paused and looked down at him.

"Did you know that in Texas it is illegal to graffiti

a cow?" Ace said.

Glen roared with laughter at his son's odd question. Lilly's laugh was one of respite; she wasn't sure how long Ace had been sitting there and dreaded any questions he might have concerning them. She continued walking up and into the house, leaving Glen and Ace to their unusual conversation about cows.

Lilly headed for her bedroom, eager for a little breathing space. She could feel her heart quickening and her breath become shallow and rapid. She shut the door behind her and fell sprawling to her bed. *Deep breaths. Deep breaths.* She coaxed herself into calming the anxiety rising inside her. She hugged her knees tightly to her chest, fighting the impulse to lose control and weep. The detachment she had maintained all these weeks while planning and plotting her escape finally broke as the enormity of what she was about to do dawned on her. *I'm leaving my children!* the voice in her mind cried. She tightened her grip around her legs and began to rock her body back and forth, attempting to comfort herself as she fought with her mind over what she needed to do for her survival, and the sacrifice that lay before her. She told herself she would see them again – *It's not goodbye forever.* She told herself they would be with her wherever she goes – *It's not goodbye forever.* She told herself she was a good mother and that she had tried for so long – *It's not goodbye forever!* Then she told herself she would not end up like Samantha. And this thought soothed her and she regained her resolve. Her breathing returned to normal and the turmoil in her mind eased.

She sat up now, feeling the turbulence drain away while the wheels in her mind shifted into gear for the strategic undertaking she was about to commence. Thanks to the approval of the personal loan she had applied for some weeks ago, she could buy herself a car. She had parked it at the end of their street, and every night when Glen was at work and the kids were in their bedrooms, she would take a few of her belongings to her car, filling it enough at a time so her missing belongings would go unnoticed and she wouldn't have to pack her things all at once on the night of her departure.

She had been in contact with an old friend from school on the Gold Coast for help with covering her tracks. This friend was Scott who she had known throughout her adolescent years and into her early twenties, before she had packed her then few belongings on a whim and headed south to Sydney to pursue her dream career in modelling. Her aspirations died a slow death when she was faced with closed doors to the glamorous world reserved for models. She couldn't go home with her tail between her legs. Instead, she found herself sharing a small dingy Sydney apartment with two aspiring out-of-work actresses who resorted to turning tricks on the side to pay the rent. Working dimly lit city streets was not Lilly's style. She opted for long, tiring nights working at a rowdy pub in The Rocks to make ends meet. Enter Glen, and all of a sudden, the misery that had engulfed her young life became alive with romantic rendezvous tinged with a hint of mystery and excitement. She was hooked. Her move to Sydney had a purpose; she was to be somebody's mother and not a failure after all.

Lilly knew from snippets of gossip over the years that Scott had kept allies close in a world that abided no rules of the law. When she contacted him and explained her situation, he was eager to help his old friend escape her husband. He arranged, for a price and a promise of a drink together when she arrived back on the Coast, a new identity for her to slip into. The transition to her new life would then almost be complete. But first she had to see her ageing parents. She decided that she would explain everything to them and seek their blessing. Ready or not, Albert and Margaret Winston were about to discover the whole unvarnished truth of her life with Glen. And their pleas from all those years ago, that she take baby Millie and leave him behind would be instantly validated.

Her thoughts were interrupted when she heard a soft knock on the other side of her bedroom door.

"Mum?" Millie called through the flimsy plywood separating them. "Can I come in please?"

"Sure Millie," she said wearily.

Millie gently closed the door after entering and faced her mother hesitantly. "Can I talk to you about something?"

Lilly beckoned her daughter to sit beside her on the edge of the bed. She caught the apprehension in Millie's expression when she glanced at the bed. She knew she had avoided her bedroom since that dreadful afternoon when they had found her there. She reached out and took Millie's hand, pulling her closer. "It's okay sweetie," she smiled. "What would you like to talk about?"

Millie perched awkwardly beside her mother. Her eyes fell to the floor in deliberation before she glanced back up and cleared her throat. "Well … don't think I'm crazy, okay." She gave a little nervous laugh and twirled her hair nervously. "I was wondering about our thoughts … you know, people's thoughts."

Lilly gave a little nod, encouraging her daughter to go on. She herself had briefly pondered the subject in earlier years.

Millie felt encouraged and continued. "Do you think that the thoughts people have can influence the way their lives turn out? I mean, do our thoughts have some kind of attracting power? They must have some function other than the automatic day to day boring stuff, right? There must be more to humans than that."

Lilly considered her daughter's words for a few moments, unsure how to satisfy the profound questions that spilled from her mouth. She was both surprised and impressed with Millie's depth of thinking. She looked at her thoughtfully, searching for the right words.

"I recall reading a book years and years ago. The book was called *The Marriage of Heaven and Hell* by William Blake." She paused, noticing Millie's eager expression to hear more. "Over the years, I always remembered one comment William Blake made in the book which relates to what you are asking me now, Millie-pie." She smiled openly. "He said, 'What is now proved was once only imagined'."

Millie was silent for a few moments as she absorbed the words of that petite sentence. She started to be aware of a tingling sensation crawling its way through her spine and up around the back of her neck. She immediately understood that the words her mother had just spoken held significant importance.

"That means that everything comes from our imagination first," she said.

Lilly, warming to the discussion, swiftly remembered another quote she hadn't thought of in years that might be of some help with Millie's inquiries. She smiled and her eyes lit up as the memory flooded to her.

"There is something else that comes to mind!" she said. "Albert Einstein said, 'Imagination is more important than knowledge. Knowledge is limited. Imagination encircles the world'."

Millie felt exhilaration sweeping through her, rushing through every cell, every molecule and every particle that made up her body. She closed her eyes for a moment, allowing the divine power she felt to seep into and through her, revelling in the feeling its influence bestowed on her. For the first time since these visions and experiences began, Millie was grateful for them. She knew she wasn't going crazy at all. She knew everything was going to be just fine.

She opened her eyes to look at her mother again. "Then thoughts do have great power, just as I suspected. Thank you, Mum." She leaned in and hugged her, giving her a slight squeeze. "I love you," she murmured.

"Love you too," Lilly crooned as she held her daughter for a few moments. Then, as the struggle within her bubbled to the surface again, she pulled away. "Now, you have a big date to get ready for and I have lots of things to do today!" she said.

Millie took her cue and left, leaving Lilly with her ponderings again.

My thoughts have got me this far, Lilly mused. *Not exactly where I wanted to be... So*, she thought with a speck of a thrill racing through her, w*here will I have them take me now?* She switched to thoughts of the wooden box filled with secrets hidden in her closet. It was a box of truths that were thought to be destroyed a long time ago. They were truths she knew would certainly put her life in jeopardy when they were revealed. *Pandora's Box*, she thought with repugnance. *What to do with the box?* She decided she would bury the box deep under the giant avocado tree in the backyard before she left that night, and leave a letter for Millie to await further instructions in the future. *She's not yet ready for the absolute truth...*

When the letter to her daughter was complete, she fished out the key that hung in all its obscurity on the end of a gold chain. She placed the key with her letter in an envelope and sealed it closed with a lick of her tongue, then hid the envelope safely until she was ready to retrieve it later that night when she would leave it for Millie to discover within the pages of her much-loved journal.

Ace called out loudly from his bedroom, "Muuummm, I'm ready for bed now!"

Scooping up his favourite worn out teddy bear, Benny Boy, Ace flounced among the bed sheets and blankets of his bed, all set to snuggle down for the night. Placing Benny Boy gently on the pillow beside him, he leaned towards the short tight curls of the bear and planted a small kiss on the tip of his hard black nose. "Good night Benny Boy," he whispered.

Lilly appeared at his doorway, breezing in with a smile. "Teeth all brushed?" she asked.

"Yep."

The fine hairs of a critical right eyebrow raised. "Blow," Lilly instructed, leaning over his face to smell the breath that escaped from his mouth as he exhaled on demand. A warm minty breeze wafted over her senses as his breath trailed around her nostrils. "Very good," she said.

She sat next to him and waited while he went about arranging his pillows and sheets just the way he liked before settling his head into the soft pillow beneath him. Eyes that reflected her own gazed up at her with a sleepy smile when he was all done. Lilly looked down at her son wistfully, aware that this was to be the last time she would tuck her son into bed and wish him the sweetest of dreams. Lilly gazed upon eyes awash with an innate faith that her presence in his young life was unwavering. She could hardly endure these last moments with him, savouring each one of them and drawing out the bedtime process longer than usual. Wrapping his little body in her arms, she held him close and tight against her bosom. Nuzzling her nose into the tufts of his hair, she breathed deep, filling her nostrils with the unique smell that belonged to him. The faint aroma of floral-scented soap combined with the sweetness of the passionfruit tart dessert invaded her senses. Feelings of nostalgia seared her, settling over the tremor of her body like a heavy cloak, as she swore this moment would be with her forever.

"Listen, it's important to keep your teeth clean, okay," she quipped as she began to fuss about tucking him under the blanket. "And be good to your big sister; she loves you lots."

Ace crinkled his nose up at her.

She leaned closer. "I love you baby boy," she whispered into his little ear as her eyes moistened.

Ace giggled as his mother's warm whisper tickled through his ear, activating tiny shivering tingles all the way down his spine. "I'm not a baby, Mum," he reminded her between giggles.

The ripple of his laugh prompted Lilly to continue murmuring, whispering cherished "sweet nothings" – a special little game she would play with her children at bedtime when they were very young. Ace's laugh was contagious and Lilly found herself giggling along with him, while relishing the moments of delight she had persuaded from him.

When their laughter had finally subsided, a shadow of sorrow crossed her eyes as they moved longingly over her son's features for the last time. Shaking the loose blonde tresses of her hair, Lilly gulped back the flood of tears that threatened to spill as she said her final goodbye to her son. "You will always be my baby boy, Ace. Remember that I love you very much."

She walked over to the door of his bedroom and paused one last time to look upon her content drowsy son. "Sweet dreams," she choked.

"Good night, Mum. I love you too," Ace said dreamily with a faint smile on his rosy lips. Then he turned his back towards her, hugging Benny Boy close to his chest, and closed his eyes.

As she shut Ace's bedroom door behind her, Lilly quietly leaned against the flimsy plywood of the door, fighting the urge to crumble in a heap to the floor. She resisted the intense impulse to scoop her sleeping son up in her arms and bundle him away with her into the night. *I can't!* Lilly wrestled with herself, *Glen will surely hunt me down!*

Squeezing her eyes shut, she willed herself to press on with her plans. Then, with all her might, she steeled herself against the ache in her heart and practised the detachment that had been her comforting friend through her ordeal, and sprang into action. There was not much time.

CHAPTER SEVEN

Millie walked back to her room with a breeze of elation after her conversation with her mother. She leaped on her bed and laughed. Blowing loose strands of hair away from her mouth, she stilled herself in her doona and examined the peeling cream-coloured paint on the ceiling. *Ahh, life is good!* she thought, milking the pleasant peacefulness within her. She had wanted to stay in the room with her mother longer, as there were other things she wished to discuss. She was certain now the special bond they had shared would regain its strength over time.

She smiled. "Imagination encircles the world," she said with wonderment to the ceiling. Those words felt good to her. Really good. "All I need then is my imagination. And so it shall be." A confirming tingle ran up her spine while she thought about thought. Her smile broadened in the deliciousness of the feelings this trail of thought produced in her. Millie was unable to explain why or how, yet she did not feel the need to. She was learning to trust the tingles that surged through her being on occasion, even though she did not completely understand it. Somehow, she had developed an inner knowing that the impressions she perceived within herself were a key to another dimension. *Perhaps a secret to life*, she mused. She recognised that there was a higher power she could learn to tap into at will, and that higher power had always been there – *A power that is available to anyone willing to open themselves to it.*

"Anything is possible!" Millie squealed out loud.

She leaped up and reached for her sketchpad. A surge of inspiration overtook her fingers as she sketched out the image of her mother in her mind's eye as she saw her a few minutes ago. Feathery strokes captured the soft smile crinkling the corners of her mouth and lighting up the blue hue of her mother's eyes, and the tumbling locks of gold framing her face as she tilted her head, completely immersed in her daughter's questions. Millie's hand flew in a flurry of movement, not ceasing until her portrait was finished and her mother, captured in an expression of fascination, was permanently portrayed upon the page of her art book.

Millie gazed down at her work with astonished pride, amazed with her accomplishment. She had portrayed the beauty of her mother perfectly. Each stroke and shading of her pencil reflected an integrity reserved to the talented few. For Millie, this was a moment she would know forever. For the first time, she felt limitless.

A light tapping at her bedroom window burst into her contemplation. She peered up from her cross-legged position on the floor to spy Emily's grinning face staring back at her.

"Hey Miss Millie." Emily lifted a bag up and shook it a little. "Ready for your hot date tonight?" Her grin was wide enough to almost split her face in two.

Millie threw her head back in laughter. She had been looking forward to a girly afternoon with her friend. "Sure am!" she called out.

She dashed out to meet her friend at the front porch. Poking her head around the corner of the house, she watched Emily as she made her way towards her on the front porch.

"Let's do this," she grinned.

Millie remained as still as she could on the floor with her back facing Emily who was sitting on the bed's edge while she rolled long dark locks of hair into hot rollers some twenty minutes later.

"So, how will I know if he's having a good time?" Millie asked with a hint of uncertainty. "What if I bore him?"

"Are you kidding me? Have you seen the way he looks at you? You will not bore him silly Millie!"

"How will I know though?" Millie persisted.

"If he's having a good time?" Emily smoothed another long strand between fingers while balancing a very hot roller. "Ouch!"

"Hmm," Millie confirmed, "And be careful please!"

"Well," Emily began. "If his breath is hot and heavy on your neck and his crotch is bulging, he's having a good time."

Millie blushed. "Emily!"

Emily peered back at her without flinching, and placed her hands on Millie's shoulders. "What? And you're lucky I wasn't rolling your hair then."

"Well, I didn't mean it like that!" Millie retorted, still blushing.

Emily shrugged, then gently twisted Millie's head around again so she could continue working on her hair. Millie obliged and both girls fell into an awkward silence.

Minutes passed while Millie mulled over her friend's words. She didn't know much about sex, and while the subject intrigued her it was also a topic she found disconcerting. *Nobody has ever spoken to me about it*, she thought.

Unable to contain her curiosity a second longer, she broke the silence between them. "Em, how do you know all that?"

Emily stalled her answer while intentionally concentrating on the delicate task of twisting the last strands of Millie's hair into a roller. She picked up a can of hairspray. "Cover your eyes," she instructed, then pressed an index finger on the nozzle.

The fumes of the hairspray filled the air around them in a mist. Both girls gagged and coughed, waving hands wildly about in front of them in an attempt to escape more consuming vapours.

Millie, moving away from her spot on the floor, was not thrown off her intent, as she suspected Emily had hoped. She stilled herself against the bedroom door, bringing her knees up against her chest and hugged them to her. She watched Emily from across the room as she busied herself tidying up loose rolling pins that had littered the bed. Millie could sense Emily was feeling uncomfortable, but still, she persisted.

"Are you going to answer my question, Em?" she asked.

Emily stopped fussing about for pins and looked at Millie. Her China-blue eyes held Millie's for a moment before she looked away. A single tear rolled down her cheek, falling where her eyes stared down into her lap. Millie jumped to her feet and rushed to her friend on the bed, enfolding her in her arm.

"I'm sorry. I didn't mean to upset you," she said, frowning.

"It's not you, Millie." Emily's voice was barely a whisper. "It's my stepfather." She leaned against Millie's chest and embraced her. Her body began to quiver as she wept.

Millie was bewildered at her friend's sudden outburst. She did not understand why the usual upbeat, playful Emily she knew, was so upset. *What does this have to do with her stepfather?* she mused. Millie tried to console Emily as best she could.

When Emily's sobbing subsided, Millie pulled away gradually for a better view of her tear-stained face. "I don't understand," she said.

"You're the closest friend I've ever had." Emily's voice broke into a sob.

"Me too." Millie's frown deepened as she nodded for her friend to continue.

"About a year ago, my mother had to go into hospital for a few nights... 'women's problems' they told us."

She took the tissue Millie offered to her, paused to blot tears and blow her nose. "One night I was sleeping in my bed, and he came in and laid next to me." She took a deep breath. "He hushed me when I stirred, telling me he needed a cuddle because he missed my mother so much, and that he was so lonely without her."

Millie watched Emily struggling with her words. As her story began to unfold, the significance of her friend's traumatic experiences at the hands her stepfather slowly dawned on her. She took Emily's fidgeting hands and held them firmly between her own to reassure her.

"I felt uncomfortable right away. I asked him to let me sleep but …" Her eyes skipped to the ceiling in an effort to contain her tears as she relived the past, "but he didn't go; he didn't!" Emily cried. Her eyes met Millie's. "He told me it was my fault for being too pretty. He told me because I was pretty the boys would like me, and it was his job to teach me what the boys wanted so I would be ready for them." Her tone hastened and grew in pitch. "After he was done, he told me it was our secret because if anyone was to ever discover what had happened, I would be deemed a sinner and my mother would disown me … and I know he's right, my mother would hate me for this!" Emily's tone dropped to barely a whisper. "And he keeps coming, Millie, at least once a month. Sometimes more ..." Pausing, she searched Millie's face for her reaction.

"Oh Em," Millie shed tears in empathy, "I'm so sorry. What are we going to do?"

She studied her friend while trying to think of a solution. At a loss for words, she hugged Emily close to her again and both girls wept together in each other's arms. Millie could feel every emotion Emily was experiencing, almost as if she herself was subject to the ugliness of Emily's stepfather. She could feel the desperate powerlessness engulfing her friend. Her small trembling body reflected her terror, burden and helplessness.

"I'm here for you, Emily," Millie said, reaching for more tissues. "I'll always be here for you."

She blew her nose on the soggy folds of a damp tissue with a loud snort, sparking an explosion of giggles. Their mirth lifted the gloomy air around them, alleviating the weight of the sordid information Emily had shared with her best friend. Both settled back into the bed, hands clutched together, feeling relieved to escape the emotional roller-coaster they had just ridden.

They heard a thud against the bedroom door.

"Millie, can I come in?" Ace called from the other side.

"Yes."

He threw open the door and paraded into her room ready to report the new close developments he had witnessed earlier between their parents, and the progressive appearance of gifts left under the

Christmas tree. He stopped short when he saw the girls laying together on Millie's bed.

"What are you guys doing?" he said, puzzled.

He shuffled closer to them. "I saw Mum and Dad hugging," he boasted.

"Really?" Millie and Emily exchanged glances. "Well, that's different!"

"Yeah, it's good," he said.

"Hmm... yeah," Millie said absently. "Now, you got to go Ace; I have to get ready okay?"

His little face dropped. "Well," he piped up, "Have you seen the new presents under the tree? Mum is putting them *all* out early this year!" His eyes were wide and bright again.

Millie reluctantly drew herself up from the bed. "I'll have a look later, okay."

"Okay," he moped.

Millie placed her hands on his shoulders and turned him around towards the bedroom door. "Off you go now."

He squirmed loose from her and screwed his face up at her. "Oh!" he said, turning to face the girls again and smiling, "Did you guys know that a cat has thirty-two muscles in each ear?"

Millie swung around for a pillow and threw it at him. The pillow smashed into his face. "Out!" she commanded.

He was gone before she drew her next breath.

Butterflies were alive and well in the pit of her stomach, and fluttered about with nervous excitement. Millie cast a sceptical eye over her reflection one more time as she heard his knock on the front door. *This will have to do!* she thought. Long, dark brown curls swept up and cascaded against the soft white fabric of her dress, and tumbled down to reach her lower back. Her face showcased charcoal-accentuated eyes and full gloss-pink lips. The new dress her mother had given her slipped over her slim curves and hugged the bronze glow of her skin. *Whatdoyouknow! Emily was right*, Millie thought with a twirl in front of the mirror. *The bangles work fabulously!* She was ready for her first date with Damon Richards.

The broadest smile Millie thought she had ever seen greeted her when her eyes first came to rest on him. A dozen long stemmed red roses, *which must have cost a fortune*, Millie speculated, were balanced in his outstretched hand. His eyes, creased with a soft smile, reminded her of a calm, dreamy blue lagoon. *Just the way I like them*, she thought.

"Hi." A murmur escaped through her trembling lips as she accepted the flowers. "Thank you, they're lovely." Millie focused on the roses resting in her arms in an effort to curb her shyness.

"Not as lovely as you, Millie." His voice was husky and deep, and a sweet melody on her ears as her name rolled deliciously over the curve of his tongue.

She lifted her skittish eyes to meet his, and recognised the gentleness there. This time, her smile was a little bolder. "I'll go put these in water," she stammered. "Be right back!"

She turned away and rushed down the hall to the kitchen where she rested against the bench-top while trying to soothe the butterflies. She then set about finding a suitable vessel for her flowers. She flung open cupboard doors in a frenzy to find her mother's vase.

"What are you looking for?" Her mother's voice sliced through her frustrated frenzy.

"Your vase," she said, still searching.

Lilly spotted the roses laying on the kitchen bench. "Oh, Millie!" she gushed. She sauntered casually to a cupboard high over the stove, and pulled out a vase. "They're beautiful."

Millie gave a relieved sigh when she saw the vase in her mother's hands. "Thanks Mum," she said.

"He must really like you," Lilly said. "Here." She smiled as she reached for the roses. "I'll take care of the flowers for you." She stretched her arms out, beckoning her for a hug.

Millie stepped into her mother's embrace and hastily wrapped her arms around her, giving her a quick, tight squeeze. Pulling back, Millie smiled up at her. "Gotta go!" she quipped, missing the guilt that tore at her mother's heart as she turned her back on her for the last time.

"Have fun Millie-pie. I love you."

Her mother's voice trailed after her, barely heard over the screeching creak of floor boards beneath running feet.

Damon caught Millie's swinging hand as they ambled down the street towards the bus stop. Clasping graceful nimble fingers between his thick ones, she was conscious of feeling safe and cherished as his fingers encircled and held her own. Millie enjoyed the way he collided his hand against hers, and she loved how it felt to entwine her fingers with his. She started to relax more as they walked. The more they talked and laughed, the more the fluttery, nervous noise inside her began to slide away. She shot him a sideways glance while he guided her across the street, weaving through the evening twilight traffic. The contour of his lean, masculine physique was clad snuggly in denim jeans, while a casual white Cold Chisel emblazoned T-shirt showed off his solid bronze-toned arms. Thick dark brown hair fell in wisps over his eyes, framing the square set of his jaw and lips that frequently broke out into the widest of smiles.

When they reached the bus stop, Damon slowly drew his hand away from hers and tentatively let it fall around the small of her waist, watching closely for her reaction. Her heart quickened at his intimate gesture, and she gazed at him with the softest of smiles playing in her eyes. Emerald eyes met his before tracking lower and lingering over the swell of his lush lips. Dreamy eyes examined every line and curve of his face without any curious onlookers gawking and whispering in jealous tones around them. Her eyes finally rested again on lips that seemed to have some kind of magnetic power over her. A warm shiver shook her. *I can't wait to feel those lips against mine again!* Millie mused. He gave her a cheeky grin, as if reading her mind. *Am I drooling?* she thought in sudden alarm.

Damon pulled her closer to him. "Do you like vampires, Millie?" he said, still grinning.

"I guess," she said, puzzled.

"Good," he said, as the bus came to a halt in front of them. Taking her hand, he led her through the automatic doors of the bus. "Because I'm taking you to see *The Lost Boys*."

Millie smiled as she looked out the window of the bus. She couldn't remember when she had last been into the city at night. The waters of the bay rocked languidly back and forth, illuminated with the glimmering reflection of lights. She soaked in every detail as they passed the bay, and closed her eyes to take a mental snapshot. *This, I shall paint one day*, she vowed, and prayed silently for canvas and paint this Christmas.

They ate at a small, cosy cafe before the movie started. Conversation between them was light and easy as they enjoyed their food and each other's company. *Turns out*, Millie thought, *Damon is really quite nice under the cocky confidence he portrays at school*. He was much more mature than other boys his age, and showed his maturity with his gentlemanly manner. His attitude towards her was sweet and thoughtful, and he made her feel special. She couldn't imagine any other place or person she'd rather be with in this moment.

Hmmm … well perhaps Michael Hutchence might give Damon a run for his money! she thought with private amusement while they munched down their burgers and hot chips.

"So, how does Amelia Anderson view the world?" Damon grinned when their dinner was demolished.

Her eyes widened. "Whoa! Deep question. I'm impressed," she smiled.

He watched her with intrigue.

"Well, I'm learning that not everything is always as it appears. That angels live among us. That the core of our essence is love … and maybe the world isn't as tangible as we think it is."

Damon traced a finger lightly over her hand. "Hmm … you're feeling pretty tangible to me!" he laughed. "Perhaps angels can be tangible too," he whispered.

"I'm no angel!" she said blushing. "I mean in the creative sense. What if we can deliberately create our lives with our thoughts?"

"Then I would create an abundant future with you by my side!" he said extravagantly. "You are unique, Millie." His expression became serious. "And you take my breath away."

Her blush deepened as she lowered her eyes. "How about you? How does Damon Richards view the world?"

He grinned. "That's easy. Absolutely breathtaking!"

She leaned forward to rest her chin in her cupped

hands. "That is easy!" she laughed. "Let's go see this movie."

He held her close throughout the movie, offering her popcorn, Fantails and slurps of an oversized Coke they shared periodically. She was full to the brim by the time they were on the bus heading back to Rockton.

Damon watched as Millie held her belly in mirth, cracking jokes about how she'd have to roll instead of walk home, "Or, you'll just have to carry me home, Damon" she declared. "But no biting!" Millie waved an index finger at him while the brows of her eyes furrowed in mockery.

"I'll bite when you tell me to bite." He smiled playfully. Damon's eyes grew serious as he looked at her. "Millie," he said as he gently touched her hand, "I enjoy your company very much."

She stopped giggling as she returned his gaze. Her heart did a flip and her mouth became dry as she bit down on her bottom lip and brought her free hand up to grasp the ends of her hair. *How does he do this to me!* she thought, mildly irritated with herself. Although secretly, she liked the effect he had on her.

"Me too." She could feel her cheeks blushing red. Then, avoiding his stare, she flicked her eyes towards the window and the passing traffic.

Damon cradled her face in his large hand and lightly turned her head to face him. "Come here," he said. Peering deep into her eyes with longing tenderness, he bent his face down to hers. Their eyes locked as their lips met in a gentle collision of anticipated passion. Her eyes closed in sync with his, and their lips united for a few moments with his hand still cupping her jaw. He lightly pushed his tongue through her parted lips, setting her heart racing as her body responded to him in ways she had never known existed. His tongue became hot and urgent against her own, and for a moment she thought she might have died and gone to heaven. She clasped her arms around his neck, entwining her fingers through the thick tousled curls of his hair. Their kiss deepened as lips and tongues explored unfamiliar territory with the flame of passion ablaze. The bus arrived at their stop too quickly, and with a last few desperate pecks, their lips reluctantly parted.

They alighted from the bus clutching one another's hands and walked quietly back to her house, savouring their intimacy and strolling slowly as to delay their arrival. Pausing beneath the dim glow of an old street light a few metres from Millie's home, they turned to one another to say their goodbyes.

"Thank you for a lovely first date, Damon." Millie took each of his hands in hers and swung them lightly together.

Damon returned her grin. "Since we got off the bus, I've been thinking."

"Oh yeah?"

A glint of mischief crossed his eyes. "I have to know, where on earth did you learn to kiss like that?"

"It belonged to thought first," she whispered, biting down on her bottom lip and feeling herself blush.

"It was a fine thought, Millie." His smile became

gentle. "I liked it a lot."

"Me too." *This is all I imagined!* she thought. Only it was better than anything she had previously conjured up in her private visualisations about Damon. She delighted in the knowledge she had of co-creating this deliciously intoxicating part of her life.

"Can we do that again sometime?"

"I'll put some thought into it!" she joked. Her eyes locked onto his as her laughter subsided. "I would like that."

"And so it is." He took her in his arms and kissed her again.

After their lips parted, they held each other for a while. Raising herself up on the toes of her white laced kitten heels, Millie wrapped her arms around his neck. Bodies moulded together and hearts beat against each other to the rhythm of their newfound love.

"And so it is," Millie whispered into his ear.

When Damon had finally left, Millie floated up the steps to the porch, oblivious to the darkness that fell over the house. She was drifting along the tail end of a brilliant white cloud that silently sailed through an azure sky. She let herself in through the front door and quietly made her way to her bedroom where she switched on the bedside lamp and let herself fall back on the bed in a breathless heady plunge. A smile played on her lips as she thought about her date with Damon and what had transpired between them. She replayed over and over the scene on the bus when they had kissed passionately, and his question to her before they had parted. Her heart soared when she luxuriated in thoughts of the desire in his eyes and the urgency of his tongue against hers. *This is the best night of my life!* she thought.

Millie propped herself up on her bed. Her face began to ache from smiling as she took her journal out of the top drawer of her bedside table and settled herself against her pillows. She was eager to record this highlight of her life before falling asleep. She opened her book, still smiling, and grabbed her pen to start writing. She was startled from her reverie when an envelope fell from between the pages of her journal. She picked it up and turned it over in her hands, recognising her mother's handwriting with the simple inscribed word on the cover of the paper – "Amelia". Her first thought was of the possible breach of privacy this envelope represented. Puzzlement replaced annoyance as it dawned on her how unusual it was for her mother to write a letter to her.

She ran her finger under the sealed lip of the envelope and pulled out a folded piece of white-lined paper. Unfolding the paper with her mother's handwriting scrawled over it, she was surprised when a small, old brass key on a chain of gold was revealed within its folds.

She held up the chain with the key, allowing it dangle in front of her. She watched the key swing for a moment, glinting gold as it reflected the light of the lamp beside her.

Brows furrowed at what this odd little key unlocked and why her mother would place it in an envelope with a letter for her. And as she watched the key, almost mesmerised by its haunting pendulum motion, a feeling of dread washed over her, extinguishing the joy she had cherished. Placing the key beside her near the lamp, Millie finished unfolding her mother's letter. Instinctively, she took a deep breath as she began to read the words written for her on an ordinary piece of notepad paper.

CHAPTER EIGHT

Dearest Millie,

The moment I laid eyes on you and held your tiny body in my arms, my heart was stolen. I became a mother for the first time, and for the first time I felt my life had purpose. I had a family of my own. You will understand one day, when you hold your first child, how it feels to really love another unconditionally and devote yourself to your family. And devote I did. When your brother came along, it was perfectly complete, and we were happy for many years. But nothing stays the same. Even when you feel joy surging through every part of you and know in your heart contentment, and wish you could feel this way forever, still it doesn't stay the same. Everything is always changing, Millie; wanted or unwanted, the change is relentless. I thought about your questions today, about how much power we have over our lives, and the power of thought. I realise now that all this time I have created my life by default so far, because I have attracted a situation I wish to participate in no longer. I hope you can find it in your heart to understand why I have made the decision to start over, and this time I will be much more conscious of my repeated thoughts and attempt to create my life how I desire. Thank you for bringing to my attention the power we all possess over our life experiences.

I cannot take you and Ace with me, Millie, as much as I would like to. Your father will surely look for us. You don't know him as I do; he will not stop and I cannot live my days looking over my shoulder in fear. He loves you and Ace very much, and I know he will make sure you two are cared for and happy.

I have enclosed a key with this letter. This key is very important, Millie. I want you to keep it somewhere safe and tell no-one of its existence. The information it unlocks will one day be paramount to you, and when you are older, I shall write to you and direct you to the keyhole it will turn.

Leaving you and Ace is not easy for me, but I must leave. When you finally come to know the information the key holds, my dear Millie, you will understand. Until then, know that I will never stop loving you and Ace, and some day we shall reunite again.

Remember my beautiful daughter, you are standing on the brink of the rest of your life. Create it as you want it and always listen to the whisper within you.

Albert Einstein said "Knowledge will get you from A to B, imagination will take you everywhere".

Use your imagination wisely my sweet Millie. You are special. And you can have anything you desire.

With Love,
Mum xxoo

The last words of the letter found difficulty penetrating through the numbing disbelief that engulfed her. Her breath quickened with her heart, as a dizzy sensation clogged her mind. Her body became heavy, pressing into the mattress beneath her like lead. *I can't move!* Millie panicked. She willed her legs to move, and they wiggled with a little twitch under her gaze. She ran her eyes to her pink polished toes. *Funny toes*, she thought. *Not like my mother's long slim skinny toes at all. Where did these toes come from?* She perused her toes, as if seeing them for the first time. They were shorter than her mother's, and the ends seemed to bulge out slightly like ugly little light bulbs. Tears toppled over her cheeks while she studied her toes. *Not like Mum's toes at all. And I will never see her toes again.* Millie's thoughts became frantic. "I hate these toes!" she yelled. *How can she leave us? How?* Confused, distorted thoughts battled with each other in her mind and all thoughts of toes vanished as she erupted into deep sobs. *How can this be happening now?* The best night of her life had also become her worst. She cried for the comforting arms of her mother. The familiar emptiness in her stomach drowned in a hollow void of abandonment. *She can't leave me!*

She leaped up from her bed and ran to her parents' room. She flicked the light switch and flung open her mother's wardrobe to inspect the contents. She paused frozen before the wardrobe as she realised that most of her mother's belongings were missing, confirming what was written in the letter. She collapsed onto the soft covers of her parents' bed, scrambling to the side her mother had favoured. It was the side of the bed she had found her beaten up and bleeding only weeks before. Millie slumped over and clutched at the hanging strands of her hair, trying to comprehend exactly what was happening and what this would mean for her and Ace. The noise in her mind overwhelmed her as she rocked forward, gripping and clawing at her head. She didn't hear the footsteps falling on the tired floorboards over the commotion in her mind, nor her father's entrance into his bedroom after a long night at work.

Glen paused in the doorway, awkwardly juggling a brilliant bouquet of lilac lilies and his dirty old work bag, when he saw his daughter sitting on the edge of the bed. She was still dressed in her new white dress that bore witness to the night's blossoming romance, now creased and crumbled around her as she bent doubled over.

"Hey Millie-pie," he said, frowning. "What's up?"

Startled, Millie jerked up in response to the deep voice of her father. A look of vague surprise was in her eyes as she looked upon the big man cramming the doorway.

Glen gasped when he caught a glimpse of his daughter's tear-stained face. He dropped the work bag and flowers as he hurried over to her. "Millie, what's wrong? Are you hurt?"

The vagueness in her eyes shifted as she regained her composure and glared back at him. He stopped in his tracks, stunned that she could give him such a look. She motioned towards the open wardrobe, bare of her mother's belongings. "Are you happy now?" she said, her voice an almost inaudible whisper.

He followed her gesture with clueless eyes towards the wardrobe. After a moment of staring blankly at the almost empty closet, it slowly began to dawn that his wife's belongings were missing. He looked back to Millie, struggling with the truth of his wife's absence. He was unable to speak as he stood dumbfounded and rooted to the floor while he looked at his daughter in a state of shock.

Millie's lips pursed and her eyes flared as she witnessed her father's understanding become complete. When he turned to look at her, she was livid with anger. "She's gone Dad. She's gone!" Her voice became shrill. "This is all your fault!"

"Millie," Glen retorted.

"No! Don't you dare try and explain this away with lies. I know it was you that beat her up and left her here for dead. My mother has abandoned us because of you! You! I hate you!" she screamed. "I hate you!"

Millie leaped up and lunged for him, beating small clenched fists vainly against his chest while she yelled at him with tears streaming down her cheeks.

Glen was unprepared for the double-whammy heaped upon him by Millie's outburst on top of his wife's departure. He clutched at the flying balled-up fists of his daughter, easily restraining the slim wrists while trying to soothe her anger with calm words of reassurance. Her knees buckled and she sprawled down, sobbing heavily while he guided her gently to the floor at his feet. He kneeled and stroked back long strands of the hair falling over her face. He watched, patiently waiting for her to catch her breath and regain her composure.

"I'm so sorry, Millie. I didn't know that she would leave us," he said, at a loss for anything more to say.

He scooped her up in his big arms and cradled her against his chest, just like he did when she was a baby, then carried her through the dark hallway to her room. As he lowered her onto her bed, she turned away from him and curled up in a ball.

He sighed heavily as he stood over her bed. "I love you, Millie-pie." He turned and quietly left, disappearing into the hall.

Back in his room, Glen slumped on his bed in front of the empty wardrobe that gaped in accusation at him. He sighed as he thought of Millie, so grief stricken and angry. *What have I done? She hates me.* He blinked through tears at the lilies dumped and forgotten on the floor. *I bought her flowers. I thought everything was going to be okay. How can she do this to us?* He stared at the flowers and the empty wardrobe, trying to process what had happened. He pulled himself up off the bed and strode up to the bouquet. He snatched up the flowers and brought them up to his nostrils. He breathed in deep, taking in the sweet scent of the lilies. Memories of Lilly instantly arose as he remembered her in their early days together. She was working long shifts at that rowdy bar at The Rocks in Sydney when they met. She was like a dainty lost angel, with a halo of gold swept up over her head and sad broken wings. He had watched her working that bar, warding off drunken, sleazy men with a hard-on for anything that moved with a certain weary grace. It was clear to him she didn't belong there. He recognised the naivety in her youthful azure eyes. She could be moulded into a perfect wife for him, and mother to his new baby girl. *After everything I've done for that bitch, she's betrayed me.* He steeled his heart against any feeling for her and vowed to get back at her for what she had done. Hatred rose in him like a black snake, filling him with its venom and rearing up ready to strike with deadly intent. He knew the ugly monster that lay dormant inside him could be tamed no more. He knew, as he embraced the inner beast, as it lingered over and settled itself firmly in his soul once again, that he would not stop until he satisfied its need for revenge.

"That fucking bitch!" He crushed and tore the lilies to shreds and forcefully threw them to the floor. His sudden outburst ended just as quickly as it had begun when every lily lay in a mangled mess over the bedroom floor. A cold calm permeated through him as he allowed the black serpent to spread its poison through him.

"Hello old friend," Glen said. A crooked grin spread across his face, and a yellow blaze flickered in his eyes.

"*Millie.*" A soft whisper beckoned her. "*Millie.*" Arms outstretched in welcome from a streaming light all around. The warm voice beckoned, soothing. She tried to move towards the light and the voice that dripped like smooth folds of honey on bread. She loved bread and honey. Wings appeared, slender and translucent, rising behind outstretched arms. The wings spread open and stretched out like an emerging butterfly, dazzling in their glistening colours.

"I am coming!" Millie cried out.

"Millie! Millie!" The voice rose in volume. "Millie, wake up!" The voice shattered her winged vision which now faded as she was forced into consciousness.

Millie lay still as the events of the night before filtered through to her mind. She rolled over as fresh tears formed, and turned her back to Ace who was on his knees beside the bed.

Ace gave her shoulder a little nudge. "Millie, you should see under the Christmas tree this morning. There's heaps of presents!" he said as he stood up and sat on the edge of the bed.

"That's great," she forced herself to say.

"Come see!" He nudged her again. "Come on!"

His eyes wandered to her bedside table where he

spotted the little key on the chain laying on top of the letter her mother had left behind for her. He leaned forward to pick up the key, curious. "What's this for?"

"What?" Back still turned, she had forgotten the letter and key was still in plain sight on her bedside table.

"This key?"

Millie flipped over in a flash and snatched it from her brother's grasp. "It's nothing," she said. She gathered up the letter and replaced them both inside the envelope.

"What's it for?" Ace persisted.

"I told you, it's nothing. Now, let me get up in privacy and I'll come out and see the presents okay," she said, clutching the envelope to her chest.

He scrunched up his face then shrugged. "Okay, but hurry up!" he said on his way out.

When Ace was out of sight, Millie rose out of the bed and tucked the envelope beneath the mattress. Satisfied with her choice of hiding place, she trudged over to the mirror and peered at her reflection. *Well, I'm glad I didn't look like this before my date last night*, she sighed. The skin around her eyes was puffed up and blotchy. *I look like a gold fish*, she thought. *I feel like a goldfish.* Goldfish were clueless little creatures. *I must be a goldfish! Didn't see this coming. How am I going to tell Ace?* She felt the sting of fresh tears rising again as she thought of her brother. She knew his innocent child's heart was about to break and the security of his world was about to be swept up from under him. And there was nothing she could do to protect him. "It's not fair!"

Millie cried out to her image. "It's not fair on him!"

Ace's voice cried out from the lounge room, breaking into her thoughts. "Millliieee! Hurry up!"

Wiping her damp face with a tissue, she called back. "Coming!" She dashed for the bathroom to bathe her face in some cold water before facing her brother beside the Christmas tree.

He was waiting with a smile, and bounced up to her as she entered the room. "Look at all these presents!" he said. He gestured under the tree with wide arms, his face animated in delight. "Look at this big one, Millie. It has your name on it." He kneeled before the gifts assembled under the tree, his sandy blond head bent and his eyes wide as he filtered through the presents.

Millie eyed the gifts under the tree. Their mother sure had gone to some trouble playing Santa Claus this year. *To compensate her abandoning us*, she speculated. *How could she do this to us at Christmas time?* Her eyes shifted to Ace who was now watching her closely, expecting her to share in his excitement like she normally would on any given Christmas. But this Christmas was different. This Christmas she could find no flicker of excitement to share with her brother. This Christmas they were motherless. *And he doesn't even know yet,* she pondered.

She forced a smile. "That's great Ace."

Millie sat down on a lounge chair and felt exhaustion consuming her. She could feel her body aching and her mind going around in weary circles. *Is this how I will feel forever?* Her eyes glazed over the

Christmas tree. It was all lit up with the vibrant, glowing colours of the glittering bulbs and twinkling tinsel. Christmas had always been her favourite time of year. She loved everything about Christmas, from the magical stories of Santa Claus to the delicious Christmas lunches. *I used to love Christmas … but no more.*

"Why has Mum put all these presents out now?" Ace quizzed.

Millie dragged her eyes from the tree over to where her brother sat. Big blue eyes stared at her with inquiry. She was unsure how to answer his question. "Ummm … I …," she started, her voice trailing. Her brain strained as she attempted to produce a suitable explanation. She shook her head from side to side and grasped a thick lock of hair, twisting. She felt her heart thumping, and her breath became short as the room started spinning.

Ace's brow knitted into a frown as he watched her. "What's wrong? Are you alright?"

He got to his feet and cautiously approached where she was sitting. He perched on the arm of the chair and awkwardly circled an arm around her trembling shoulders, patting her gently. His gentle act of compassion was enough for the floodgates to break. He pulled her close to him, and held her clumsily while she cried against his little chest, finding comfort in her baby brother's arms. Ace stroked her shoulder as soothingly as he could until her sobbing broke into gulps of broken air. He handed her a nearby box of tissues and looked to the floor uncertainly as she wiped away the tears that had swamped her face.

"I'm sorry, Ace," Millie said quietly, observing his attitude.

"It's okay," he replied.

They sat together on the lounge chair in silence for a few minutes. Both sets of eyes fell on the tree again, both minds a world apart. Hers was a whirlwind of tormented anguish, and his muddled somewhere between confusion and elation. After all, it *was* almost Christmas time.

Between the background jargon of the television and the emotional interlude the siblings had just shared, they had failed to hear the faint clanking of spatulas on pans emanating from the kitchen. The two looked at one another when the aroma of pancakes wafted through to them in the lounge room. Empty stomachs began to rumble and mouths started to water in anticipation at the prospect of maple syrup laden pancakes for breakfast.

"Yum!" Ace said, licking eager lips. Eyes flashed towards Millie. "Mum is up early cooking pancakes!" He bounced up from the oversized arm of the lounge chair and scurried out of the lounge room before Millie could respond.

She pulled herself up with much more effort than usually required, and followed her brother out to the kitchen. Unsure of what to expect of her father after her hysterical accusations and attack against him the night before, she approached the kitchen with light footsteps. She paused when she reached the doorway, hand buried firmly in a twist of long hair. Leaning against the wooden skirting for a moment, she watched Ace and her father, feeling her nerve ends jitter all over. They were pulling out plates, cutlery and maple syrup from the cupboards and placing the items on the table ready for their breakfast. The mood was light and joyous; smiles played on both lips as they gave one another affectionate jabs as they passed each other around the kitchen. Watching her father wisecracking with Ace irked her. *How could he be so happy after last night? After our mother had left because of him? How?* She stalked into the kitchen with a deliberate, indignant thud.

Glen looked towards Millie as she entered the kitchen and sat down at the table with the unmistakable air of displeasure. "Good morning, Amelia."

He didn't miss the stern look she flashed at him, nor her intent to ignore his greeting. He exhaled patiently and tilted his head as he smiled at her. "Pancakes sweetheart?" The smile grew broader.

She ignored her father with a flick of her head, and turned to Ace. "Pass the syrup please, Ace."

Ace passed her the maple syrup between stuffing gulps of pancakes and ice-cream into his mouth.

"Err … thanks," she said dryly.

She grimaced as she accepted the sticky bottle from him. Her father seemed pleased she was eating the breakfast he had prepared for them, and this bothered her even more. *If I wasn't so damn hungry!* Millie shot her father an angry sideways glance. He was still smiling her way. *Geez … what's with the dopey grin? That's gotta hurt.* She directed her attention back to her brother and noticed with a trace of surprise that he had stopped eating – a feat when it came to soaked-up maple ice-cream pancakes.

He was looking at their father thoughtfully. "Where's Mum?" Ace asked.

Millie bit down hard on her bottom lip as she dropped her cutlery to the plate below her. She also looked at her father, awaiting his reply with dread. Her heart began to thunder again.

Glen chewed on a mouthful of pancake, purposely savouring the tasteful sensations the sweet syrup evoked on his tongue. He took a long slurp of hot coffee, considering the question posed to him. He replaced the steaming hot mug on the table next to his pancakes and looked at Ace.

"Ace," Glen perched his chin on the end of his bent arm, grinning, "You're a big boy now. My big boy, right?"

Ace nodded and returned his father's grin.

"Last night, Millie and I discovered that your mother has left us," he announced in such a matter-a-fact fashion that he might as well have been talking about the weather. "It's okay though, because we don't really need her anymore, right?" He turned his gaze to Millie for reassurance. "Right Millie?"

Without waiting for her reply, he picked up his mug of coffee again and drank from the steaming liquid. "These pancakes sure are good!" he remarked to a spot suspended on the wall.

Watching her brother, Millie's eyes teared up as

the bombshell her father had so casually thrown at Ace fell on confused ears and an uncomprehending heart. His eyes glazed over in a stupefied haze as he tried to understand his father's statement, and small eyebrows knotted together in an attempt to recognise why his father would be so offhanded. He looked to Millie for clarification while their father continued his breakfast unperturbed.

"Millie, where's Mum?" he asked again with a sense of urgency. His lips started to tremble as he looked at his sister and saw the fresh tears falling from the corners of her eyes. "Where's Mum, Millie?"

Millie gulped back the hard lump that had wedged in her throat. "She's gone," she rasped.

Ace shot up abruptly, sending his chair hurling noisily to the floor behind him. "She wouldn't leave us!" he cried, and raced out of the kitchen towards his parents' room. "Mum!" he yelled on his way down the hallway. "Mum!" He flung open the door to the room and found it empty. He rambled out loud as he searched the room. "Where is she? She is supposed to be here, sleeping in. Mum!" He hastened back into the hallway. "Maybe she's in another room, or outside. Mum!" His voice rose in tone.

Millie chased after him as he came out into the hall. He pushed her aside and ran through all the rooms of the house while calling out. He flew past his father, who was still eating his breakfast at the kitchen table, and headed out the back door to the porch and backyard. The worn screen door slammed. "Mum! Mummy!" He crumbled down to the cobblestone steps of the porch, whimpering. "Mummy? Mummy, please." He clutched his face and wailed as his father's words began to ring true to him. "No, no, no!" he repeated between sobs. "Don't leave me, Mummy."

Millie came up behind him and captured his small quivering body in her arms. She rocked him back and forth while ignoring the pain gnawing through red-raw knees on the hard, rough cobblestones.

"I want my mummy," Ace sniffled.

"I know," she replied with a heart so trodden with grief, she could barely stand it. "Me too."

CHAPTER NINE

December 25, 1987

Dear Journal,

It has been exactly nineteen days since our mother has left us. And it has been the hardest nineteen days of my life. I try so hard to be strong and keep it together for Ace. I lay beside him every night until he is asleep, and then I go to bed and cry myself to sleep. Will she ever return to us? Does she miss us as much as we miss her? Life seems empty without her.

Today was the first Christmas I have ever spent without my Mum. Her absence was felt by me and Ace profoundly. We have never experienced such a depressingly dull Christmas – ever. Dad tried to make it as joyous as he could, and for him I actually think it was. He doesn't seem too fazed by our mother's elected disappearance at all. When I look him squarely in the eyes, which is rare because I seldom talk to him, a cold chill springs to life right at the top of my spine and runs all the way down. Although he is acting quite happy and joyous, he is different. And with every inch of my body, I know that it's not a good different.

Our mother has abandoned us because of our father. I know she is scared of him, because she mentioned as such in her letter. I have the most dreadful feeling she has every right to be frightened of Dad, even though she has left Ace and I here with him. I fear that choice has made no difference in my father's thinking.

She should have taken us with her. I don't want to be here with him. I hate him! I hate her for leaving me! I hate the world! I hate everything!

She brought me an easel and canvas set for Christmas, with the most beautiful paints and brushes. I can't imagine I shall ever use them now. I can't imagine ever picking up a pencil to even sketch now. Without her, life is meaningless. Sketching and painting is meaningless. I hate this place!

I miss my Mummy.

Millie xo

Lilly rolled over in the bed, kicking one slender leg out from the tangle of sheets in an effort to cool herself from the morning heat. She had forgotten the intense heat of Queensland summers. Squinting towards the digital alarm clock, she struggled for a moment to focus on the red LED digits displayed on the bedside stand. It was 8 o'clock on Christmas morning. She turned flat on her back, vaguely staring up at the ceiling of her parents' guest room. *The kids would be opening their gifts now*, she mused. A parade of tears trickled down to her ears. She wiped at her ears with the backs of her hands. She blindly clutched for the tissue box that she knew was on the bed beside her where she had left it the night before. She had made her way through a mass of tissues in the last nineteen days, and had come to think of them as her comforter. In fact, tissues were her new best friend. She consciously ensured there were always a handful of tissues within reach. Handkerchiefs would be of little use to her in this state.

Lilly could hear the faint sounds filtering through the window of her parents carrying out their summer morning ritual. Every morning they sat together at the table and chair set under the outdoor awning overlooking the canal that backed onto their backyard. They were chatting over morning coffee and the newspaper in hushed tones, enjoying the sunlight that managed to streak through and around the awning above them, and relishing the fresh breeze that gently sprung from the glistening waters of the canal. *The kids would love it here. Mum was right! I should have brought them with me!* Rolling on to her side, Lilly curled up into a rigid ball and squeezed her eyes shut tight as if the action could erase her misery. The past couple of weeks flashed through her mind like a wild wind as she relived the events leading her here – back home – running scared like a little lost girl. And worst of all, running away from her babies.

After she had buried the wooden box for Millie under the avocado tree, she had cleaned up and collected the remaining items she wished to bring with her, piling them together on the floor beside the front door. Aside from her clothes and necessities, Lilly had remembered to bring treasured school work the children had made for her when they were little. Tiny hand-dipped handprints with poems that had melted her heart, Mother's Day artwork and handmade birthday cards scrawled with love were all part of the collection she had kept safe and cherished over the years. And photographs! She took as many as she could – a few examples from every year of their lives so far.

After she was done collecting all she could think of to take with her, she did a last stroll around the house while memories of her babies growing throughout the years flooded back to her. Images, happy and sad, haunted her. *I will not miss this damned old house!* she thought, steeling her heart and pushing sentimental feelings away as she passed through the kitchen, glad to see the last of the beat-up old screen door. She paused as she made her way along the hallway to her son's room. She opened his bedroom door quietly, and tiptoed to his bed. She gazed down at him while he slept soundly, and reached out to brush back a lock of damp hair that had clumped against his forehead. "I love you," she whispered, bending to kiss his forehead.

As she drove away in her new car from her old life that night, Lilly blinked through a stream of tears that obscured the view of the road before her. However, she didn't dare stop once as she knew she would turn back. She knew one stop was all it would take for her to easily sweep back into her old wearisome life. She drove all night. She drove mile after mile, and hour after hour. She drove until the air changed from stiff urban stuffiness to soft country freshness. She drove until it was necessary for her to stop for more petrol, and by that time her resolve had strengthened and she knew in her heart there was no going back.

When she had arrived at her folks' doorstep some thirteen hours later, her legs almost buckled beneath her at the opening of the front door. A fine mix of devastation and relief washed through her at the sight of her parents. She fell exhausted physically and emotionally into the comforting arms of her mother.

The sudden arrival of their only daughter had sparked concern along with elation. They had longed to see her and their grandchildren for many years, but each attempt had been met with Glen's cold shoulder. Albert and Margaret Winston had to settle for brief phone calls every now and then, and a Christmas card each year. They had been happy to see their daughter again, and even happier when she had told them she had finally left Glen.

Lilly had sat them down and explained the whole story from what she knew of Samantha to the recent events of her life.

"It was the demon that lurks within him that acted so maliciously towards Samantha, the same demon that almost beat me to death."

They understood Glen was much more dangerous than they had first imagined, and both were concerned for the children left behind with him.

"But don't you see," Lilly pleaded. "He cannot

bear to be without his children … if that were to happen I know that demon will overcome him again." Tears stung her eyes. "He would hunt me down. He terrifies me!"

"There has to be a way to get them away from him," her mother proposed. "They can't be safe with him; he's too unpredictable."

Lilly had acknowledged her mother's uneasiness about the safety of her children, but assured her of Glen's love for them.

"He wouldn't ever harm them, Mum. Their presence with him will be my safety net, I just know it."

"If you're sure," Margaret said, frowning towards her husband.

"Perhaps we should call the police?" Albert said, resting a hand on his wife's shoulder. "Then we can collect the children and bring them here, a fresh start for all of you."

Lilly shook her head. "Are you not listening, Dad? We are not dealing with a sane man here! Even if he were to be charged and locked away for a while; eventually he will be set free, along with the demon that lives inside him. He would come for his children, and he would kill me!" she cried.

Her parents grudgingly accepted her word, and spent the following days comforting and consoling their overwrought daughter who had deteriorated into a shaky bundle of nerves.

Lilly lay in her bed, struggling with her thoughts. *I chose this!* she told herself. *This is how I wanted it. Now, get up, get strong and get on with your new life!* She decided to take a snippet of the recent conversation she had with Millie concerning the power of thought and direct her thoughts to better feeling subjects. *I can at least try!*

"Today, things get better," Lilly said out loud.

She sat up in her bed and resolved to enjoy the day with her parents as much as she could. She told herself she had done the right thing for her. She vowed to never look back again. Tomorrow was her planned meeting with an old school friend who would give her a golden passport to the new exciting life. Tomorrow, she would have that requested drink with Scott and collect her new identity. But as intoxicating as all her tomorrows promised, she couldn't help but feel the dangerous gnaw of her husband behind her. She knew it would take a while before she could relax enough to stop looking back over her shoulder.

Scott Perry gritted his teeth as he circled the club's parking lot. "Damned tourists!" he muttered under his breath. This time of year it was nearly impossible to find parking anywhere on the Gold Coast. He spotted a car backing out of a space over in the next laneway and pushed his foot down hard on the accelerator, almost sliding his 1985 Mazda RX7 as he glided around the corner to ensure he would claim the newly vacated space. Mission accomplished, he killed the roaring engine and tilted the rear-view mirror to reflect on his image. *Looking good!* he grinned to himself. He smoothed back light brown hair and his grin turned to a scowl as he spotted a silvery thread taunting him. Dark brown eyes narrowed as he plucked out the unwelcome strand. Turning his head from side to side towards the mirror, he inspected the rest of his hair for unruly greys. Finally satisfied, he grabbed a thick yellow envelope beside him then bounced out of the red sports car, strutting with a spring in his step towards the main doors of the club.

Elton John's *Rocket Man* danced around his lips in an out-of-tune hum. He and Lilly had spent many hours smoking weed and giggling together in the carpark at the beach to the background of the well-known tune. Her recent contact with him had come as a surprise. Somehow, he had always known she would come back into his life again. It was just a matter of when.

He picked up his pace as he approached the big glass doors. *Tonight is a good night,* he thought. Tonight, after fifteen long years, he would again meet the woman he had always wanted, his "Lilly Pad".

He had arrived early in the hope that his favourite little table in the back of the beer garden would be vacant for them. He ordered a scotch on the rocks then sauntered outside to the garden, throwing greetings to familiar faces along the way. He poised at the doors to the garden, scanning the outdoor area with interest. The lush foliage of the overhanging ferns and palms were scattered around oversized hand-carved wooden benches and tables, and appeared almost fluorescent bright green as the fading sun joined them in one last dance for the day. A local band scrambled about, setting up for an evening of entertainment in one corner of the garden. Varying groups of people laughed and chatted amid the festive fairy lights and tables lit in the glow of candles.

Scott's gaze fell on his favourite table opposite the band, snugged intimately in a corner of the outdoor area. It was empty. He broke into a broad grin as he wended his way to the table. *Tonight is a good night!* He sat down at the side of the table which offered the best view of the patio drinking area, and directed his gaze to the garden's entrance. He took a generous sip of his scotch, and waited for Lilly to arrive through the double glass doors.

He did not have to wait long. He recognised her immediately as she pushed through the heavy doors to the beer garden. He caught a sharp breath and held it unconsciously for a few moments as he realised that Lilly was there again in the flesh. He watched her glance over the bustling beer garden, searching for the old familiar face that was him. Her glance seemed edgy to him, even from his viewpoint at the furthest corner of the patio. *She is still a beauty*, he thought, drinking in every detail of her with dark brooding eyes, while she stood by the doors exploring the garden with wide-eyed blues. She was wearing a simple A-line black dress which cradled perky breasts that strained against thin material and skimmed over the rest of her slim body. Golden hair cascaded past narrow shoulders, and a simple pearl necklace encircled her slender neck. Scott smiled and waved to her, beckoning her over to him. She returned his smile, and kitten-heeled black sandals pivoted in his direction while heads turned as she walked over to him with an air of uncomplicated elegance.

Scott stood up as she neared the table. "Lilly Winston!"

"Scott Perry," Lilly smiled.

She spread out her arms for a hug and eyed her old friend curiously. After fifteen years, she was surprised to find the years had been kind to him; the deeply set lines that crinkled along his forehead and speared the edge of his eyes suited him. She realised, in that moment, just how much she had missed him. She allowed her eyes to sweep over him. Light brown locks licked his white polo shirt. Blue Levi's hugged firm buttocks and surfer legs, and coffee coloured eyes gleamed at her. *He has certainly matured into a charismatic, handsome man*, she mused.

She inhaled his soft masculine scent. "It's so good to see you," she said, her warm minty breath tickling his ear while they embraced.

Scott held her at arm's length, inspecting her thoroughly with mockery scrawled over his features. "Hmmm … let me see," he teased, as if in deep thought and making a spectacle out of his analyses. "Yep. You are still the same Lilly Pad," he said with a wink.

Lilly laughed. "I can see you're still the same jokester," she retorted, as they settled down at the table. "Maybe quite the romantic now?" She gestured around at the dim magic of the garden.

"Wasn't I always?" Scott's whole face beamed.

His heart swelled with the old familiar affection he had felt for her all those years ago. He felt like a huge Cheshire cat in her company, content and happy to be near her again. *Now, if only I get to lick the cream this time around.*

They fell effortlessly into the familiar, comfortable bond they had once shared. Theirs was a bittersweet reunion. After exchanging polite chit-chat, Lilly detailed her life with Glen. She revealed the deep-seated fears that Glen would come after her despite leaving the children with him. She confessed the desperate, heart-wrenching yearning eating at her and the overwhelming guilt for abandoning her children she had felt since arriving on the Coast.

Scott listened as her story unravelled before him. He found himself in unfamiliar territory as endearing and often shocking words fell from her mouth. He was unsure of the reawakened feelings she had evoked in him. All he wanted to do was to hold her close to him and whisper words of loving reassurance.

When she was finished, she dabbed her moist cheeks with tissues plucked from her small black handbag. Lilly felt grateful then for the intimacy the corner table offered them.

"Oh Lilly," Scott shook his head, "I wish I could have helped you … and your children," he said, stumbling over his words.

His face clouded over as his eyes darkened. "He's monstrous!"

They sat in silence as minutes passed, sipping on refreshing beverages and falling into the habitual warmth they had known together years before. There was no need for them to voice their strong reconnection, as they recognised it in each other's eyes. It felt like they had both come home.

Lilly couldn't help but smile, as she was the most contented she had been in a long time. She felt safe and it was a surprise that she hadn't counted on nor even contemplated.

"I couldn't thank you enough, Scott. This is just what I needed," she said.

"Thank you, Lilly." He picked up the thick yellow envelope. "Or should I say, 'Kate'." He handed her the package.

Lilly's expression darkened as she took the envelope from him with shaky hands. Her heart began to skip. This is why she had come here, and a huge piece to the puzzle of the future she had been planning and working towards for the past months. This was the security she needed. And yet, as she held the envelope in her hands, she willed her overwhelming apprehension to leave her. Long supple fingers gently pushed their way between hers, hiding her hand within his. His touch tamed the tremble of her fingers. It was a touch so simple, yet when she looked up into his smiling face, she knew it conveyed the depth of their renewed friendship.

"You're not alone." Scott's dark eyes glimmered with his affection for her.

Her weary blue eyes held his like a lost little girl

trapped in a womanly body.

She squeezed his fingers. "I really appreciate your help with this … but..." Her voice trailed off for a moment.

"But what?" He seized the break she allowed in her speech and searched her face for clues as to what she might be thinking.

She tore her eyes away.

"Lilly?" he urged.

She turned back to meet his gaze again and forced a smile. "Scott, I can't stay here. It's too risky to stay on the Gold Coast. If he did decide to look for me, this is the first place he'd come."

Scott's smile returned. "I know, Lilly. There is nothing for me here," he said, gesturing broadly at their surrounds.

Since he and Lilly had parted fifteen years ago, his had been a high-flying life on the Coast. He had tried the nine to five variety of jobs but found them too mundane. He just didn't understand how people lived in such a way. One balmy Queensland afternoon, after getting high in his car, he grabbed his beach towel and sprawled on the white sands of the beach. Dark, bloodshot eyes were concealed beneath sunglasses as he lay watching fluffs of clouds reshaping in the breeze that licked over the shores of the beach. A few moments later he pulled the little silver tin that housed his stash of weed out of the pocket of his Hawaiian printed board shorts. He eyed the dried out green buds and broke a little away for the joint he was about to roll. He decided then that he would grow copious quality weed and auction bulk amounts to the highest bidder in town.

He found an investor and started growing his first crop. The money started to roll in and life was good for the most part. He worked at producing the best quality weed in town, and damned if he wasn't proud of that fact at the time. Drugs, booze and blonde women with big tits were at his disposal. He noticed that he was selecting women who reminded him of Lilly. Some nights, he would lay with a woman in a hazy drug induced daze and whisper lovingly in his "Lilly's" ear. But no blonde could fill the tear in his heart.

After a decade passed with no sign or word from her, he decided it was about time to move on with his life and forget about his beautiful "Lilly Pad". Letting go of that vision was difficult, yet he realised it was necessary. He jettisoned his lucrative marijuana business and opened his own nightclub on Cavil Avenue. The club thrived, filling his bank account so much more than he could have ever possibly imagined. The blonde women faded and were replaced with a healthy new lust for elegant brunettes. Eventually, he tired of the constant parade of nameless, faceless women through his jaded bed and yearned to find someone special to share his life. A partner in crime, so to speak. But she had eluded him – until now. His "Lilly Pad" was back, and he was not about to let her walk away from him so easily this time around.

He watched and waited for her answer. He waited like a little worm on the end of a fishing line, dangling helplessly for its fate to be decided. He waited for what would next pass through those pink-glossed lips of hers.

She sat near to him, her brow knitted together in deliberation while she contemplated what he was trying to express to her. She was unaware that his happiness hinged on her response.

"What exactly are you saying, Scott?" she asked. The intensity of his stare began to unnerve her as she fidgeted with her fingers.

She isn't going to make this easy, Scott thought with a trace of irritation.

"Lilly, I am saying I want to come with you. Let me be the man you need in your life. I promise I will never hurt you like him; I will never let you down."

There! She made me say it out loud. My pledge. My vow to her. Does she even realise how much she means to me?

She gave him a genuine smile. "I need some time to think, Scott," Lilly announced as she rose to her feet. "It's just too early to bring anyone else into my life just now."

Scott nodded. "I understand," he reassured her with a smile. "The envelope contains everything you need to secure a bank account, passport and driver's licence. You'll find a birth certificate, a medical and social security cards; hell, there's even a school certificate. You have been imbedded into the system as Kate Hunter."

"Kate Hunter," she whispered. Her new name sounded foreign to her.

He walked with her to a little green Datsun in the club's parking lot, hugging her close before she got into her car and drove away. Scott continued to watch long after her little green car was out of sight. He wondered if her dissolve out of his life was to be a hasty one this time around. He chided himself, as he had done many times over their years apart, for not having the courage to tell her how he felt. He turned with a long sigh, and dawdled to his own car, hoping that he would see her before she disappeared again.

CHAPTER TEN

December 31, 1987

D ear Journal,
It has been almost three weeks since she's left.
Ace and I are slowly and grudgingly
beginning to accept that she's not coming back. I had
hoped she might have missed us so much that she just
had to come back or die. But I guess she doesn't miss
us at all. I guess the whisper inside her is much
stronger than her love for her children. And I guess
that I was wrong in thinking love is the only way.

I have been passing through the school holidays
a mere shadow of my former self. Waiting. Hoping.
Breaking. Feeling empty. But being strong for my 8-
year-old brother, who thinks he has done something
terribly wrong for our mother to leave us. Dad has
been trying to make a happy home for us. I am stuck
between hating him and needing him at the same time.
He works a lot though, and when he's home through
the days, I spend much of the time with Emily and
Damon. I have learned to cook dinners for us too,
which keeps my mind occupied somewhat. But
regardless of how much Dad tries, I am feeling lost and
emptier than ever, and I know Ace has been left with a
hole in his little heart for our mother too.

Dad says he has to go away for two to three nights to Queensland for work soon, which is odd because he has never before had to go away for work. He will be leaving me here to look after Ace. I am a little frightened at this prospect. And what if he doesn't come back? What if he leaves us too? What then? I'm scared.

It is New Year's Eve. Dad will be working a double shift, and since I can't leave Ace alone, I have decided to have Emily and Damon here. Thank God for friends. They help in keeping my spark dimly lit.

If I focus hard enough and love hard enough, 1988 might just bring our mother back.

Maybe.

Millie xo

Emily leisurely stretched coconut oiled limbs on a towel as she soaked up summer rays. She pointed her slender toes while rolling over to her stomach in a provocative motion, deliberately trying to catch the attention of a group of teenage boys strolling past them on the beach. The frilled waistline of her yellow bikini fluffed about slightly as she turned over, settling just below her tight rounded little bottom. The boys gawked at her glistening slender body, nudging each other and wolf-whistling in approval. She swivelled around to gaze at them with eyes obscured beneath dark sunglasses, and flashed them a broad smile. She glanced over at Millie who lay beside her in a pink and lime green bikini. Emily rolled her eyes when she noticed her friend's disinterest. Walkman headphones were clamped on Millie's head, blasting INXS tunes into ears oblivious to their admirers who had set up camp near them.

Emily nudged her. "Millie," she said, trying to break through her world of beating drums, guitars and the voice of Michael Hutchence. She nudged her again. "Millie." She reached for an earphone and pulled it away from Millie's ear. "Hey! Pussy-cat! Are you there?"

Millie pressed the stop button on the Walkman and shot Emily a puzzled look. "Pussy-cat?" she asked, raising darkly defined eyebrows.

Emily grinned, much like a Pussy-cat with mischief on her mind. "Yeah, and I like it. It suits you." She discreetly gestured towards the group of four boys who were now bare chested and grooming themselves with oil. "Check it out," she instructed.

Millie propped up onto her elbows and gazed at the boys. "And?" she asked, before dropping to her back again and reaching for the headphones.

Emily snatched them out of her reach. "Uh-ah," she whined. "Talk to me, Millie! I'm kind of getting bored over here."

She pulled two cigarettes from the pack laying between them. "The one with the wild brown curls is cute," she said, delicately placing the two cigarettes between her lips and lighting both. "What do *you* think?"

Millie glanced back at the boys. "Yeah, I guess,"

she said, trying to sound interested for her. *I would've been interested in this conversation a few weeks ago*, she thought, sighing and taking the smoking cigarette from Emily. She inhaled deeply, allowing the smoke to drift into her lungs, then exhaled, studying the smoke ring appear in front of her.

Emily eyed her friend sharply. "Tsk! You are not much help."

"Sorry," Millie muttered.

Emily noticed the downhearted expression written all over Millie's face. She knew Millie was feeling lost and down since her mother had left, and she tried so hard to be supportive for her, only her way was trying to pry smiles and lift spirits. She had never been good at the mushy, nurturing side of things.

She placed her hand on Millie's arm. "No, I'm sorry Pussy-cat." Emily's face softened. "I know you're going through stuff. I just miss your happy face lately."

Millie put her hand over Emily's and gave her a little squeeze. "Thanks Em," she said, showing a hint of a smile. "Can I tell you something?"

"Sure," Emily nodded.

Millie paused and looked over at her friend with hesitation. Would Emily understand what she wanted to share with her?

"Every now and then I have these visions. I see beautiful angel wings," she began, taking a deep breath. "It feels as though someone or something is attempting to communicate with me. When they come, my whole body comes up with goose bumps and tingles … it's a nice feeling." She paused, trying to judge Emily's reaction.

Emily nodded for her to continue.

"I think the messages are about love and … well, connecting to some sort of higher all-knowing part of me. A part of myself that has a creative force using my thoughts. I kinda think it might be *the* creative source or angels reaching out to me … or even maybe a part of me that *is* the creator." She twirled her fingers in the ends of her long hair. "You probably think I'm nuts. It's stupid isn't it?"

Emily sat beside her in silence, gazing out to the aquamarine waters of the bay. She thought of all the years her mother had forced her to attend Sunday morning church. It was something they had never practised when her father was alive. Some of those verses still stuck in her head, and she was keen to encourage Millie to keep talking.

She turned towards Millie. "First of all, I don't think you're nuts. I would have picked up on that by now! Second of all, when you mentioned the part where a part of you *is* the creator, it reminded me of a verse in the Bible when Jesus says, "It is not written in your law, 'I said, 'You are gods?' John 10:34." Emily paused as she meditated on another verse related to Millie's announcement. Matthew 19:26 – "Jesus also told us, 'With God all things are possible'." Emily smiled as she looked at Millie again. "Something to think about maybe?"

Millie considered Emily's quotes from the Bible, a book she had never picked up, nor contemplated doing. "I might be right then. A part of me *is* the creator? That would explain the power of thought then," she murmured as her body began to tingle.

Emily shrugged. "Interpret it as you want Pussy-cat, but I guess we all carry a part of the creator, whatever we choose to call him ... or her," she said, grinning. "I think it's pretty cool you have those visions though. Wish I saw angel wings."

Out of the corner of her eye she saw the wild-haired boy strutting in their direction. "Oh, look out!" She nudged Millie with a soft squeal before he was standing in front of them.

Light blue board shorts hugged strong upper legs and toned buttocks. A dimpled bright-brown eyed smile beamed down at them. He carried a can of soda in one hand and a lit cigarette in the other. "Hi," the boy said to Emily, his voice wavering.

Emily returned the smile with an enticing tongue flicked over moistened cherry lips. "Hi, I'm Emily, and this is Millie." Emily gestured towards her friend.

He acknowledged Millie with a brief "Hi" and turned his attention back to Emily. "I'm Ryan. Want to go for a swim?"

Emily felt conflicted as she glanced at Millie. She really wanted to go for a swim with Ryan – *He's a hunk* – but felt obligated to stay with Millie and finish their conversation.

Millie noticed how Emily looked at the boy, and smiled. "Go," she said, holding up her Walkman, "I have to get back to my date with Michael anyway."

She welcomed some time alone to ponder the verses Emily had just brought to her attention. And how they might fit with all she was trying to figure out.

Emily was on her feet in a flash. "Let's go!" They walked off towards the water together, already engaged in excited chatter. She turned briefly to glance at Millie. "See you soon Pussy-cat," Emily called over her shoulder.

Millie watched Emily and Ryan as they started running to the waiting waves. She noted his physique. *Hmmm ... strong masculine calves. He's got to be at least eighteen.* She could hear Emily's laughter while he took her hand, leading her in deeper before they plunged into the salty spray of the waves. Millie took in the view of the beach as she sipped on a bottle of spring water. Her attention was captured by an elderly man at the water's edge. The long brown slacks that covered his dry old skin were pulled up to wobbly knees. He was standing in the water, digging his feet into soggy sand while the wavelets of the bay collided gently with his legs. Greying eyes that had seen a lifetime, peered out as he stood enjoying the simple feeling the sand and salty air gave him. Millie watched mesmerised as he closed his eyes and tilted his head, catching the warmth of the sun. He smiled to himself as though finding a secret. As she watched him, she realised the significance of the simple smile he offered the world. He was displaying the same appreciation as she had of her garden and the emerging life within it. Her eyes now saw the beach afresh. She saw the clean white sand, and she breathed in the cool salty breeze that blew across the tiny hairs of her skin. She saw the wide reach of the bay, and the heads that stood sentinel to the ocean behind. She too closed her eyes, feeling and absorbing her environment with all her senses, and for the first time since her mother had left, she began to feel appreciation. And for a fleeting moment, she was at one with the man standing in the shallows, and all her surroundings. *I am ok*, she thought purposely. Then she lay back down on her towel to enter another oasis – INXS.

Emily broke away from Ryan's strong playful grasp in a fit of giggles. She hastened towards one of the two floating pontoons enclosed within the shark nets of the bay. Long swimming strokes propelled her to the deserted pontoon. She glanced over her shoulder between strokes, squealing to see him hot on her tail. Thanks to years of swimming lessons, Emily was confident in the water, but he was a strong swimmer too, with longer arms and stronger legs. She swam faster, determined to reach the pontoon before him. She looked ahead almost out of breath as the pontoon came within an arm's reach. She reached out in triumph to the chrome railings that edged the green slimy stairs that led to the pontoon platform. As she began to haul herself out of the water, she felt a strong arm encircle her waist and tug her forcibly back into the deep. She held her breath as she went under in a flurry of bubbles. She kicked against him, trying to escape his unyielding grip. He guided her up to the surface to catch a breath, both of them laughing as they splashed in the water.

With his wild hair stuck wet against his face, Ryan pulled her closer and looked into her eyes. "You're very pretty," he said.

Emily returned his gaze with a hint of challenge. "And you're very cute." She circled her arms around his neck, tangling small fingers among wet curls.

Ryan paddled them to the steps of the pontoon, holding her petite body close to him. Balancing himself on the edge of the bottom step for support, he positioned her on him in a straddle and brought eager salt-tarnished lips down on hers. Emily's lips obliged at once, parting as lips and tongues came in contact. His hand groped at her bikini top as he flicked the yellow swimsuit material easily up over her breasts, revealing provocative deep pink nipples that swelled in invitation to his mouth. He took one large nipple between his lips and began to suckle gently, flicking the erect flesh with his tongue. Her blonde head fell back as she pushed her breast into his mouth. A low blissful moan escaped her lips, encouraging his desire. He reached down and slid her bikini panties to the side. The pulsating hardness of his groin entered the soft, sweet well between her legs before she realised what was happening. He grasped her hips firmly and thrust into her with grunting force. Pink nipples danced in front of his face while he tried to catch one between eager lips. Moments later, he peaked in a groaning climax, burying brown curls between her nipples as he lost himself in the intensity of the moment which was over as quickly as it had begun. Emily pushed off him, allowing herself to sink beneath the water while she adjusted her bikini in a mixed state of bewilderment. *What the hell was that?* Her mind raced as she fought conflicting feelings of loss of control and the alluring power she had over him. She broke the surface as she came up for air, and pushed past him to haul herself up to sit and rest on the pontoon.

Ryan came up to sit beside her. He was grinning broadly at the score. "Hey, that was fun!" he remarked boyishly.

She didn't respond as her eyes stayed fixed ahead of her. "Are you okay, Emily?" He pried, a little uncertain now.

Emily turned to him coolly. "Of course!" She flashed him a curt smile. "It *was* fun." She stood up, stretching her slim pale body, now turning a little crimson in the sun. "I have to get back."

"Wait! When can I see you again?" he said.

Emily shrugged. "My friend's house tonight if you'd like?" she said, feeling more certain of what had just transpired between them.

Besides her stepfather taking liberties, she had never been so intimate with a boy before. *I guess Drew was right after all*, Emily thought of her stepfather's disturbing whispers. This *is* what boys wanted and expected of her. But she was learning fast that she could use her alluring qualities to her advantage.

"Great!" Ryan replied, as she glided away from him and dived back in the water.

Emily swivelled in the water to look back at him. "You ain't seen nothing yet! My loving will make you weak at the knees!" she shouted with a grin, and swam off in long strokes back to the shore.

"It already has," Ryan said to himself.

Ace looked up at his big sister from his pillow. "Millie, since tomorrow will be the beginning of a new year, do you think Mum will come back to us?" Benny Boy was clutched in one arm and optimism filled his young eyes.

Millie stopped fussing around with his bedding, readying herself to lay beside him as was their bedtime ritual since their mother had left. She recognised the innocent faith held in those eyes watching her with expectation. She smiled and wished with all her heart that she could make his world right again. "I hope so," she said, climbing into the bed beside him. She leaned towards him and planted a big kiss on one rosy cheek. "Love you."

Little arms encircled her neck and held on tight for a moment. Ace buried his face in her long tresses and took a deep breath, closing his eyes briefly as he did so. He breathed in the comforting scent that reminded him of the mother he missed so much. He pulled away gently to bask in the love of his sister's tender smile, realising with an unwavering sense that she would never abandon him as his mother had. Millie had filled the role his mother had left open. She was his rock – his safe place.

"Did you know that seeing somebody else smile actually makes you happier, Millie?"

"Well, when I see you smile it makes me feel better, so I guess that makes sense," she said. "Now, time for sleep," she commanded, as she settled her head on the pillow next to him.

"Your smile makes me happy too," he mumbled before turning his back and drifting off into a restless sleep.

Millie stared up at the ceiling. She was tired of feeling so serious lately. She was tired of hate and sorrow. And she was tired of this old crappy house. But she felt powerless to do anything about it. She remembered Emily's quote from the Bible earlier that day – "With God all things are possible". She thought about her visions and the overwhelming feeling of love that accompanied them. Her mind wandered over the fleeting feelings of her own presence within her and previous thoughts of tapping into another higher dimension. *Perhaps that is where I can find this God?* she pondered. *Inside of me. And if inside of me I find love, then God must be love.* Millie silently left the bed where Ace slept, deciding that tonight she would not be Miss Serious, Miss Sorrow, nor Miss Miserable. Tonight she would be Miss Fun. After all, it *was* New Year's Eve. And Emily made for a perfect accomplice.

Walk Like an Egyptian played in the background while Emily carefully measured out a shot of Southern Comfort for each of them. Feet twitched to the beat as she added ice and topped each tumbler with Coca-

Cola. Mission accomplished, she let loose, allowing the music to penetrate through her and guide her feet and body. Millie laughed and swayed along with her. A warm tingly feeling made its way through Millie's body. It was the first time that she had tried alcohol, and so far, she was enjoying the lightheaded numbing feeling it provided. *Plus,* she thought giggling to herself, *I think I could do anything now!* All her concerns, fears and worry were slipping away, leaving in their place laughter, happiness and love. Damon arrived all spruced up in blue Levi's, a black T-shirt and his dreamy eyes.

"Come hither my blue lagoon," Millie beckoned as he strode through the lounge room door.

"On my way my exotic queen," Damon played along.

Tonight she wore blue bubble-gum jeans that clung around her bottom like a glove, and he could just make out the shade of the lacy lilac bra that cupped already generous breasts under her simple white singlet top. Oversized gold hoop earrings hung from her ears, and black charcoal underlined her green eyes. Damon wrapped her in his arms, squeezing her tightly. He looked down at her blushed, smiling face upturned towards him and planted a full kiss on her welcoming lips. He knew he was hooked, but the line he dangled on felt good and it was a line he thought he could dangle on forever.

Ryan knocked on the door a few minutes later, and the foursome continued drinking and dancing, chatting and laughing together as 1988 made its inevitable entrance at the stroke of midnight. A chorus of "Happy New Year" broke out at the strike of midnight, and hugs and kisses were exchanged in abundance.

Even in her alcoholic haze, Millie soon realised that her father was due home from his late shift. She began to hustle them out and remove any evidence of alcohol consumption that may be in sight. She even managed a hasty, albeit tender goodbye with Damon before pushing him out the front door, lopsided grin and all.

The house descended into quiet darkness as Millie scooted to her bedroom with a tall glass of water, recalling Emily's advice that she would need it through the night. She flung herself into bed, feeling victorious. *I did it!* she thought as she lay in the dark. *Dad will never know.* She had enjoyed her night of Miss Fun, and as she lay there, she vowed she would do it again soon. *Life was meant to be fun, right?*

Millie was drifting into the comforting world of sleep when a familiar shrill voice broke through the murkiness of her heavy head. She sat up in a daze as her ears listened for the sound that had disturbed her slumber.

"Leave me alone!" a voice rang out.

Millie knew for certain that the voice belonged to Emily.

She leaped out of bed and skipped over to the window of her bedroom that overlooked the street. There, under the scant light of the street post stood Emily and Ryan. Ryan had his arm around Emily's narrow waist and she clung to him as if for her life. Millie moved the curtains aside and peered around the dim deserted street some more. *Who could she have been yelling at?* her thoughts muddled. Then she spotted a figure in the dark shadows in front of Emily's house. She squinted in an effort to make out the ghostly figure lurking near the trees of the pavement. The dark figure approached Emily and Ryan, and Millie could just discern that the tall lanky figure belonged to Drew Kent, Emily's stepfather. He was saying something inaudible to Emily as he approached her. As he came under the glow of the street light, her view of him became clearer. She could plainly see the short mousy coloured hair that slicked his scalp and the horn-rimmed glasses that perched on a long pointed nose. *He even looks creepy!* she thought as her body stiffened and her heart began to thump in growing alarm.

"Just go away!" Emily yelled at him as he continued to move closer to them. She was visibly weeping now, her body trembling against Ryan's protective chest.

Millie switched on her lamp and scampered to find her sandals. She raced out the front door with a loud thudding bang as the porch screen door slammed behind her. The noise startled them all, as they turned and saw Millie running on wobbly legs towards Emily and Ryan. She positioned herself in front of them like a lioness ready to fight to the death for her young cubs. Regarding the man half hidden in the darkened street, Millie was unafraid.

Drew chortled at the sight of Millie's small,

gallantly placed frame blocking his step-daughter. Millie thought that the noise that came from his lips was the most ugly, sinister laugh that had ever touched her ears. But she wasn't scared. And as she stood there, listening to his cackle ringing through yellowed chipped teeth, she felt nothing but contempt for him. She was no longer sweet little Millie. She was no longer somebody things just happened to. For a fleeting moment something twisted through her like an evil black serpent, flickering with golden flames in the backs of her green murky eyes. Millie felt she had more control than she otherwise would have.

She began to laugh, bending in a snicker then building up to a chortle that even surprised her, before dying away just as suddenly. "What?" Millie said with an unnerving calm. "You don't think I know who you are?"

The gape of Drew's mouth closed as he glared at Millie. He then decided to ignore her and brought his attention back to Emily. "Get inside now young lady!"

Taking her cue from Millie, Emily lifted her chin in defiance. "You're not my father!"

Drew took another step towards them. The street light cast inky shadows over the hollows of his features, creating an eerie image.

"That's right. You're not her father are you? No, you are a sick, perverted horrible man that likes to hurt girls," Millie said. "You are nothing!" she hissed.

Drew grasped at Millie's shoulders with long bony fingers and began to shake her. "Who do you think you are little girl? How dare you speak to me like that!" he snarled.

He brought his hand up to his face as the headlights of a car shone on him, and the car screeched to an abrupt halt alongside them.

The car door flew open, revealing Glen's towering bulk as he sprinted towards them with breath seething. He didn't utter a word as he tore the lanky, mousy man from Millie and smashed a huge balled-up fist into the man's long thin nose, sending his glasses flying while he buckled down to land on knobbly knees. Drew held his busted bleeding nose as he grimaced from the pain that shot through his shattered nasal bones. He whimpered at Glen's feet in shock.

Glen glowered down at him. "If you ever touch my daughter again I'll kill you," he said. He turned to Millie. "Let's go inside," he said while taking her arm.

"Wait!" Millie shook free of her father's hand and leaned over Drew. "And if you ever touch Emily again, I'll have my father kill you. And no amount of praying to your God will save you," she hissed in his ear.

Millie took her father's hand proudly to begin their short walk to the house. She glanced back at Emily, who was watching them with mouth agape. "Bye Em," Millie called out, giving her a small wave.

Emily smiled back as she mouthed the words *"Thank you"*.

CHAPTER ELEVEN

January 29, 1988

Dear Journal,

I have been thinking about my recent outbursts of rage. So unlike anything I have ever experienced before. I mean, sure, I would sometimes become angry, but this is different. It feels like a black cloud hovers over me, then I am consumed in a dark haze of rage. And yet somehow, the rage is one of controlled, calculated coldness. I know this might sound strange … perhaps even wrong of me, but when this cloud consumes me, it feels powerful. What a contrast to the powerful feelings of love I experience with my visions! I guess the more concentrated my feelings become either way, the more they are magnified. And to be honest with you, dear journal – the cold rage cloud does not provoke lovely feelings within me. It's even kind of frightening actually. Where does it come from?

If we hold the power to use thought and imagination to determine our future, then how can we avoid unwanted situations or circumstances? However much we imagine a life wanted, we cannot exercise our personal imaginations to control others. There must be more to this idea than I know. And I will some day figure it out!

I would much prefer concentrating on feelings that make me feel good. And I'm getting there. I just need to forget about Mum a little more. That last goodbye. I brushed her off because I had wanted to get to my date. It has been haunting me every day. If only I took the time to really hug her close and tell her how much I loved her, she may have stayed. If only.

My father has left us now for a couple of days or so. He left super early this morning. I am worried about being alone here without him. Especially with creepy Drew Kent next door. What if he realises I am here alone with Ace? Luckily I have a super cool boyfriend who will be keeping us company. I think I need to stop worrying! It provides me with nothing, and just ruins today. Emily's stepfather hasn't touched her inappropriately since the night my father punched him. I guess there is a silver lining to that rainbow after all.

So, enough with the "if onlys" and the "what ifs." I will try my hardest to fill my thoughts with only things of loveliness – like my little brother's beautiful smiling face. It feels better that way anyway!

Millie xo

Since Lilly had left, Glen found himself going through his days just as he had done so before her chosen withdrawal from their family. Only now, every waking hour was spiked with a skilfully concealed feeling of hatred fuelled by his fierce need for vengeance. Today however, there was nobody around to hide the vicious feelings that tormented him. Today, he was all alone with his thoughts of revenge. A smile, contorted with the hell in which he found himself captive, crossed over thick lips as he gunned his brown Holden Premiere at high speed along the Pacific Highway. He hoped that this night his black snake of malice would find what he sought – his wife. *Oh, and when I get my hands on her!* Images of his large hands gripping her slender neck paraded through his mind. *No longer will she be beautiful! No wife of mine leaves me! She, of all people, should know that!* He drove on fixed in resolve, and took as few stops as possible. He turned up the volume to the radio, and as ACDC's *T.N.T* blasted from the speakers, he thought about the weeks that had passed since his wife's departure.

One of the first things he had done was to pay a visit to the pharmacy where Lilly had worked. He had strolled in there one morning to hear the gasps of the women who worked the floor as they were startled at his unexpected appearance. The first person he approached was a dowdy, pretzel-stick brunette stationed behind the counter.

"Hi Jenny," he said after reading the name tag pinned on her white dress.

It was clear to him his presence had almost turned the woman into a nervous wreck, which baffled him. After all, he had never met her before this moment, so he didn't understand her stilted reaction. And why was she fidgeting anxiously with her wiry glasses? He silently cursed Rockton where everybody knew everybody else's business. This woman had been of no help to him at all, so he asked politely to speak with the manager.

Harry Cornell, who had been hovering behind the medicine shelves beyond the counter listening, reluctantly came out at Glen's request. He took Glen aside to a corner of the pharmacy, and disclosed to Glen that Lilly had told him two weeks prior to her desertion that she would be resigning.

"I thought you knew," he mumbled awkwardly, as Glen explained how Lilly had left him and their children.

Harry had handed him an envelope addressed to Lilly which had arrived at the pharmacy some weeks after she had left. The envelope displayed the Rockton Bank logo and it was marked in bold as "Confidential". Glen took the envelope with rising interest.

He wondered why Lilly would be receiving a letter from the bank. He managed all their household finances; she had no personal business with banking as far as he was aware. Glen saw this as a breakthrough in his search for her, and when he was out on the street, wasted no time tearing open the envelope to find a letter containing information about repayments for a small personal loan of $10,000 in the name of Lilly Anderson.

"Fucking bitch!" he swore, taking out his rage on a garbage bin that was near to him on the street curb. The bin broadcast a resounding boom as his boot connected with the thin metal. The garbage bin was anchored to a post, but the impact of his kick put a large dent in it. Passers-by quivered at the sudden noise resonating through the air around them. In a reflex, he smoothed back his hair in a moment of embarrassment as he regained his composure, and strolled off down the street as if he didn't have a care in the world. He knew she would run back to those nosey parents of hers, and now he knew how she found the funds to get to them.

His next move was obvious, but he didn't want to give the game away just yet. He avoided calling his in-laws as he wanted her to feel safe. Let her think she's home free. Let her think he wouldn't come for her. She did leave some insurance behind for her safety. She left her children, and he knew her enough to know that she was not the kind of mother who could let her children go that easily, and he was well aware why she left them with him. What he didn't know was how she thought that it would be enough to stop him from coming after her. She was the only person that truly had an inkling of what he was capable of. She could never outsmart him. He would allow a few weeks to pass before making his next move.

He pressed his foot down on the accelerator as he drove down the highway as he recalled an article he had read in the previous day's newspaper. The article detailed recent arson attacks to the homes of residents on Queensland's Gold Coast. Some of the arson attacks had resulted in a number of fatalities. It hadn't taken long for the beginnings of a plan to pierce through his mind after reading about the attacks. The corners of his mouth twisted again. He was eager to arrive on the Gold Coast, just as she had done the month before him, to land on Albert and Margaret Winston's front door. Only this time, their visitor would be of the unwelcome variety.

The Winstons were just about ready to leave for their weekly Friday bistro dinner and pokies night. After giving their white toy poodle fresh water and her nightly feed, and checking their house was secured, Albert sat in the lounge room waiting for his wife. He was always waiting on his Margaret, and after 45 years of marriage, he found his waiting on her still managed to irk him most of the time. He picked up a crossword and a pen lying on the solid mahogany coffee table in front of him but he could not concentrate on solving it. His empty stomach growled.

"Oh for God's sake!" Albert slammed the pen and paper back on the table. "Margaret! Are you ready yet?"

Margaret flowed into the lounge room on cue with an air of daintiness, dressed from head to toe in a recently purchased linen apple-green three-quarter pants outfit. The gold stitched fabric glided around her figure as she strode into the room. She had chosen to accessorise her new clothing with a long golden rope that fell in a thick twist around her neck, and matching gold rope around her wrists, with metallic gold sandals on her feet to complete her look. Short hair wisped about her head in loose waves, showcasing the golden hooped earrings that hung from her ears.

She looked up at Albert with a broad smile. "Yes, I'm ready," she said.

She soothed his impatience by performing a dramatic pirouette in front of him. "You like?" Her pencilled-in eyebrows were raised in amusement awaiting his response.

Albert eyed his wife with a pout. "You look like a piece of fruit," he said as he lifted himself up off the lounge chair to leave.

"Hmmm … does that mean you'd like to eat me?" she teased.

Albert made an unintelligible grunt before allowing his annoyance to dissolve into a smile. He could never stay angry with her for too long. "You look lovely dear. Now let's get going, shall we?" He reached out to take her hand in his when they heard the ringing of the doorbell.

They looked to one another other equally puzzled. It was odd for somebody to visit on a Friday evening. Albert envisioned his bistro dinner being delayed yet again. "Now who could that be?" he growled.

Margaret shrugged in response as she turned towards the heavy oak entrance and made her way to open the door. The doorbell rang again as she reached the threshold, alerting their poodle which bustled to the door with chirpy little barks. Margaret picked up the dog. "Shhhhh, Cha-Cha." She stroked her tightly curled head. "It's okay." Margaret smiled down at her pooch as she swung the door open.

Her smile froze on her painted face for an instant before fading as her eyes saw who was on the other side of the door.

Glen smiled his best fake smile. "Mum!" he said. He opened his arms and enveloped her in his embrace before she could regain her composure.

Margaret pulled herself away from his grasp. "Hello Glen. We weren't expecting you," she said with a scowl.

Albert dawdled up behind his wife to investigate, and stopped short when he caught a glimpse of his estranged son-in-law. It was all he could do to conceal the shock of Glen's untimely and unwanted appearance. He greeted him in a flat tone, ignoring the hand extended out to him.

"What do you want, Glen?" he said.

"Oh, that's an easy one, Albie. I want my wife," he said with a smile.

Their skittish glances confirmed his suspicions that Lilly had been there.

Albert gently pushed his wife out of the way. He was dwarfed next to Glen, but he wasn't about to be intimidated nor would he give him the information he wanted. "She's not here. You've wasted your time coming here."

Glen looked around them as if in deep thought. "No, I disagree Albie; time spent seeking the love of my life is time well spent." His smile began to waver as annoyance crept in. "May I come in for a minute?"

"Actually, no. We were just on our way out for

Friday night dinner and pokies." Albert turned to his wife. "Get your purse dear." They pushed past Glen, securing the door behind them, and ushered themselves into the car.

Glen followed them to the car and tapped on the passenger side window. He watched Albert nod to his wife, at which she then partly unwound her window.

"Please," Glen begged, "The children … they just want their mother back in their lives. It's unfair on them …" His voice trailed off.

He could see Margaret's expression soften as he spoke of her grandchildren. "They need their mother," Glen said, even managing to bring tears to his downcast eyes. "I just want to talk to her. That's all." He shook his head in mock sorrow.

Margaret hesitated. "Are the children okay?"

"Enough!" Albert cut in. "You should have thought of that before you beat our daughter and left her for dead. Now, if you'll excuse us, we are leaving, and please don't come back here again or I'll call the police."

Before Glen could respond, Albert put the car into gear and sped out of the driveway. Glen watched the car disappear out of sight before walking back to his car. *They think they are better than me! Pompous old fart.* His mind churned as he sat in his car mulling over his next move. And as thoughts formed in his mind, a part of him cried out, urging him to go home to his children. *No! I can't let it go!* He fought the light. *I have to get back at her. She must be punished.* The serpent had the upper hand, holding rein over his thoughts like a vice. A plan materialised before him – almost as if he were watching a movie. He knew what he had to do.

The V8 engine roared to life as he accelerated down the street. He felt empowered by the darkness. He felt control. And the more he fed the dark serpent, the more black thoughts came to mind, gaining momentum until the shadow of a light that urged him to good, dissolved in the murky cloud that clogged his mind.

He roared towards his hotel feeling lightheaded. And when darkness fell upon Broadbeach later that night, Glen would send the serpent free to perform its duty. *But first I need to release some of this powerful energy*, he thought as he felt a stirring in his groin.

Glen squinted over at the digital clock near the bed. It was midnight. A peroxide-blonde woman lay asleep beside him. Her breathing came in short, shallow breaths against his shoulder. He had picked her up earlier at a bar down on Cavil Avenue. He had bought her three drinks and she had been ready to fall over with her legs wide open. *Easy pickings, but weren't they all?* he thought as he gave her a sharp nudge. She had given him what he had desired. But now he desired for her to get out of his hotel bed. He nudged her harder and slowly she began to stir. Big silicone-stuffed breasts moved obediently with her and stood up to attention as she turned over. False eye lashes blinked, bewildered. He eyed off the large nipples that peaked and strained towards the ceiling. Fake or not, Glen loved big tits and he had missed out on them for so many years, having to make do with Lilly's little B cups. He reached out and caressed the boobs, circling them with his large hands as they bulged out beneath them. *I can't even get my hands around them*, he thought, chuckling to himself. Then he pinched her swollen nipples hard.

"Get the fuck out now, sweetheart," he said.

The woman squawked and retreated. Talon lavished fingers cupped her breasts and cursed him, but stopped short when she caught the flicker in his eyes. She threw him a cautious glance when she had dressed herself. She studied him for a moment before hastily scooping up her belongings and leaving without another word.

Glen rolled out of bed and headed for the shower. After scrubbing himself clean, he strode naked through the cheap hotel room. He felt like a different man, and indeed had taken on a different alias when checking into the hotel. This was the kind of hotel that rented rooms by the hour, hosting a constant parade of hookers with their clients, as well as junkies and general street garbage. The management weren't too concerned with the comers and goers that visited their rooms daily. This suited Glen as he wanted to keep a low profile while he was in town. He dressed and threw the rest of his belongings in his overnight bag, and left unnoticed.

A steamy January night gushed prickly air through his unwound car windows as he drove with care back to the Winstons' home in Broadbeach. He pulled up at their street intersection in an effort to minimise any association with them at this early hour. He slipped quietly out of the car and light-footed it to their sleeping home, carrying with him a large black backpack strapped to his back. The Winston backyard was in darkness against the glistening reflection of the moon on still canal waters. He jimmied the flimsy lock to the internal laundry window, releasing the rusty latch with ease. He climbed through with as much stealth as the bulk of his body would allow, careful not to topple over laundry detergents that sat along the sill of the window. His joggers landed on the tiled floor with barely a sound, only to be met with the snarling growl of Cha-cha who was guarding the house. Without a single thought, Glen collected the surprised poodle with gloved hands and swiftly twisted her neck until the dainty bones snapped between sturdy fingers. He tossed her limp body aside like a rag doll, and crept through the house, searching for signs of Lilly's presence and where she might have gone. He slinked past the sleeping couple's room and paused at the doorway for a moment, watching as they lay snoring and spluttering like the overbearing pigs he considered them to be. *So, where's your police to save you now, Albert?*

He continued down the dim hall to the guest room where he knew she would have slept. Finding the guest room neat and tidy, with not a trace of her recent presence, he laid on the bed *she* would have occupied. Burying his head in the plumped up pillow, he inhaled the faint musky scent familiar to him that lingered on the soft fabric. *She hasn't been long gone from here*, he noted. He stalked back through the house again, and was making his way back to the laundry where he had left the jerry can of fuel that he had brought along with him, when a scrawled-on notepad caught his attention. It was on the bench in the spacious kitchen, and simply read "Lilly – Kate Hunter" in blue ink. He tore off the page with the inscription and shoved it into the folds of his cargos. He then retrieved the jerry can and sprinkled the house with petrol, paying particular attention to the hall that led to the bedrooms.

When he was done, he stood silently at the front entrance, breathing in strong petrol fumes that seemed to feed his frenzy. He reached into a deep pocket of his pants and took out a box of matches. He casually struck a match and threw it onto the carpet. He watched for a moment as the beginnings of a fire took hold of the carpet and the furniture littered about the house. Flames licked at the curtains and the walls, mirroring the golds flickering in his eyes. He smiled as the black serpent rejoiced at the blaze that quickly took hold.

He left the Winstons' home for the last time, taking long strides along the shadows of the street, satisfied at the completion of his task. He had taken from Lilly the only security she had left – her beloved parents.

CHAPTER TWELVE

Emily chatted over the commotion of the school bus, her face animated as she enthused about the new love in her life – Ryan Green. "Oh, and Millie, the slightest touch sends shivers down my spine … and he's sooooo passionate!" Her voice lowered as she concealed her mouth with her hand. "And horny!" she added with a cheeky glint in her eyes.

Somewhat preoccupied with a weekend before her without her father home, Emily's last secretive words erupted through Millie's mind with a jolt.

"Horny?" she asked, her face screwing up in surprise. "You mean, you guys do it? Already?"

"Shhhh," Emily chastised.

She looked around the bus self-consciously. She couldn't afford this piece of vital information to get around *this* school. She would do anything to avoid the name she had throughout her time at her old school. Her mother's words ran through her mind – *Loose lips sink ships!* It was one of her mother's favourite annoying sayings.

She nodded back at Millie. "Yes!" she said, and leaned closer. "Don't you tell a soul. You're my best friend and I trust you."

"So, who's the pussy cat now, huh?" Millie

taunted. "Meow," she purred playfully.

Emily narrowed her eyes at her friend. "Millie!" she cautioned.

Millie laughed as the bus grinded to a stop in front of the big iron gates of the school. "You know your secret is safe with me."

"I know," Emily said. She cherished her bond with Millie, and she was slowly adjusting to a little bit of the mushy stuff too. "Let's go to school, shall we Pussy-cat?" Emily grabbed her backpack and slung it over her shoulder.

They joined the hustling traffic of teenagers spewing out of the bus and filing through the iron gates for their second day back at school after the long summer break. Not much had changed over the holidays. The cool kids were still cool. There was the surfer-cum-skater crowd, nicknamed "The Skegs". They liked the beach and surfing, and adorned themselves with labels that represented as much. Millie was sometimes uncertain how many of them actually owned a surfboard, much less used one. The ethnic kids stuck together within their own nationalities, and were also known throughout the school as "Wogs", an Australian slang word used to label immigrants. These groups usually comprised people from southern Europe and the Middle East. There were also the geeks and general misfits. Millie was never quite sure where she belonged in this student social scene. She never felt cool enough to be cool and not geeky enough to be a geek. She just seemed to drift along, like a leaf blowing aimlessly in the wind, spending much of her spare school time to herself.

However, something had changed over the holidays for her. This year she had two firm friendships on her side within these iron gates, and outside of them. The fact that the most sought after boy at school was now securely off limits hadn't gone unnoticed among the female students, but didn't seem to add to her popularity status, *But hey, who cares about the opinion of others anyway?* Millie thought, as she caught the death stares from the "cool" girls hovering at the gates. She thought it quite amusing that people behaved in this manner; you can't force others to behave in a certain way as much as you cannot control the weather. *Freewill is a beautiful tool bestowed upon us,* she figured, and she was certain freewill was the ultimate gift of creation available to us, because it gave people the freedom to choose their desires, and in doing so, alter the course of their lives. She knew it all tied in with the power of thought; she just needed to uncover the right way to use this power.

She threw a taunting grin at the group of snide girls, who she knew would watch her enviously as she walked into Damon's waiting arms. Soon, any thoughts of those girls vanished as his arms fell around her waist and she revelled in his closeness.

She smiled up at him. "Hi," she murmured. *Oh, he smells so good!*

"Hi beautiful," Damon said. He lifted her chin and they kissed.

His arm lingered around Millie's waist as they trailed through the gates and into the school grounds.

He had no further need for the ego-driven persona he had previously embellished; he let go of the false self that he had allowed to occupy his thoughts. Thoughts about social status, coolness or impressing girls no longer plagued his mind. He found he was just happy to be just as he was. Damon knew the change in him had something to do with Millie. The energy she radiated felt beautiful. And the more time he spent with her, the more he felt at ease with himself. There was something special about Millie that he had pondered over for hours at a time. He could not entirely grasp what it was, so he decided to let it slide and just enjoy her company.

He gazed down at her as they walked arm in arm. "So, did your dad leave for the weekend?" Damon asked as Millie listened to Emily's bubbly chatter.

"Yeah, he left super early."

"Right. So Emily will keep you company tonight." He cast a glance at Emily who nodded her agreement. "Then I thought tomorrow, you, me and Ace could spend the day at the beach, and I could stay with you guys for the night," he tested. "On the couch, of course," he added, feeling a little apprehensive that Millie might get the wrong idea.

"Of course!" Millie laughed. "You guys have it all figured out, huh?"

She felt her heart go out to Damon and Emily. "I love you guys," she blurted.

The next morning Millie scampered to answer the knock on the old wooden front door.

"Beautiful day for the beach I'd say!" Damon greeted her with a towel flung over one shoulder and a broad smile.

"Huh?" She stared absently around him.

Her attention was drawn to the hazy rainbow of colours that surrounded him in a drifting cloud.

"Earth to Millie. Hello?" Damon laughed with a wave of his hands.

"Oh!" She said, blushing. "I'm sorry, come in."

The colours caught her off guard, as she hadn't recognised such a phenomenon since she witnessed the colours surrounding her mother the day she had given her the white dress. However, Damon's rainbow aura extended out at least a metre all around him in a glistening cloud that left her awestruck. At the same time, she also felt something inside her lift and linger in tingling waves at the top of her skull. It was almost as if the spirit inside her elevated to a higher level. The sensation stayed with her deliciously, hovering with her and through her as she led Damon into the kitchen where Ace sat eating breakfast.

"Hi Damon," Ace chirped between mouthfuls of Weetbix topped with brown sugar.

Ace liked Millie's boyfriend, and he had been looking forward to spending the day with him since Millie had told him of their plans. It was the first thing he had really looked forward to since his mother had left him. Ace secretly hoped that when they grew up, Millie would marry Damon, and then he would have a real brother, just like he had always dreamed. They would do cool things together like go fishing and share stories and jokes. And it would be just the two of them most of the time because Millie would be too busy looking after their kids. *Kids. Oh, that would make me an uncle!* Eyebrows knitted as he mulled over that quite unsettling thought. *Okay, I'm not too sure about the kid thing yet, but Millie would be busy doing something ... surely!*

Damon greeted Ace with a smile and rustled his hair as he took a seat beside him.

"Damon? Do you like kangaroos?" Ace asked.

Damon grinned. "Sure. Why's that Ace?"

"That's good, because did you know that there are twice as many kangaroos in 'stralya than people?" Ace said. He was sure the knowledge he gained from an old book he had found lying about the house would impress Damon as much as it had impressed his parents and Millie.

Damon's eyebrows lifted. "Really? I didn't know that. It is a good thing that I like kangaroos then."

Satisfied he had impressed his mark as planned, Ace wasted no more time demolishing the rest of his breakfast and racking his brain for the next odd fact he could share with Damon. Plus, he was eager to get down to the beach so he could show off his excellent swimming skills acquired after the many hours of swimming lessons his mother had forced him to take.

It was early afternoon and the three of them were sitting on the edge of the jetty relishing their ice-creams. There was a broad mix of people on the jetty. Fishermen balanced lines at the end of the timber wharf, patiently waiting to hook a big catch. Some even ventured precariously down the slime ridden steps that trailed into the deep at the wharf's edge, in order to gain a better advantage over the other amateur fishermen littering the jetty. As far as Millie could gather, those that chose to undertake the slippery steps never seemed to reel in anything better or bigger than those who decided on the safer option. Along the lengthy boardwalk of the jetty, children were hurling themselves off the jetty and squealing as they dived into the water, only to haul themselves up the knotted rope ladder to jump in again. A group of teenage boys were holding a bombing competition. Millie, Damon and Ace watched them with amusement, neglecting fast-melting ice-creams that dripped down their arms and into their laps. They laughed as the boys teased one another while they judged each other's efforts with a critical eye.

They had bought fish and chips for lunch from the fish shop across the road, and devoured the paper-wrapped hot food in a hurried battle against the local seagulls that scavenged the beach with beady red eyes. After lunch, they sat around and relaxed under the shade of the boardwalk, gulping down fizzy Coca-Cola and listening to Ace recall cheesy jokes between well practised burps. Millie chastised her brother for not minding his manners, but he and Damon laughed while Ace told them he could burp the alphabet for her if she so wished. Her look of warning was enough to deter him from performing this feat.

Later, Millie and Damon caught a brief time alone while Ace swam out to the pontoons with some kids he knew from school. And while Damon lathered Millie's back with coconut suntan oil, she spoke of Emily's sleepover the night before. She told Damon of the new golden sweetheart necklace Emily had proudly shown off to her, and how much Emily loved the delicate gold twisted chain with a small 24 carat diamond encrusted heart at its end.

Damon's hand paused longingly over the small of her back, while his eyes admired her small rounded buttocks.

"You sound worried?" he asked.

Millie admitted then that when she had questioned Emily about her new necklace, she had told her it was a gift from Drew. An early birthday present, he had told her. Emily had also told Millie that Drew had apologised to her, saying that he had never meant to hurt her. This latest information unsettled Millie. There was something she didn't trust about Drew, and she was suspicious of his sudden act of generosity. She wondered what he might want. *Would he hurt her friend again?*

Damon followed the impression of the line that ran down between her bottom and toned thighs and allowed his hand to linger lightly on her buttocks, and then he followed with his hand towards her thighs, pausing just under her bottom cheek for the slightest moment.

All thoughts of Emily and her stepfather disintegrated from her mind at the intimate touch of Damon's hands, as they concentrated around her buttocks and thighs. She closed her eyes, focusing on the exquisite shivers his light touch had provoked in her. Swivelling around to face him, she gazed into his eyes. To her his eyes were a lagoon that she wanted to explore and become lost in forever, surrounded by its clear comforting waters. She grinned at him through white rimmed sunglasses, and pulled him gently down with a hand that clasped the back of his neck, guiding him towards welcoming lips. His lips met hers willingly. He tempted her with his sensuous tongue, kissing her with a trace of the deep urges he felt for her. She felt him grow hard against the side of her thigh, and it was enough for her to pull away from his embrace as a sudden feeling of shyness overwhelmed her. Millie wasn't anywhere near ready to go that far yet, and luckily Damon understood that. He told her he would wait for her forever if he had to, laughing it off as a joke. But she knew he meant it.

Then, he brought his mouth down next to her ear and whispered the words she wanted to hear. "I love you, Millie."

Her spirit soared as she basked in the purity of the love shining through Damon for her. And she basked knowing that this moment shared between them was not unlike the love that created all things. A fleeting thought crossed her mind. *If thought and imagination shape our experiences, what would happen if every person in the world would deliberately focus their thoughts on love and nothing else?* Surely such a phenomena would cause a shift in mass consciousness. Surely this could change the world. *Where do these thoughts come from?* she wondered.

Millie shifted her attention back to Damon, rewarding his heartfelt revelation with a lovesick grin.

"I feel the same, Damon," she said.

"You deliberately created this moment, didn't you?" he teased.

She laughed and tangled her fingers in a wisp of hair. "Oh yes I did … so, you better watch out mister!" Her eyes dropped to the grainy sand under them. "I love you too, Damon."

"And so it is." His smile was tender.

"And so it is," she repeated.

They sat in silence side by side on their beach towels, clasping hands and watching Ace swim. There was no need for words; all was perfect in their world for those precious moments.

"Now remember," Millie reminded her brother, "Not a word to dad about Damon staying on the couch, okay."

"Okay, I promise," he reassured her.

Ace didn't understand why she had to keep

reminding him of the same thing over and over. He rolled his eyes as he walked off to the lounge room to see what the television offered at 2pm on a Sunday.

Millie hit the play button on the red rectangular boom box she kept in the corner of her room. She plopped back on her bed while Cyndi Lauper's *True Colours* filtered through the stuffy air of the room. She felt like she was skimming lazily on a golden leaf along the calm waters of a blue lagoon filled with love and harmony. They were peaceful waters that to her felt deliciously endless. His close embrace still lingered on her skin, and she could still feel his lips as they pressed against hers and idled over her slender neck, kissing their way up to gently suck on the lobes of her ear. The intimate look in his eyes remained fresh in her mind. She wrapped her arms around her chest and shivered in pleasure. *How sweet is life when love visits!* she thought.

She heard a car door out front slam shut with a robust bang, interrupting her daydream. Peering out the window, Millie caught a glimpse of her father as he walked briskly through the opened short gate of the front yard and bounded up the stairs to the porch.

The front door slammed behind him. "Where are my beautiful children?" Glen bellowed.

He dropped his overnight bag in the hall as Ace ran into his arms. A broad nose buried into his son's hair as he held him. He shut his eyes as he breathed in the unique smell that was Ace.

Millie lingered at the door to her bedroom. "Hi Dad." She threw him a brief smile and bit down on her bottom lip. *He'd kill me if he knew Damon stayed overnight!* She silently prayed he wouldn't see right through her.

He released Ace and walked over to her. *Oh my goodness he knows!* she cried out to herself while her heart flipped. He enfolded her in a bear hug. "Hi Millie-pie. I missed you guys."

"We missed you too, Daddy" Millie said, feeling relieved. "How did it go?"

Glen shrugged, and leaned down to fetch his overnight bag. "It went well, I think," he said with a smile. "Boy, am I tired after that drive. How about pizza tonight?"

"Yay! Yes, please!" Ace shouted.

"It's settled then. I'll go clean up." Glen retrieved his overnighter and made for his bedroom.

Millie watched her father head down the hallway, mesmerised and unsettled as she noted the dark cloud that accompanied him. She felt a sudden sense of dread creep through her, clogging up her senses with a perception of fright. It was so overpowering that she felt nauseous. She followed her father to his room, curiosity beckoning her forward. And as she neared the half closed door, she could hear the sound of faint sobbing from within the room. She snuck up and peered through the crack in the door. She saw him doubled over and hunched on the floorboards in a corner of the room. Large hands cradled his head and pulled at his hair while he rocked back and forth on his heels, whimpering between sobs.

"No more! No more!" he chanted over and over.

Millie noiselessly entered the room, concerned. "Dad? What's wrong?" She stood feeling helpless as his despair seeped into her as though it was her own.

Glen glanced up startled, his eyes luminous with tears. He looked up at her as if in bewilderment. She noticed the shift in his eyes as they slowly adjusted and focused on her in the dim light.

"Samantha?" he murmured.

Millie moved a step closer. "Dad?" *Who is Samantha?* Her face scrunched up in confusion. She had never heard that name spoken between these walls before; the only Samantha she knew featured on a TV program called *Bewitched* – One of her favourite TV shows.

He continued to stare at her as if seeing a ghost. "Samantha," he whispered.

"Dad, you're scaring me?" Her eyes widened.

He threw up his big hands in front of his eyes and he began to whimper and sob again as he lowered his head into bent knees. "I'm sorry, Samantha. I loved you … I'm sorry!" he repeated in an almost inaudible babble.

The mass of his huge body crunched up in the corner of the room appeared odd and awkward to Millie. She had never seen him with such loss of control. Her heart beat faster as she struggled with what assailed her father. She rushed to his side and cradled his head in her arms, holding him close.

"It's okay, Dad," she said, rocking with him. "It's okay."

Tears began to sting her eyes and trail their way

down her cheeks. She trembled at the thought of what might have happened to her father.

Millie's soothing words penetrated him like a bittersweet blade slicing through the dark serpent that gripped at his chest. His eyes were like ash after a fire as they settled on Millie, and her presence began to dawn on him.

"Millie?" The slightest sound fell from dry thick lips.

He felt the dense coils of the serpent loosen, and he crumbled against Millie. His body began to shake as he wept and gulped for air. He could barely breathe as feelings of the hell that had captured him began to ease. He held onto Millie's hands with desperation. For a few moments, the child became the carer, the rock on which he leaned and greedily fed. He quenched the fire with the grace that emanated from her. For a few moments Glen was free of the hatred that drove him to carry out unthinkable acts of violence. And for those moments, the light within him ignited again in rejoicing. His thirst for this light drained his daughter as she weakened and slumped down in exhaustion.

CHAPTER THIRTEEN

April 6, 1988

D ear Journal,
I realised today that it has been five months
since my mother has left us. It's funny how
life just keeps going on. Each day had ended and each
night has begun, over and over for five whole months
without her bright blues eyes to watch over us, laugh
with us, cuddle with us. She has missed Ace's 9th
birthday, my first real kiss and the unwelcome arrival
of my period (I think Dad had a hard time dealing with
that one!). The point is, as much as we are missing out
on her, she is missing out on a whole lot more of us.
Precious moments that can never be plucked out of a
memory tree to relive and experience again. It has
dawned on me more and more the consequences of her
choice to leave us behind, and I find myself wondering
at times how easy that decision had come to her. Did
she look forward to a life without us? Is she missing us
at all? Her silence is deafening, and if I allow myself to
dwell upon it for too long at a time, her silence
becomes unbearable. I have read her departing letter
over a thousand and one times, just to be sure I haven't
missed anything important. Perhaps she meant to let
me know when she'd return to us.

Back in February, not long after my Dad went to Queensland and returned acting all kooky and calling me Samantha – Still don't know what that was all about! The police came to our door looking for our mother. They had come to tell her that her parents had perished in an arson attack. Apparently there had been a series of these attacks on the Gold Coast, and later I saw on the news that the police had caught the people responsible for the fires. My father had been horrified. He explained to the police that she had left us and assumed she would have gone to stay with her parents.

My poor grandparents. I wish I had got the chance to know them better.

This leaves me baffled about two things: First of all, why wouldn't my father tell me and Ace that our mother probably went to her parents? Maybe we could have tracked her down and convinced her to come home. And second, if my mother didn't go to her parents, then where did she go?

Between all of these thoughts, indeed life keeps going. And between all these thoughts, I often wonder who it is that observes the thoughts that seem to flow through my mind in a never-ending stream. Now, that is a thought to behold.

Millie xo

Balancing a crystal glass tumbler in each hand, Scott negotiated his short journey from the hull of his 37 foot

Espirit Cruiser up to the top deck. The few scotch on the rocks he had already consumed, combined with the gentle rocking of the yacht, made for tricky navigation. Nevertheless, it was worth it when he reached the top of the stairs and caught a glimpse of her profile against the setting sun.

She looked like his sweetest dream come true. There were times over the last few months when Scott had to pinch himself to convince himself it was real. And whether he was sleeping or awake, she remained at his side. He took a deep breath of sea air, and watched her with admiration. She was propped back on her elbows, lounging on the gloss white fibreglass of the bow. Her hair, swept back off her face, glowed gold in the light of the sunset. She wore a white lacy bikini bottom that barely concealed her small rounded buttocks. The bikini bottom was paired with a simple white cotton tank top over her breasts. Her petite face was frozen in the moment as she gazed into a horizon where a cerulean ocean met the smouldering orange of the sun. Scott drank in the image of her, which was more intoxicating than any beverage to wet his lips.

They had been anchored off a group of islands in the Whitsundays, off the northern Queensland coast, for the last two days after following the tropical coastal waters of the reef south towards Rockhampton, their next port of call. He would need to stock up on supplies tomorrow at Airlie Beach and stay on the mainland for a night or two in the best hotel in town. There, Lilly would be able to try calling her folks again, a task that was becoming near impossible since their time at sea. Lilly had tried contacting them several times when on land with no success. Scott knew she was worried, but he kept her on the water for longer periods at a time as he did not want the outside world bursting through their intimate bubble of paradise. He could sail away with his lovely Lilly Pad, keeping her all to himself forever.

However, Lilly had other plans, and her eyes betrayed her feelings as they reflected her restlessness and remorse while she gazed out at the calm glistening waters, as if they held the answers she wanted. Thoughts of her family were suspended when Scott leaned in behind her and handed her a tall tumbler filled with an icy cocktail concoction of tequila and grenadine mixed with freshly squeezed orange juice. She hung her head back and gave him a smile as he handed her the drink. She took it with eager lips, savouring the alcohol's numbing warmth.

Scott feathered little kisses on her neck, and tickled her ear lobe with his tongue.

"A sunrise for your sunset, madam," he said.

He skimmed his eyes over her nipples straining beneath the flimsy fabric of her top. Lifting her chin with gentle fingers, he brought his lips down to hers. His kiss was deep, and she responded accordingly, allowing his yearning tongue to explore her mouth, returning his urge with her own passion. Freshly made drinks were forgotten as the arousal gained intensity. Her hands clutched his hair and gripped it with feverish fingers. She dared not let him go as desire raced through her. She felt the rock hard shaft concealed within black board shorts press against her thigh, and moaned while thoughts of him filling her roamed through her senses as a delicate, titillating tingle of pleasure seized between her legs. Legs parted willingly to the fingers that found their way down between her thighs. Lilly groaned when she felt the sensually exquisite touch they imparted on her, in her, as experienced hands lifted her to new heights. Golden hair draped the deck as he lowered her down and entered her. Hips lifted from the floor of the deck to feel as much of him inside her as she could, as she grinded against him while their bodies united in a raw embrace. She rocked with him, holding his body close as he thrust himself deep within her. Lilly wrapped her legs around his flexing buttocks and gripped him as she neared orgasm. She groaned in ecstasy at her climax, while he joined her in an erotic eruption. A growl of fulfilment passed his lips as he buried his head against the nape of her neck, panting and bathed in the glistening sweat of their love-making. He cradled her head in his arms while they recovered from their moment of ecstasy. They held onto each other, breathless as the yacht rocked with the tide and a red blaze was all that was left on the western horizon.

Lilly looked up at him with sleepy eyes. A smile crossed her lips as she stretched, still buzzing with pleasure. She pulled herself up, reached for her drink and handed Scott his scotch.

"The sunset was missed … but the sunrise is not," she murmured, lifting her glass to clink against his.

She turned and looked into the dark waters and lit a cigarette. Wearisome thoughts impinged into her bliss, extinguishing the lingering passion as she breathed in the smoke and took a sip from the glass balanced in her lap. *How did I get here?* Lilly thought, considering these new habits that had accompanied her new persona. She was aware she was drinking a little bit more than she should since they boarded Scott's yacht, yet it seemed the only way to endure the days without her children. She considered the last few months since she had left her parents' home to join Scott at sea. *Why could she not get through to their phone?*

It hadn't taken long for her to decide to leave with Scott after their first meeting in the beer garden that December evening. He had pursued her with an intensity she had not experienced since Glen. He showed up at her folks' house the next day with an arm swathed in flowers, chocolates and expensive white wine. Her parents had been pleased to see him after many years, and had invited him to join them for dinner that night. "He's so handsome now," her mother had whispered when they were serving up dinner in the kitchen. "He's always had a crush on you, Lilly," Margaret had added with a wink.

Lilly couldn't help but feel flattered by his affections for her, and she had confided this much to her mother. The more time she spent with Scott, the more she allowed herself to relax, revelling in the unwavering attention in which he bathed her. The freedom she had longed for had arrived, and she started to realise a new person lurking within her. Scott had an uncanny knack of making her feel like a woman, and the little girl inside her faded into the background of the woman she was born to be. It was easy to embrace the new Lilly without Glen's overpowering shadow controlling her.

One afternoon, Scott took her down to the docks at Southport and presented her with a new Espirit. His brows lifted as he told her of his plans to sail her away. She found the proposal tempting right from the start. He kissed her then, and when she looked into his expectant eyes, she knew that she would be safe with him.

Lilly spent many hours deliberating on her next move before she gave him the answer he sought. She knew she couldn't stay with her parents much longer, because as much as she loved them, they all needed their space. And what if Glen should look for her there? She started to relax more as the weeks passed. She figured if he was going to track her down, he would have called her folks by now. But he remained silent, and Lilly began to assume that Glen was going to let her go gracefully after all. However, despite this hope, a niggling feeling of dread remained, and she knew it would be better and safer for everyone if she left town.

When she told Scott she would join him, he swept her up and twirled her around. They left for Cairns that same day, marking the beginning of a new chapter in Lilly's life. The woman who lay dormant within her for all of those years with Glen, was unveiled. She was finally able to release her past inhibitions as she yielded to the delicate art of love-making.

Lilly fell prey willingly to the seductive brooding eyes that had her captivated. She embraced the erotic encounters in her new life as she discovered a sexual side to herself awakening with vigour. She secretly yearned for his eyes to desire her, and for the slightest touch of his bronzed skin against hers, sending shivers through her body. She had fantasised about their love-making and anticipated their next passionate session as they sailed the Queensland coast.

The months they spent at sea blurred into one another in a whirlwind of romantic encounters, tropical islands and cocktails. At first Lilly's intention to move forward and forget about the life she left behind became easy while she slipped into a new life of freedom and adventure, enjoying the loving attention Scott shone upon her. He made her feel like she was the only woman in the world. He confirmed this one night as they sat together under a blanket of stars as he pledged, "I don't need the world, Lilly Pad, I need you." Bittersweet tears had filled her eyes, as she knew she had travelled a stormy road only to find her true love where she had left him all those years ago.

As the months rolled on, Lilly found the love of a man was not quite enough to keep her happy; even a man such as Scott. Even in the light of his love, she could not shake the uneasiness within her. How could she truly love another if she couldn't love herself first? If she couldn't love humanity first? She knew Scott was having the time of his life with her at sea, but she knew he did not have to bear the burden of a past where she was forced to discard the children she loved. She had contemplated whether she could really love when she carried around so much guilt, as the whisper within her told her that God was not guilt; God is love.

She decided she spent too much time thinking, and welcomed the relief that alcohol provided as it drowned out the whisper. The price she paid was to surrender her self-confidence to the flow of the currents below the yacht as she became more dependent upon Scott and the booze. Between the alcohol-induced highs, Lilly discovered that the freedom she had sought meant nothing to her while she carried guilt. And as much as she tried to suppress those thoughts, she could not. She was also aware, as she recalled her conversation with Millie not long before she had left, it was those thoughts that condemned her. It was those troubling thoughts that would create the world she experienced.

And here she was, months later, living a life she had only ever lived in whimsical dreams. She was floating on a cloud known only to lovers, and drifting among a tropical paradise of islands and reefs yet she did not feel blessed. She fought back tears while she gazed into those dark waters, and saw Ace smiling in the reflection as the lights of the yacht skimmed across its surface. She knew she would have to find some way to live with the consequences of her actions and make peace with herself. *At least I still have Mum and Dad*, she consoled herself. She knew she needed to go back and see them again. She was looking forward to calling them tomorrow from Airlie Beach, and while rummaging through her baggage a few days earlier, had encountered the phone number of her parents' neighbours. It was a forgotten gesture her mother had placed deep into the pockets of her handbag before she had left – "Just in case," Margaret had chirped.

Lilly remembered rolling her eyes at the time – "Still so cautious mother," she had teased. Now, she was so thankful for her mother's overzealous, nurturing traits. *Yes, tomorrow I shall finally speak with them!* Lilly thought as she dragged herself up on her feet and followed the aroma of sizzling steaks trailing from the hull of the yacht. She was famished, and besides, her glass was long empty, and that just would not do.

Legs accustomed to the constant swirl of the sea fought to adjust to *Terra Firma* as they hurried through a rain-drenched Airlie Beach the next morning. Shaky hands clutched an umbrella over her head while the heavens opened over them. They scrambled together, laughing with the carelessness of children to the welcoming shelter of the hotel that would be their home for the coming nights.

Scott ushered Lilly through the heavy glass doors with protective arms leading the way. They stood in the lobby for a moment, drenched and dripping. Lilly pulled at blonde wisps glued to the sides of her face as she surveyed her surrounds. Dark leather lounges were placed strategically around the large candlelit room on plush piled maroon rugs. Each reclusive sitting area was accompanied with large solid oak coffee tables adorned with mini crystal chandelier candle holders supporting vanilla-rose scented candles. Large green palms and ferns added a tropical ambience to the decor along with the thickly carved dark timber privacy screens that added a sense of intimacy.

Lilly inhaled deeply. "Mmmm … smells so nice!"

She looked around some more, allowing her gaze to rest on the thing she sought. "I'll meet you in the bar after you check in," she said.

She stood up on her toes to brush moistly swollen lips against his, then turned towards the bar, leaving tiny puddles on the polished marble tiles.

After checking in, Scott stood at the entry of the bar watching her while she sat, sinking comfortably into a plumped lounge chair among handcrafted pillows. She appeared relaxed as she sipped on a chilled glass of white wine. He checked his watch. It was barely past 10am. A crease appeared on his brow as he regarded her again. This was not the Lilly he so fondly remembered, and he'd be damned if he was just going to stand by and watch her lull her life away with booze. It was then, watching her nurse her wine in a hotel bar in the hours before noon, that Scott knew he needed to do something to help her.

He sauntered into the bar, hardly noticing the appreciative glance of the young waitress as she threw him a flirty smile and checked her appearance in the mirrors that stood behind sparkling rows of coloured spirits and liquors. He came up next to Lilly and watched her take the last of the wine between eager lips.

He took the long stemmed glass from her and smiled. "Let's go up to the room now, Lilly Pad." He tugged at her hand. "Call your folks."

An hour had passed. Freshly showered, Lilly, clad only in the fluffy folds of a white robe, sat at the bay window of their suite to make her phone call. The call to her parents' house was met with a robotic "disconnected" notification. *I must have the wrong number noted down*, she thought, feeling somewhat dismayed as she pulled out their neighbour's phone number from her handbag. She punched in the numbers, hoping they would be home and her call would be met receptively. *After all, I have only met them briefly during my stay there.*

Scott emerged from the bathroom and breezed into the room as Lilly made the call. He sat across from Lilly while she listened to the speaker on the other end of the phone. His dark eyes were alive and sensual with the passion they had just shared in the ample confines of the glassed shower. Her face paled and a sudden look of alarm crossed her face as the phone dropped from shaking hands. He got to his feet as she slumped into a heap and wailed, tears tumbling down her face. Scott caught her in his arms as she teetered forward from her chair and fell into him, clasping onto him as they both spiralled towards the carpeted floor.

"Lilly? What's happened? Tell me!" he said.

Her instincts told her that her parents were dead because of her. She struggled to meet Scott's eyes as her heart shattered.

"Mum and Dad are dead," she cried.

"What?" Brows furrowed. "Lilly. What happened? How?" he stumbled.

"It was a house fire. An arson attack ..." Tear-stained eyes struggled to focus on him. "This is all my fault! I just know it is!" she wailed.

He cradled her head in his arms as she trembled. "It's not your fault, sweetheart." He soothed.

"If I hadn't left Glen and gone to them, he wouldn't have killed them," she said between sobs.

"How can you know that? You said yourself it was an arson attack. I recall all those arson attacks on the news a few months back, Lilly," he said softly.

She gazed up to him grimly. "You don't know him like I do. You don't know the black serpent," she whispered before falling against him again.

Scott held her for a few minutes, smoothing back damp golden locks from her reddened face and hushing her gulping quivers. He scooped her up on her feet and placed her down on the king-sized bed in the bedroom. His heart ached for her, and he wanted to convince her of her innocence but knew the time was not right for her to talk.

After she finally calmed down enough, Lilly looked up at him with a mask of resignation. This was the future she had chosen – one of misery and a private hell. His face dropped and the ache in his chest worsened, as a chill shuddered down his spine when she opened her mouth to speak in a whisper, and requested a drink.

FOUR YEARS LATER ...

"Then what is the truth about hate?

The truth about hate is love.

Hate is simply love moving in the wrong direction."

U.S. Anderson

CHAPTER FOURTEEN

October 10, 1991

Dear Journal,
For the last four years, Ace and I have learned to live without a mother, and my father without a wife. As the years have passed, so too has it become easier, though not one of those days have passed that I have not missed her. I have grown into a young woman without her. I have looked after and cared for my younger brother as if I were his birth mother, and I know as much as he has loved me over the years, still I remain only his sister. He doesn't say much about her anymore, but I know in the deepest recesses of my soul, he aches for her every day, more than I ever had. And as my 18th birthday calls upon me tomorrow, as a new phase of my life begins – Adulthood; so too have I decided to be rid of some long held childish habits and dreams... and they are:

1. After four long years, the woman who gave me this journal with the noblest of intentions to forge a record of my dreams and desires, I leave behind the fiercest of childish dreams; the return of the woman who called herself my mother for 14 years.

2. I leave behind the grudge I have nursed towards my father for her abandonment. I realise, although he may have played a part in her decision, it was *her* decision.
3. I leave behind my childhood dream to go to Disneyland. It never happened.
4. I leave behind the question my father never answered, even though I asked several times; who on earth is Samantha?
5. And last but not least, I leave my journal behind. Although the sweet and the sour have been shared, it is time to move on Dear Journal as I become a woman. (Please don't take it personally; I did so enjoy you!)

I bid farewell to these old dreams as I welcome new much more exciting dreams! And as for my mother, I wish her love and I hope she is happy... but I don't need you anymore either.

Much love and goodbye,
Millie xo

"Oh my God!" Millie squealed as Glen grinned at his daughter's reaction at the presentation of his gift. "Thank you, Dad!"

She planted a kiss on his cheek and ran towards the 1987 maroon Mitsubishi Magna to check out every nook and cranny of its grey interior. *A new car! Woo hoo!* She had not, in her wildest dreams ever thought she'd get this for her eighteenth birthday. Now she wouldn't have to commute to art school in Darlinghurst every day next year. *No baby, I shall drive in style!* She threw Ace and her father an inquisitive glance as they ducked their heads through the car doors.

"Wanna go for a quick spin?" she said.

She turned on the ignition and listened to the quiet purr of the engine. "I'm going to call her Maggie," Millie announced as Ace and Glen joined her in the car.

Millie drove them through Rockton, looping around the outskirts of the town and detouring past the bay on their way home. Glen watched the road like a hawk in his seat beside her. Millie noticed his knuckles turning white while he gripped onto the door next to him.

"Relax Dad!" she laughed.

"Watch the road," he warned, wiping at the nervous beads forming on his brow.

He glanced back at Ace who was also laughing. "What are you laughing at?" he demanded, barely concealing a smile as both children giggled. "Alright, alright," he muttered, "let's go home. We have to get ready to go out for your birthday dinner."

He was really going all out this year. After all, it was her eighteenth birthday. It had taken him some time to save so he could buy her a car, and he knew she would appreciate it. She never asked for much from him, and she had been so much help with Ace since Lilly had gone.

Since his return from the ugly weekend he had spent in Queensland all those years ago, Millie had also unknowingly helped to keep him on track again. It was the grace of his daughter that had kept the black snake tamed; and the thoughts of revenge that had ravished him when Lilly had left, faded into the background. Millie had managed to soothe the dark force within his soul just enough for him to grasp precariously to the lifeline she had thrown him. Months of battling and pacifying the torment inside him followed, for the deadly serpent did not concede easily. After all, Lilly was still out there enjoying the freedom she had so obviously yearned. Yet, he clung to the thread of light he knew still existed within him, pushing aside the unspeakable actions he had already orchestrated.

Glen felt his daughter deserved to be spoiled a little, and tonight he had planned a real treat for her. He was going to take her, Damon and Ace out for a seafood dinner. He knew she enjoyed seafood, and along with her car, he was proud to give this back to her. He fastened his grip on the door handle as she turned a corner a little too fast for his liking.

A few minutes later they were home safe.

"See you soon, Maggie," Millie gave the car roof an affectionate stroke as she closed the door and locked it.

"Are you driving Maggie to dinner tonight?" Ace asked.

"No," Millie and Glen chorused.

Millie raised an eyebrow at her father. "Hmm,"

she murmured at him, realising the reason for his answer after his tense experience next to her in the car. She flicked her hair at her father with mock indignity as she turned her attention to her 12-year-old brother. "Tonight Ace, I am legal to drink alcohol," Millie announced with a smile. Then with a grin to her father, "And as such, I shall have a glass of champagne for my birthday. Right Dad?"

Her grin was a little too devilish for Glen, who grunted a reply to her.

Ace skipped up the stairs to the porch, taking two at a time with long strides, and turning to face them when he reached the top. "I can't wait to eat seafood tonight! Did you guys know that a lobster's blood is colourless, but when it is exposed to oxygen it turns blue?"

He screwed up his nose as he contemplated what he had just said. "Eww! I think I'll skip eating lobster tonight!" he said.

Glen and Millie laughed at Ace as they shuffled inside the house.

A little later Millie was dressed and ready, and sat out in the backyard, gently rocking back and forth with Emily on the swing chair her father had acquired from a work mate. They both dragged on a cigarette in silence while they observed the beginnings of a clear spring evening. The sky above was a blanket of deep blue, as it gradually revealed the glistening of the first stars. The only sounds came from the cries of the last birds as they settled down to roost for the night, and the awakening night creatures that dwelled within the trees nearby. Millie thought dusk held a certain magic that inspired the creative side in her. Like the dawn, she had often thought the whispers of the universe could be heard within those quiet hours, if we were inclined to listen. Millie felt an overwhelming feeling of worship spiral through her as she felt the bond of the earth and all of life saddle in close to her. A sense of unity engulfed her, and she basked in appreciation while gazing into the emergent night, savouring these special moments that fell between the ordinary ones every now and then.

Emily's voice startled her as she broke through her contented emotions. "You look lovely, birthday girl," Emily said, blowing smoke lazily from ruby lips as they curled into a warm smile.

Millie contemplated her friend's compliment for a moment. She felt lovely sheathed in a thin flowing floral dress that fell almost to her ankles, under which she wore a fitted white T-shirt with cute short fitted sleeves that hugged her arms. She wore her long hair loose, and silver hooped earrings clung to her ears and around her both wrists.

"Thanks Em, and thank you again for the concert tickets!" Millie embraced Emily, as she recalled the Concert for Life tickets she had received earlier that day. She was looking forward to an INXS concert headlining in March the next year in Sydney's Centennial Park, along with an array of other Australian talent. She couldn't wait to tell Damon when he arrived soon.

"You are very welcome, Pussy-cat" Emily

grinned. "Steven and I are looking forward to going with you and Damon." Eyes glazed over as she spoke of the latest boy to hold her interest for a little more than five minutes. "Hmmm," Emily pondered, "Concert sex!" she laughed.

Emily enjoyed teasing Millie about sex, because her friend was still a virgin, and to her amusement, became uncomfortable about the subject at times.

Millie rolled her eyes and sighed. "Seriously? Is that all you think about, girl?"

She was quite used to Emily's sexual shenanigans by now, but she just didn't want to hear about all the details every single time.

"Mmmm ... most of the time!" Emily teased. "And you might too if you hurried up with the cherry thing and all!"

Millie landed a mock punch to Emily's upper arm. "Talk about peer pressure! Sex is a sacred expression of love ... and there is no doubt that I love Damon, so it will happen when it happens. Until then, shut up about it okay!"

Emily pouted at Millie with wounded eyes. "So, you think I abuse sex then?"

"God no, Emily," Millie's hastily said. "I didn't mean that at all. After all, it is more passion and love that will undo the world's hate. But I don't think you will find the love you seek from external forces, Em."

She took Emily's hand and placed it against her friend's chest. "First you need to find it here, the love that links you to the universe." She gestured towards the velvet sky above them. "And everything in it."

"How do you do that?" Emily whispered as she felt the strong presence of a divinity she did not understand.

Emily was astonished at her sudden feeling of emotion as her eyes filled with tears. She had always known Millie was a deep thinker, and she was aware she received messages from another dimension, but this was the first time she had ever felt the presence of a divine power bigger than her.

"Do what?"

Emily could feel the eternal truth in Millie's words resonating in her soul, and she had a fleeting sense of the spiritual essence radiating between them. It was a sense of transcendence that for a brief moment revealed her own divine nature which was at one with the universe, a perfect creation of God. And it felt wonderful! She recalled with tears of joy the words of Jesus – "God is love; He dwelleth within me, and I in Him".

"Know what you know, be what you be; think how you think!" Emily's voice rose as tears streamed down her face. "I mean, how do you do that?"

"Hey! Birthday girl!" Damon's throaty voice cut through their conversation like a gust of wind. Both girls turned in his direction as he sauntered down the cobblestones.

Millie's face lit up as she jumped from the swing chair to greet him in a whirl of hugs and kisses.

Damon laughed under her affection. "Aww, you only just saw me yesterday!" he teased, enjoying the attention she lavished on him.

"Yesterday was too long ago," she murmured near his ear.

He nuzzled against her as his arms encircled her neck. "Happy birthday, Millie-pie."

Emily watched them for a minute before she leaped up from the chair. "My cue to leave!" she announced, walking towards them. "Have a lovely birthday dinner Pussy-cat!"

She paused to hug her friend. "You are so very special, Millie."

Emily leaned up close to her ear. "Love you," she whispered.

"Love you too, Em."

They smiled at each other for a moment before Emily left in a skip down the path. Millie turned back to Damon who presented her with a small silver wrapped box, complete with a shiny red bow on top. Quick fingers hastened to open the small package under Damon's watchful stare, and when her eyes caught the first glimpse of the jewelled golden heart and the fine twisted gold chain on which it hung, her breath caught in her throat.

"Oh! It is beautiful, Damon. Thank you!"

Damon reached into the box and took out the necklace. Holding the heart in his hand, he carefully broke away one half. "One half for you, the other for me. We carry each other, you see. My heart belongs to you, Millie; it always will."

He turned her around gently as long thick fingers fumbled with the delicate clasp of the fine chain and secured it around her slender neck.

"And mine belongs to you, Damon," she pledged while a hand reached to caress her half of the diamond heart which now plunged proudly to her décolletage.

She looked into his eyes, which lacked the calm that was usually there. Her blue lagoon had been transformed into a churning ocean.

"Is everything okay, Damon?" she asked.

He threw her a dazzling smile, trying to conceal the trouble that lingered in his eyes. "Everything is fine, Millie-pie. Oh!" He revealed a white envelope, "almost forgot; this was in your letterbox. It's addressed to you."

"Do you make it a habit to check people's letterboxes?" she teased as she took the envelope.

Damon grinned. "Only the ones that belong to beautiful girls," he said grinning.

Her father popped his head through the back door to announce it was time to go to dinner as she scrutinised the envelope. Her eye glimpsed the handwriting on the front face of the envelope, making her catch her breath. Glen's boisterous words echoed through her ears while she felt the world closing in and suffocating her in a moment of turbulence. The elation of the day dimmed as she recognised the blue inked scrawl as the unmistakable handwriting of her mother.

Millie cloaked her dismay with a flash of a smile and an "okay" as her father peered at her from the doorway. She hastened up the cobblestones and through the hallway. "Be right back," she called, reaching her room where she hid the letter under her mattress beside the first letter her mother had left for her almost four years ago. Millie struggled to pacify her racing heart and hold back the tears that threatened to spill over at her distress. *Stop it! Damn it!* she silently cursed herself. She had said her private goodbyes, and had finally allowed her long held hopes for her mother's return to fade peacefully into the background of her life. *I wasn't supposed to hear from her now!* she thought, stamping and kicking the floor. The heel of her foot caught the edge of something solid, making her cry out as her temper began to get the better of her. She bent over to inspect the source of the pain, feeling around until she located the object. She pulled it out, revealing her old sketch pad.

A thick layer of dust cloaked the hard cardboard cover of the art book. As she reviewed the first drafts contained in her dusty old sketch pad, all antagonism fell away. Her ears pricked as she heard the commotion of the men in the house drawing closer to her room. She skimmed the pages, knowing her time was limited and she could reacquaint herself with this book later that evening. However, one glimpse of the last sketch entry caught her attention. She sighed as she observed the skilfully shaded strokes she had created of her mother, sitting on the edge of her bed as she saw her when they had last exchanged a meaningful conversation. It was the day she was sure everything would be okay, only to discover it was far from it. It was the day she had experienced the most magical evening of her life, only for it to end in despair and torment. It was the day her mother had left them. She remembered now why she had thrown the sketch pad deep under her bed to be forgotten, for the life-like sketch of her mother had been too painful for her eyes to dwell on.

"Millie! Let's go!" Ace called through her bedroom door, startling her out of her memories. She gratefully returned to the present as she heard the rustling of the men assembling on the front porch.

She threw the sketch pad aside and hurried out to join them. She steeled herself against sad reminders and broke into a grin as she joined her father, brother and Damon and headed out for her long-awaited birthday dinner.

CHAPTER FIFTEEN

illie woke up with a start. Propping herself up on an elbow, she reached for the switch on the bedside lamp, willing the eeriest of feelings to leave her as the room around her flooded with dim light. Drowsy eyes blinked, struggling to push away the unsettling fragments of emotions left from the dream world she had just visited.

"Samantha," Millie whispered. She bit down on her bottom lip while the grogginess of sleep began to fade. "Who are you?" she said, as if addressing an unseen presence. The name, distinctly spoken to her in her dream state, reverberated through her mind accompanied by an inexplicable sense of loss. She took a sip of water from the glass she kept beside her bed, and drew in a deep breath. As she allowed the warm breath to exhale slowly through her nostrils, all at once it occurred to her that it was no mistake nor coincidence that her father had called her by that name those years ago. She remembered vividly the odd way his eyes had seen her when she had come to comfort him. They had fallen on her as if she were a ghost. She recalled the vague sense of fright mixed with guilt his eyes had revealed when he struggled to comprehend who she was as she came nearer to him. And the repeated, almost inaudible utterances of "I'm sorry" as if from an insane person.

She struggled to piece together all the chunks to this puzzling story, and how this had any significance to her. A faint chill made the hairs on the back of her neck stand up as it dawned on her that the woman she had seen in her dreams all those years was Samantha.

"Who are you?" she whispered again, half expecting a reply as she scanned the silent room where a palpable presence seemed to linger.

She slumped her head back onto the pillow, gazing upward as she silenced her mind for a moment. Millie knew it was *her*, this Samantha that had visited her frequently throughout the years. A flicker of a light behind the curtains that were drawn over the window caught the corner of her eye. She slipped out of bed and crept in bare feet across to the window. She cautiously drew the curtains back, uncertain of what might confront her. A small pang of disappointment rang through her as she looked upon the darkened street. There was nothing out of the ordinary. A heavy sigh fell from her lips as she was about to draw the curtains closed when, in the clear black night she glimpsed a searing light soaring across a velvet sky. She unlatched the lock to the window and pushed the pane up as far as it could go. She poked her head out for a better view and her heart flipped when another shooting star blazed across the sky, so close as it burned a radiant wake through darkness. She gasped with awe. She laughed as yet another meteor shot across in the opposite direction. Tears of elation rolled silently down her cheek as her heart beat faster and her head felt light with tingles. She knew this meteor shower was created for her, and she was not alone to tread through the days of her life. The eerie feeling that had awoken with her revealed there would be a struggle ahead, yet Millie knew where to find the strength to overcome it. All she needed was to have faith in her divinity, have faith and trust the source of all creation, the source most people call God. In her stillness, she heard the words resonating through her and settling in her heart with clarity – "I love you"– whispered words instilled within her. She knew the words came to her from Samantha. "I love you," she whispered back, and it seemed confirmed as another meteor blazed through the sky.

Daylight filtered into room when Millie awoke again. She felt energised, and bounded out of bed reflecting the invigoration that raced through her bones. She cleaned up, dressed and ate a speedy breakfast before grabbing the keys to her new car and setting off to pick up Damon. He was eager to go for a drive in her new car, so they had arranged for her to pick him up that morning for a cruise around town. Pulling up in front of his apartment block, Millie caught sight of him leaning on the rails of the large balcony that wrapped around the corner apartment he shared with his parents two levels from the ground.

She had seldom made the trek up those two

flights of stairs in the four years they had been dating. And the times that she had, Millie had been met with an over-protective mother who made for little conversation, and a father that attempted to over-compensate for his wife's obtrusive manner. Uncomfortable with his mother's behaviour towards Millie, Damon had kept her away from his home for the most part. And he had confided in Millie that his mother's rudeness was nothing personal towards her, and that her over-protective demeanour was due to the loss of her first son, his older brother, who had died with a severe case of pneumonia when she was pregnant with Damon.

"Jake was barely two years old when he died," Damon had told her. "And when I'm not almost suffocating with her smothering ways, she makes me feel like I'm not good enough. For Jake wouldn't have failed in maths, surely?" He gave a bittersweet laugh. He had not spoken of his feelings about his mother and the brother he had never known. Yet, with Millie, Damon felt as if he could confess the world and still be met with the love that lingered for him in her eyes.

Millie had nodded her understanding and had never asked to go and visit with his family again. Only on the rare occasion had she made the trek up those stairs, and only at Damon's insistence. He had badly wanted his mother to notice the grace of his girlfriend and understand his devotion to her. Efforts to bring Millie and his mother together had faded over the years as he had tired of his mother's unwilling attitude towards Millie, and her reluctance to accept the happiness he found spending time with a girl he treasured dearly. Millie couldn't imagine how it must feel to Damon to have had an older brother he was never able to know, nor the grief his parents must have endured at the loss of a young child. She could envision his mother wanting to hold tight and keep her only surviving son close to her, and the reluctance she must feel at the thought of letting him fly some day. The individual spark in us all cannot really be restricted by another. Perhaps some day Damon's mother might learn to accept her son's freewill and choices; perhaps some day she might even accept Millie.

Millie gave the horn a toot in response to his wave to her from the balcony, and lowered the volume on the car radio to hear him say that he'd be right down. She nodded up to him while she speculated what might have caused the lost look in his eyes the night before. She had had no time to speak with him about her concerns at the seafood restaurant, and he seemed to pick up dramatically during their meal, as she had noticed no other signs of the disturbance that had stirred in his eyes when he had presented his gift to her. He had told her of his intentions to discuss something important with her the next day. And despite awakening feeling excited, Millie could not shake the unsettled feeling growing in her stomach. Almond eyes concealed behind dark shades watched as he bounded to her car, as if the fall of his footsteps might reveal the importance of his news.

He swung open the passenger door and secured

himself in the seat beside her.

"Hey beautiful." He leaned in for a greeting kiss.

They drove off, enjoying the breeze through their hair and skin as it blew through open windows. They exchanged grins between verses as they sang along in out-of-tune melodies to R.E.M's *Losing My Religion* from Sydney's Triple M. They drove out to the shores of a quiet tree-lined bay demurely nestled behind streets of grand mostly glassed houses in the southern suburbs of Sydney.

With arms full of supplies set for a little picnic, they trekked through a well-worn steep grassed path down towards the opening of the bay.

"Did you see Ace's eyes when the lobster was brought to the table?" Millie said with a giggle.

Damon laughed. "I thought his eyes might have popped right out of his head!"

"Me too. He makes me laugh so much."

"I think the waitress had a crush on your dad," Damon said.

Millie stopped and turned to look at Damon. "You think so?" The curve of her brows knitted.

"Yeah."

She thought for a moment. "Huh … well, it would be nice to see my father meet somebody special. I think it would be good for him."

"Oh, so he has your approval then?" Damon teased.

"I guess he does," she laughed.

They claimed a secluded patch under a willow tree near the water's edge. Millie peered up with an artist's eye at the long branches lazily overhanging their picnic spot. Willows were one of her favourite trees. *I could paint this scene*, she thought, as she looked around her, capturing every detail in her mind's eye. *Oh! Such a romantic scene!*

She watched avidly as he spread out the picnic rug, and a ripple of desire awakened within her when he enclosed his fingers over hers and she caught the burning look in his eyes as he gently pulled her down on the rug next to him. Millie blushed and lowered her eyes as she grabbed for a lock of hair. She longed for him to make love to her – to ravish her with the passion that they had withheld for so long. However, she knew Damon was waiting for her go-ahead, and she knew he would never impress his male desires on her until she allowed him. She just wasn't quite sure how to let him know that she was ready to go all the way with him, as the subject still invoked a timidness in her she herself did not understand. *Perhaps he'll bring the subject up soon*, she pondered while she gazed at the shallow waters near them. *Perhaps he will learn to read minds! Oh! Why can he not read my mind!* she thought with some amusement.

"Let's eat!" Damon's voice released the spiced tension brewing between them. He handed her the toasted chicken, asparagus and cheese focaccia they had picked up on their way, and an ice-cold soda.

She laughed at her grumbling stomach as she unwrapped her favourite sandwich. "Yum!" she said.

"I always did like a girl that liked to eat," he teased with a wink.

"Well," she said with her mouth full, "You found her!"

"Yes I did," he said as his expression darkened.

As soon as they had finished their lunch, Millie demanded to know what reasons lurked behind the trouble she saw in his eyes.

He sighed deeply as he reached for her hands. "Millie, my father has agreed to a great job opportunity. He's really excited … so is my mother."

"Okay." She nodded for him to go on.

"The thing is, the job he's taking is in New York."

He searched her face as she began to understand.

"Millie, my dad has pulled some strings. He has got me a traineeship in marketing in the same company. It's a really good opportunity for me …" His voice trailed.

Her mind seemed to spin, and the sandwich, only moments ago eaten with ravish, began to feel heavy in her stomach.

Millie jerked her hands away from his grip and slid her sunglasses to perch on top of her head. She clutched at her hair and twirled with agitation.

"This can't be so!" Her eyes darted about in despair. "We are supposed to stay together. I know this!"

She brought her trembling hands up to her face as tears began to trickle down in ugly streaks. She now understood his split-heart birthday gift. *He is leaving me too! Nooooo!* Old familiar feelings of abandonment shuddered through her.

He scooped her into his arms and held her tight

while his tears joined hers as the heartache he had been carrying for the last few days broke into an avalanche of agony. "We will always be together," Damon choked. "The traineeship is only for four years … I will be back. I promise, my beautiful Millie-pie."

They held on to one another until their sobbing had ceased and the silence between them grew deafening. They clung together, reluctant to allow the other out of arm's reach. They were desperate to prolong their precious time together, as his whispered reply had come unwillingly when she had asked him when he was to be leaving – "Tomorrow". They watched the dance between the filtering rays of the afternoon sun upon the glistening water's surface, and marvelled at the glowing display of colour through the long droopy branches of the willow.

Damon turned to her, holding her eyes hostage in the depths of his. "Amelia Anderson," he declared, with her chin cupped within his hands, "I have loved you from the start. I will love you forever."

He leaned in and kissed her with vigour. Full lips caressed against his, savouring the taste his pressing tongue provided, almost desperately as it swept against hers. Her whole body was aroused as her desire fed into his. Sensing her response, Damon explored her lips and mouth with a trace of urgency as they echoed her awakening desire. His tongue probed against hers, tasting the sweetness of her mouth like a decadent dessert. The broad palms of his hands cupped the back of head while his kiss reached an animal-like fervour. There was no escaping the yearning sexual hunger that had lingered for her all these years, now finally released to the surface. She wasn't turning back. Millie ran her fingers through the back of his thick dark hair, pulling at the ends of the strands that bounced in wisps at the collar of his shirt. She became aware of the pleasurable wet throbbing between her thighs, and longed to feel his hardness penetrate her for the first time.

Damon gently tore himself away from her, leaving her panting while emerald eyes looked to him, losing herself to the passionate caress of his eyes. And while those eyes held hers without falter, his hands came to grasp the material ends of the singlet she was wearing. She lifted her arms obediently as he swept the top up and over her head easily, then turned for him and waited as he fumbled to unclasp the hooks of the laced bra. Millie breathed in and slowly turned back to him, biting down on her bottom lip as she was seized with nervous excitement. A stirring of pleasure ran through her as she felt the intensely powerful, provocative stare of his eyes as they lingered over the ample swell of her breasts. Her breath fell from her lips in shallow bursts as she caught his face becoming intoxicated with desire, yet in his eyes remained the deep tenderness she knew so well. Willing herself on, she stood to her feet and slipped the khaki coloured shorts and her panties down over her buttocks. She gazed to where he still sat on his knees on the rug. The fullness of her bare breasts lifted and fell as her breath heaved in anticipation as she poised before him naked, waiting for the reaction she knew would come.

His eyes perused her naked body, caressing, absorbing and relishing in every detail, every curve and every line of her smooth olive skin. He had waited for so long, and he was not about to rush this moment. His eyes drank her in as he marvelled at the beauty of her body, then they swept up to meet hers, recognising the arousal he found deep within them.

"Millie, you take my breath away," he murmured.

He reached out and pulled her to him. Pressing his mouth on hers, eager lips teased and kissed as hands caressed in delighted exploration as he tenderly made his way meticulously over every inch of her body. She panted and moaned while her body awakened as his touch found the depths of places they had not ever known. She undressed him, keen to travel her hands over the taut body he offered to her. She kissed and suckled her way across his flesh with vivid curiosity. Delving in unchartered territory, naked skin twisted together, glistening in the afternoon sun, stroking and embracing each other with fingers and tongues. They explored each other until they could no longer withhold the desire that led them onwards. He positioned his hardness between her opening, holding her delicately as if she was but a porcelain shadow of herself, and slowly entered her. Her breath caught in her throat, and a small whimper of erotic pain escaped her lips as she felt the welcoming, burning invasion of him as he pushed his way, burrowing deep into her. Her body opened willingly, and she gripped him as she began to relax and rock with him as they joined together in the throes of their love while she surrendered herself and her body gushed in a climactic finale in unison with his eruption of desire.

They lay against the warmth of the rug, holding each other while catching their breaths. Sorrow weighed heavily in hearts that soared one moment, only to crash into a thousand pieces the next. They wept as they clung together, and laughed moments later, celebrating in their love for each other. They made bittersweet, tender yet desperate love under the giant shadows of the willow tree until the sun was no longer visible and the air became thin with night. Only then did they quietly dress and make the trek back to Rockton together for the last time.

It took every ounce of strength Millie could muster, as they said their farewells, to tear herself away from the potent scent that lingered on the arms that held her tightly against his chest. Her best friend was leaving her, and if it were not for the divine moments she had experienced in the quietly dark hours of the morning, she was certain she could not endure his departure from her life. Reminding herself of those feelings of love and the knowledge she was not alone in this, tears burned in her eyes as she turned away from him.

"This feels so surreal," she whispered.

"I know," he said clenching his fists against her back.

"I love you Damon. You are the best part of my life; don't you ever forget that."

He smiled down at her. "And you'll always take

my breath away, Millie. I love you."

His "blue lagoon" flooded her as she drove off into the night, leaving behind only the impression of her kiss against his lips and a broken jewelled heart that hung around his throat.

The old screen door squeaked as Millie entered the quiet, dark house upon arriving home soon after saying her last goodbyes to Damon. Her mind swirled with the enormity of her day, unable to grasp the reality of his move. She plodded down to her room and sat on the edge of her bed while contemplating the highs and lows of her day. She felt powerless to push aside her heartache, and to stop the tears, despite the feelings of limitless love she knew was available to her at any given moment. She wallowed in the depths of murky emotions while she cried at the sudden turn of events. She cried until her eyes grew puffy. She sobbed until her head throbbed and she calmed herself with the comfort of a tissue.

Now what? Millie thought, knowing her life would not be the same without its star player. It occurred to her that she had become quite dependent on Damon's presence in her life since her mother had left. She was so perplexed at the thought of his absence, that she realised she did not know who she was without him. On wobbly feet she went to the mirror to reflect upon the impression she cast in the old looking glass, and asked aloud, "Who is Amelia

Anderson?" She noted the puffiness around her eyes, then peered past the outer fleshy shell into the reflection the pupils of her eyes showed her. She was overcome with the old familiar feeling she remembered when she would look at herself when she was a child. A peculiar thought came to her – *I am here, and I am there*. "I am everywhere," she whispered in completion of her thought. A sense of serenity crept through her as she repeated the words firmly, "I AM everywhere!" The throbbing in her head gave way to thrilling tingles as she became aware of the power of this statement. The slightest of smiles crossed her lips, and she knew without doubt that the presence of God dwelled within her, and it was up to her to tap into that mighty presence. Armed with this knowledge, she decided she was ready to open the letter from her mother.

She slipped her hand beneath the mattress and pulled out both envelopes that she had concealed. She placed the first of the letters carefully on her bedside table beside the glass-panelled lamp, handling the envelope delicately as if its contents were a treasure trove. Recognising the nostalgia provoked within her, she realised just how precious this correspondence meant to her, despite previous attempts to push aside the sentimental feelings she still held for her mother. She needed to understand her mother's decision to leave them, as she knew in her heart their mother's love for them was sincere, so her reasons must surely have been vital. She took the second, unopened envelope between curious fingers and, catching a deep breath, pried open the sealed envelope.

Her breath caught in her throat as she pulled out an elaborately crafted, handmade birthday card. She looked at the front of the card for a few long moments before exploring its contents. A wave of longing gripped her while she examined every detail of the card's cover. Fine purple and pink paper butterflies had been painstakingly glued in the centre of the card, creating the illusion of fluttering butterflies. Their pastel painted wings edged in gold, spread out and fluttered with the movement of the card while their tiny bodies were painted with a fine delicate brush tip with strokes of black and gold. There were four detailed butterflies scattered over the front of the card, and as she examined each one carefully, Millie knew her mother's choice to paint butterflies on a card made for her was not a careless decision, as her mother knew of her love for butterflies.

"They are a symbol of transformation," her mother would say to her when she would marvel at them as a child, before lightly breezing a kiss on the tip of her little nose. "They remind us to keep our faith." Millie closed her eyes as she recalled old memories, which flashed through her mind like a movie, as if only yesterday she was in the garden with her mother and baby Ace bobbing and laughing in a croqueted bouncer.

In her mind she saw them playing in their backyard under the huge shade of the avocado tree, and picking daffodils and dandelions from a well tendered garden bed while watching with childlike fascination for the fluttery movements of butterflies. "Mummy, what does faith mean?" Millie had asked, with her little head cocked to one side. "Believing in what we hope for," her mother had answered with a bright smile. "Always keep your faith my little Millie."

Her mother had seemed so happy then, she thought. A wistful smile captured her own lips as Millie recalled how she felt as a child towards her mother. *Oh, how I had loved my mother! And oh, how I have missed her all these years!* Her mother's words brought to her mind that only a few years ago she was attempting to figure out the power thoughts held over our experiences, knowing there was more to it than what she knew at the time. *Faith? So, how about faith plus thought?* The idea felt so good that a shiver of excitement surged through her.

"If we take thought and add faith, and believe unwaveringly," she said, thinking out loud, "Which means we would need to feel that which we want before it has actually manifested in our lives." *That's where a healthy imagination would come in*, she pondered. "Then surely this must be the way to create with our thoughts!" Her smile broadened as the realisation of her spoken words gave her goosebumps on her arms.

She quickly searched through the top draw of her bedside table for a notepad and a pen to write down her thoughts concerning her mission to seek the knowledge of thought creation. With that done, she whispered a "thank you" to the universe, and to her mother for reminding her of butterflies and presenting to her the information resonating through her being.

Millie returned her attention to her card, slipping her fingers between the thin cardboard and revealing a white folded piece of paper that fell to her lap from the folds of the card. Before retrieving the letter, her eyes fell on the simple words written with a black felt tip pen on the inside of the card; they read:

> Dearest Millie,
> Happy 18th Birthday
> Love you always,
> Mum xoxo

She studied the uncomplicated text, and although recognising her mother's handwriting, Millie noticed the mark of her mother's script was much messier than it had been in the past. The letters seemed to have a wobbly curve to them, almost as if the writer had written these words on a boat at sea. She couldn't help but feel a little disappointed at the simplicity of the phrase written on the first card she had received from her mother in four years, expecting to have read something far more sentimental. The slightest of underwhelmed sighs crossed her lips while she unfolded the letter; *Perhaps this may convey her affections a little more tenderly*, Millie thought as her eyes began to tear up again as she began to read the fluctuant script of the letter:

> Dearest Millie,
> It is vitally important that you understand that not a moment has passed since leaving you and Ace that I have not regretted the critical decision made to not take you both with me.

Every minute of every day for the last four years I have been plagued with the images of the smiles in your eyes, and the laughter on your lips. So much so that I barely function as a normal human being anymore. I guess I have failed at creating the life I so wanted, and instead, I am left with a vast empty shell. I was a fool to think I could be happy without my children. Millie, please understand, although it won't count for much, nor bring back the past years lost … or the years ahead lost to us, this is me saying sorry to you and Ace.

I cannot imagine how you have both grown; I do try, although your childlike images are those that I see in my mind, but I am certain that you have grown into a beautiful young woman, and your brother into a sturdy, handsome teenager. He will be a force to be reckoned with, just like your father.

I know it is time for you to discover the truth, Millie. I left with you a key in the letter I placed in your journal the night I left. You were out on your first date, and I always wondered how that night went for you. The lock the key turns you will find buried about three feet deep, between the avocado tree in the backyard and the fence line. There, you will find a wooden box which I have placed within a black garbage bag before burying, to help keep it preserved. There Millie, you will find the truth. There you will find why I felt the need to flee.

No matter what you find, dear Millie, before and always, listen to the whisper within you, for there only the truth shall suffice.

Always remember, it has always been a privilege to call you my daughter.

Love you always,

Mum xoxo

CHAPTER SIXTEEN

Ace tossed and turned in his bed, trying to fight off the constant thumping noise that persisted in its efforts to rouse him from his peaceful haven of sleep. Large hands punched at the pillow as he finally gave up trying to sleep through the pounding racket. Eyes narrowed when they fell on the digits of his bedside clock. *Who could be making such a noise at 2am?* He scrunched up his face as he tuned groggy ears into the whereabouts of the offending noise. He had occupied the last of the bedrooms at the end of the creaky hallway for as long as he could remember, and for as long as he could remember, the street noise had never filtered in far enough to infringe upon the ten hours sleep he required every night. *Come to think of it, not much of the house noise usually did either*, he thought, as annoyance gave way to curiosity while his ears honed into the thumping noise that seemed to be coming from their backyard. The one small window in his room looked out to the back of the house, showcasing quite the ordinary view of their backyard. He and his father had worked tirelessly over the last few years to tame the wilderness it once was, leaving his view now unobstructed. As he listened to the noise and the pause between thumps, he realised it sounded like a shovel hitting a somewhat stubborn piece of the earth. *Oh my God!* A shiver ran through him as an absurd thought crossed his mind – *What if someone is burying a dead body in our yard?* He froze in the darkness for a moment, as he allowed the horror of the thought to grow in his imagination. *Maybe I should go and wake up Dad, after all there might be a murderer in our midst and we may be in grave danger!*

He rubbed at the sleepiness in his eyes while he sat upright, pushing Benny Boy to the floor beside his bed as he did so. "Sorry Benny Boy," he whispered to his old friend as he leaned over, fumbling to retrieve his soft tatty body and replace him on the comfort of his bed. He cocked his spiky head to one side as he noticed the noise had stopped. He decided then that before waking up his father he would brave a quick look first, just in case they tried to get away. At least then he might be able to describe the murderer to the police later. He would be quite the hero, and Ace was certain that heroes get a take-out treat, and maybe something even cooler, like a new computer. He swung solid legs to the floor and, led by the slivers of moonlight shining between the folds of the pale curtains that hung over his window, he made quiet, nervous steps to peer out to the backyard. He inspected the darkened yard, blue eyes scanning the garden bed, then further into the back reaches of the yard. *Oh! The killer has left!* he conceded, as thoughts of Hawaiian pizzas and a new computer screen faded from his imagination. While contemplating this sad plight, he remained at the window as his attention was caught briefly by the luminous shine of the rising moon that seemed to be magically suspended in a vast blackened space.

He uttered an appreciative "Wow!" as he watched the rising moon, as if really seeing the night sky for the first time. Then a flash from behind the shadow of the avocado tree caught his attention. He peered towards the tree, his chest tightening. He crouched down so the tops of his eyes were only barely able to peer over the ledge of the window, and watched with heart pounding for the first glance of the killer. He sucked in a sharp breath as he caught the first glimpse of the prowler burying the dead under the avocado tree. Finger nails dug into the crumbling old wood of the window ledge, and bare toes gripped the floorboards. He dared not breathe or make any sound in case it alerted the killer and he would become the next victim before he could alert his sleeping father. A chill ran through his spine, and Ace almost screamed when he saw the dark figure turn from the avocado tree and walk hastily towards their back porch. He shot up to his feet, catching and pulling a hanging curtain as it entangled around his hand in his frenzy. He froze and looked outside for any signs the murderer had heard the clumsy commotion at his window.

The killer froze too, swivelling on stealthy feet under the shine of the half-moon, cocking a head and listening towards Ace's window. In growing alarm, Ace watched him move deliberately closer to where he stood frozen in a tangled mess. Ace's heart was pounding so hard, he was sure it could be heard, and beads of nervous sweat swathed his brow and stung his eyes. His mouth opened past dry lips in a scream when the killer switched on the flashlight to reveal the perpetrator, and a flood of relief came in a long exhaled breath as Ace recognised that it was no killer but only Millie, and it appeared she was carrying a box.

Grappling to slide the window open, Ace poked his head through the opening. "What are you doing?" he scowled.

"Nothing," Millie hissed back. "Go back to bed," she said over her shoulder as she turned and began to walk away.

"No! You woke me up. What are you doing? What is that?" Ace pointed at the box she carried under one arm.

Millie turned back towards him. "Shhhh! I'll tell you in the morning, okay; now go back to sleep."

He mumbled a curse under his breath while closing the window, making extra sure to lock it securely, just in case. His imagination had had enough excitement for one night. He made the short trek back to bed and his waiting Benny Boy. *I'll deal with Millie in the morning*, he thought as sleep beckoned him again.

Ace stretched under flimsy faded green bed sheets as recollections of his midnight disturbance returned. He bounced out of bed and saw on the clock that he had slept in, and was missing his favourite Sunday morning cartoons. He flew into the kitchen to make a bowl of Weetbix and brown sugar before hurrying to the lounge room to take up camp in front of the television. He almost spilled milk and soggy Weetbix when he saw his sister's slight figure was already sprawled over the three-seater lounge, and the TV tuned to the wrong channel.

"Hey!" Ace protested, making no effort to conceal his displeasure.

She threw him a quick glance before her eyes settled back to the screen. "Hey what?"

"Well, it's Sunday morning," he stammered, trying to figure out how to get rid of her. "You never watch TV on Sunday morning!"

Nursing his cereal bowl, he sat down on the edge of the single lounge chair. Already tall for his age, his sturdy twelve-year-old body perched awkwardly. *What is with her anyway?* he thought, and a scowl twisted his mouth.

"Well, I am watching it now," she said, pronouncing each word with emphasis.

Ace began to scoop up big spoonfuls of cereal and cramming the wet concoction into his mouth. Then he remembered she had told him she would explain her noisy digging the night before, and he really wanted to know what was in that box. *Maybe she had dug up treasure!*

"So," he ventured, "What's in the box? Is that why you were digging last night?"

Millie sat upright and glared at him, causing him to squirm. "That is my business and none of yours."

His eyes clouded over and he frowned. "So, you don't want to share the treasure?"

"What treasure?" Her snappy reply came just as their father walked into the room.

"Good morning you two," he beamed. "What treasure?"

"Nothing," Millie muttered, throwing her brother a cautionary stare.

Ace grunted his disapproval and decided to seize the opportunity to include their father in this little venture of hers. "Dad," he began, throwing her a snide smile, "Millie dug up a box in the backyard last night. I'm sure she found treasure, but she's not sharing any of it."

Glen's face contorted as he processed the odd information offered by his imaginative son. "Oh," he responded, deciding to humour Ace's tall tale. "Treasure you say?" he grinned. "Are you telling me we are rich?" he mocked, but his humour faded as he noticed the colour draining from Millie's face. He raised a curious eyebrow at his daughter. "Millie? Why were you digging in the backyard last night?"

Squirming a little, Ace reached forward to put his empty cereal bowl down on the coffee table. The bowl clanked loudly as it made contact with the table's worn tiled top, distracting his father and Millie for a moment as both their eyes were drawn to the trembling ceramic bowl. "Sorry," he murmured. *This was way better than any cartoon!* he thought, as he watched his sister flounder under their father's questioning stare. He could see Millie was attempting to figure out how to answer, noticing the struggle in her eyes and the fingers that had flown up to twist handfuls of long dark hair. Her eyes started to moisten and Ace began to realise something was wrong. *Oh! What have I done?* He felt a lump rise in his throat and became aware, as he recognised a shift in his sister from sorrow to the clenched, angry square of her jaw and the fire in her eyes that this was not going to be good.

The struggle within her ceased, and frustrated tears cleared up to a cold stare directed at their father. "Why don't *you* tell me something, Dad?" she said.

His eyes held hers unwaveringly while his mind began to spin in warning; his daughter hadn't spoken nor looked at him this coldly since the night Lilly had left them. He knew that whatever she had dug up and discovered in the box Ace had spoken of, could not have been good. Thoughts raced through his mind as Glen tried to decipher and decide just how to handle the apparent hostility the contents of this box has brought upon them. *Upon him.*

"What do you mean, Millie?" *Play it cool*, he thought.

"Where is my mother?" She matched his light tone with a short sweet smile while she scraped her hair back off her face, tightening it into a ponytail, as if preparing for a showdown.

His laugh became a nervous jitter. "You know where she is."

"Do I?"

Shrinking back as far as he could manage into the lounge cushions, Ace gulped down the lump in his throat. *Why is she bringing up Mum now?* He clenched a tight clammy fist while another lump rose to replace the one he had just managed to wedge free. He glanced at his father, who was shaking his head from side to side and appeared just as confused as he was.

"Millie-pie," Glen said, "Your mother left us. I have no idea where she has gone. I have not heard from her." Then a disturbing thought. "Have you?"

"Yes," she said in a rasped whisper as she watched with mild fascination as this information sank its way into her father's head. "She left me a key to the box she had buried under the avocado tree."

She saw the softness in her father's eyes change and recognised the struggle as he fought to stop a scowl at the mention of their mother's connection to the wooden box. Millie knew then that he was well aware of the box she had uncovered, and its damning contents.

He was standing near the television throughout this exchange, and as his daughter's words infiltrated his awareness, it took every ounce of restraint to stop the hand, now clenched tight, from smashing the television screen. Pristinely cleaned white ivories ground together in a violent frenzy while the lustre of gold in his eyes matched those of his daughter's, as they ignited in fury. His mind, only moments before, a light-filled dome of happiness, grew dark while the serpent awakened and reclaimed its throne. He knew of the wooden box Millie had unearthed, but he thought it had been destroyed years ago. *I should never have trusted that bitch! How dare Lilly do this to me! I let her live all these years ... and this is how she repays me!* He turned away from the prying eyes of his children and looked towards the window. He knew he had to keep control over the dark force in their presence.

He sucked in a deep breath. "Ace, go to your room."

Ace seldom heard his father use this tone with him, and it sent a cold shiver down his spine every time he had heard it in the past. There was no protest he could summon when he spoke like this. Ace leaped to his feet and scampered out of the room, leaving Millie alone to meet their father's wrath.

Ace twitched as he sat on the floor at the foot of his bed. Holding Benny Boy firmly in his grasp, he attempted to concentrate on remembering the odd facts he liked to memorise. Ears pricked up as he heard the thunderous clash between Millie and his father. *Lightning ... lightning*, he thought, racking his brain as he tried to block out the storm in the lounge room. *Oh yes, lightning!*

"A bolt of lightning has enough power to toast 160,000 pieces of bread," he muttered to himself. He looked down to the stuffed toy regarding him with dull eyes from his lap. "One-hundred and sixty thousand pieces, Benny Boy! That's a lot of bread!"

He covered his ears in an attempt to block out the cyclone in the other room as it grew to a thunderous peak. *Samantha?* A word penetrated into his ears. *Who is Samantha?* he thought, unable to block out Millie's accusations towards their father. Then he heard the words that fell upon him like a molten weight on his chest and stomach.

"Did you murder Samantha, Dad?" Millie's steely voice was hardly recognisable, and was met with silence. Then her voice rose to a hysterical pitch. "You murdered my mother!"

The house fell silent. Ace's ears buzzed against the sudden lull in the house, and he felt his chest twist and tighten so much that he could hardly breathe. He rose to wobbly feet, dropping Benny Boy unnoticed, and opened the door slightly to peer through the crack. Hearing nothing, Ace strained to see further down the dim hallway. He took a cautious step into the hall, and keeping his body flush with the walls, scoured the length of the hallway towards the lounge room, feeling like a prowler and wishing he possessed the courage of one. As he neared the fully open door to the lounge room, he could hear his father sobbing. In all of his twelve years, he had never heard his father wail in such a way.

As he approached the threshold to the lounge room, his eyes met with the image of his father hunched over on the edge of a lounge chair. Large calloused hands cupped his face, and tears were dripping through the loose gaps between his father's thick fingers. Tasting the salty fluid of his own tears, Ace ventured into full view of the lounge room, and noticed Millie was nowhere to be seen. He heard the distinct groan of the front door opening, and hastily back tracked through the lounge door, glimpsing his sister slam the door behind her and disappear into a rainy morning. For a moment he was paralysed, balancing on fumbling feet, uncertain of what to do. *Should I go after her or should I comfort Dad? Surely Millie is just as upset? She needs me too!* Ace wrestled with the guilt that this was his fault.

The sound of Millie's car accelerating down the street made the difficult decision for him. He turned back to his father and sat beside him. He stretched an awkward arm around his shoulders, comforting him as best he could. And as he sat in puzzlement, it occurred to him that this was no fault of his at all. He may have brought the box's existence to his father's attention, but he had no way of knowing the contents. His muddled tears dried up and a part of his heart began to freeze over. *This is my mother's fault. She deserted us, and now she has caused this trouble! She alone has brought my father to this crumbling mess!*

And while these thoughts began to clog his mind, more thoughts like them joined in, until they gained significant momentum, and there was no doubt left to argue the new resolve which settled within him comfortably. The blue sky that shaded his lovely eyes, darkened to a sapphire burn. His mind twisted in spiteful torment while the new emotion took firm grip, it was hate's first visit. *I hate her!*

Long after the sun had drifted beyond the horizon, Ace found himself engulfed in a restless, sweaty slumber. He tossed and turned, unsettled in the dreams his subconscious played out for him.

He moaned as he discovered himself standing alone in their backyard, the sun dancing through the leaves of the avocado tree. The radiance of the sun streaming through thick leaves beckoned him closer. "Come," said a voice, as he caught a quick movement from behind the tree. "Come." He stepped closer, recognising the sweet tone of his mother. She poked her head out from behind the thick trunk and flashed him a broad smile. Her golden hair tumbled and swayed like silk. He stepped up to see her in full view. "Mummy," he uttered. His eyes fell to the earth below the tree where there was a deep hole. A shadow drifted across his mind as he remembered, and his eyes rose up to her in accusation. He watched as her smile turned to sorrow and his contempt dawned on her.

Another movement caught his attention as a black serpent with a big ugly head hissed at him, revealing its fangs. "Hello friend," said the snake. It arched back in attack mode, and grew taller until it was as tall as Ace himself. His mother stared at them with horror in her eyes. His own fear tore at his chest as his eyes stayed transfixed on her. She opened her mouth and screamed as the snake struck, sinking its fangs deep into the soft flesh of his neck and released its venom into his bloodstream. He screamed as pain scorched through his neck and felt the venom enter his bloodstream like a bolt of lightning.

Ace awoke bathed in a thin film of sweat, the scream freshly caught in his throat as he attempted to calm his laboured breathing. And although relieved it was all a silly dream, he was aware, as he lay back down on the damp pillow, that something had permanently transformed within him. And he knew, he would never be the same again.

CHAPTER SEVENTEEN

November 15, 1973

To My Sweet Baby Daughter Amelia,
How lovely you are my little girl! You are but one month old, and do not doubt me when I say; every smile, every watchful stare and every little gurgle you have given me has made every sleep-deprived night and every soiled nappy worth it. How you have captivated me with your bright emerald gaze and your rosebud pink lips! How happy I am that you have come into my world, sweet girl. From the bottom of my heart, my wish is that you understand with completion just how much I love you.

If you are to receive this letter at all, you see, life with your father has not been easy for me. Oh, I know he loves me. But there is something inside him that takes hold; something sinister. And although I have tried to help him cast this demon within him aside for good, I fear my efforts have been in vain. I fear my very life is in danger. His mind is not his own anymore, and since your birth, he has become particularly paranoid, and I have no-one to turn to for help. He refuses to help himself. I am certain he doesn't realise that he cannot contain this part of himself alone.

Millie, I have loved your father from the moment he diverted my attention away from my canvas and paint one spring afternoon in the park in Rockton. I was completely absorbed with capturing the graceful beauty of a fluttering black and deep blue butterfly when he had startled me with a most charming comment. I'll never forget the soft smile in his eyes that day, and I assure you, it took a lot for me to turn away from a work in progress in those days. Especially when it came to butterflies. Oh, but how I fell in love! The thing is, I know now that my love for him isn't enough to endure the demon that lurks below the surface and overshadows the light within him.

So, I have decided we are to leave your father, sweet daughter. Together you and I will make a peaceful existence for ourselves. Together we shall work it out. And I promise you, I am doing this for our safety and nothing more. So I write this to you now in the hope that one day you will understand the reasons why you are to grow up without the presence of a father.

And I hope the depth of my love for you will be enough.

All my love,

Mummy xoxo

P.S My apologies in advance if you find a distaste for your toes! – For you have unfortunately inherited my lightbulb endowments, and actually, they are just the sweetest little things on the tip of your perfect body.

Folding the faded pink paper that revealed her birth mother's handwriting between shaky fingers, Millie replaced the delicate letter in the worn box. She must have read the letter over a dozen times since it had come into her possession only the night before, and still the reality of its revelations echoed through her being. She allowed her sullen eyes to fall on the contents of the box, and released a heavy sigh while picking up the white-gold ring to inspect its tiny inscription on the inner circle of the precious metal. The exquisitely engraved writing read: *G&S Forever in Love. 1970.* The initials of her parents. Her real parents! A flash of anger surged through her. *How could he keep this from me?* All these years thinking Lilly was her birth mother when another had carried her within the nurturing constraints of her womb and laboured to birth her! It was a mother's love that was all too familiar to her now that she realised the significance of her divine encounters with Samantha. Fresh tears sprang to her eyes and spilled down already soggy cheeks while she placed the wedding ring on her finger. *Oh Mummy!* a numbed mind mused. *What really happened to you?*

It was a truth too harsh for her to face right now. *It can't be … not my father!* Her mind briefly wandered back to the aftermath of Lilly's brutal bashing years ago, and just as quickly pushed aside thoughts that her father was a murderer. How could she love a murderer? Yet she did love her father.

After their argument and the damning accusations she had thrown at him that morning, Millie had driven off in a tizz. She felt so alone in those moments while she pined for the arms of Damon to enfold and consume the discord that ran through her. But there were only memories as she parked outside the apartment block he had just vacated and looked up to the balcony where he smiled down at her so many times in the past. In those hours spent crying in her car in the rain-soaked street, Millie found herself in a whirlwind of emotions at the shock of discovering she was not Lilly's daughter.

The world she knew had been ripped out from under her once again, as the reality of her real mother and what may have happened to her seeped into her consciousness. And how she longed for the safety and comfort of the best friend she could no longer find. She wrestled with raw emotions about her father while the rain fell as though to taunt her. The image of his expression when she had screamed those wild accusations at him was fresh in her mind. He, the strongest and bravest of men she had known, had crumbled before her in a flood of tears. She had to distance herself physically from the deceit that poured from him as she had no idea where it ended and truth began. And by the end of a long, mentally exhausting day, she had crept quietly through the front door of her darkened home with no idea on how to handle the situation with her father, and the mother forever lost to her.

She stared unseeing at the contents of the wooden box as it perched on her bed. She closed the lid with a flick of her hand and carefully turned the small key in the lock until it fastened tight. Millie was absently examining the old delicately painted shells that had once adorned the handmade box when a tap at her bedroom window startled her. The digits displayed on the clock by her bed registered the late time of night, and she jammed the box under her bed and went over to draw the stiff old curtains that concealed the windows to her room.

She squinted through the glass to find Emily standing outside in the eerie light of the street. Even in the dim light, Millie could see she had been weeping too. Her porcelain features appeared dull and sunken. Her right eye seemed so swollen that it was almost closed, causing Millie to gasp. Her own troubles fell aside instantly as concern for her friend washed through her.

"Where have you been?" Emily whined.

Millie put an index finger up to her lips to shush her friend then gestured for Emily to meet her at the front door. She tiptoed through the hall and ushered Emily to her bedroom. She gripped Emily's arms and inspected her thoroughly. Not only was Emily's right eye swollen and bruised, but there were finger mark bruises imprinted in the pale flesh of her wrists and arms.

"My God, Em! What happened? Who did this to you?"

Emily fell into Millie's arms and began to tremble

as fresh tears fell down her face. "Where have you been? I've been looking and looking for you!" she wailed.

Trying her best to keep her own tears at bay, Millie stroked the back of Emily's hair that clung in a damp cluster to her scalp. She had been out in the stormy weather for some time, Millie figured, as she hushed her, rocking her in the unsteadiness her arms provided.

"I'm sorry," Millie said and repeated it.

There was a faint knock at her bedroom door, and she was unable to answer in time before it swung open, revealing the cloudy image of her father in the dreary backdrop of the hall.

"Is everything okay?" Glen asked with a thick eyebrow raised.

Despite the downpour of wild emotion that brewed between them earlier, Millie felt a flood of relief when she saw her father because she was certain she knew who was Emily's attacker, and she knew she was powerless to help her friend. *I will need my father for this one*, she thought, as she remembered the whispered promise she had delivered in a darkened street to Emily's stepfather.

She squared her jaw as she shook her head. "No Dad. Emily has been hurt. Look!" She pulled herself away from Emily a little so her father might catch a better view of her swollen face and bruised arms.

Glen pulled on a dust covered wire cord in the centre of the bedroom to turn on the light, and took the two long strides to hunch down next to the girls. He glanced uncertainly at Millie, searching for any signs of hostility left from their earlier confrontation. When all he saw was his daughter's look of concern for her friend, he sighed in relief and turned to take a closer look at Emily. He decided he would do anything to keep the hostility he saw that morning from returning to his daughter's eyes, and if that meant taking care of her promiscuous friend, then so be it.

He examined Emily without emotion. "Who did this, Emily?"

Emily looked up at him while still clinging to Millie, and gulped down the lump beginning to form in her throat. She recognised the contempt in Glen's eyes, yet despite the degrading feelings Glen evoked from her, his dominating presence compelled her to answer.

Forcing back a sob, she said, "My mother has gone away for the weekend with her church group." She avoided his accusing green eyes and drew a gritty breath. "I was beaten because I fought back when my stepfather raped me."

Glen massaged his chin in thought as he weighed up the information Emily had revealed. He deliberated over whether to be involved or to hand the incident over to the police, since after all, she wasn't *his* daughter. He wasn't inclined to spend valuable energy on people or subjects that held no use to him, especially when the black serpent made its home within him again. He flinched in pain as he fought for control while the serpent demanded to be in control.

He cleared his throat with a guttural grunt. "We

should call for the police; they will handle this and get you to the hospital," he said with pragmatic insight.

"No Dad! We can't hand it over to the police. That won't work for Emily; her mother will never understand," Millie protested. "Please, Dad. Can't you go have a word with him? Please."

He nodded with a drawn-out sigh as he resigned himself to conceding to his daughter's pleas, while his own eyes communicated to her a plea of their own. Both father and daughter were aware of the delicate edge between them, and both were equally mindful that the upper hand belonged to her.

Glen strode determinedly out of the room to pay a visit to his not-so-friendly neighbour. The black demon within him relished the task which would serve as a delicious appetiser for his future plans regarding Lilly. *Stupid woman!* he thought as he neared Emily's front porch. *With her meddling ways, she has sealed her own fate ... and to think, I was willing to let her go gracefully!* Thoughts of his estranged wife added fuel to the fire smouldering within him, and by the time he reached his neighbour's house, he was more than ready to vent the rage that had been brewing all day. His focus was so narrow that he failed to notice that Millie and Emily had followed him outside to watch from the steps of his own porch. And they in turn were unaware of Ace who had slipped through the door unnoticed and stood under the cover of the shadows of the porch to watch.

The inky door under the verandah of Emily's house opened slowly under Glen's persistent bashing.

The light of the cobwebbed globe that hung on the brick wall near the entrance illuminated the area with a dull-yellow glow as Drew struggled to awaken to his late-night caller. Long, wiry fingers fumbled with spectacles to gain a better look at the culprit who dared interrupt his sleep. The man's bony hands trembled as he slicked back the greasy hair that already stuck to a dirty scalp when he recognised Glen. He cleared his throat nervously while hesitant eyes met Glen's silent stare for the briefest of moments. The last encounter years before with the man that stood at his door still lingered on a bruised ego and remained fresh in Drew's mind. Glancing down at the dirty pale night shirt that slung loosely about his thin body, Drew attempted to greet his guest in the friendliest way he could muster.

"Ermmm … hello," he mumbled with a hesitant smile as his eyes strayed to the old metal baseball bat he kept in the corner behind the front door. More confident now, he steeled himself and stared back at Glen. "How can I help you at this ungodly hour? It's very late you know."

Glen grinned and his eyes flashed dangerously. "Oh mate, I'm sorry for the late call and all but I think you know why I'm here," Glen said calmly, before breaking into an eerie chuckle.

Unnerved again, Drew was unsure what to make of Glen's statement. *Surely he couldn't be here because of Emily?* As hard as it had been, he had left her alone for the most part over the years. Well, apart from a harmless little feel every now and then. But the fault wasn't his; after all, how could a man honestly contain himself with a young piece of arse like that in his face? He had just lost control earlier that evening and went too far, that's all. Nothing serious! – *And she's almost twenty years old for God's sake!* If he could just explain this to his surly neighbour, he was certain Glen would understand. Tiny beads of sweat began to cluster above the wiry bush of his mousy brow. He glanced back at the baseball bat, not entirely convinced now it would offer protection.

"Umm … is Emily okay? She hasn't been bothering you, has she?" Drew laughed nervously.

Glen's eyes narrowed as they honed in on him. "You're right! That is exactly why I am here, Drew. You see, I don't appreciate being disturbed at such a late hour, just as you don't." He chuckled again, "And I'm awake and here now because she's crying in my daughter's room because you've hurt her."

"She's no longer a child!" Drew mumbled. "I mean to say, I really didn't mean to hurt her. She was into it, I swear! She's into it with everyone else it seems." He laughed nervously. "So why not *me*?"

Glen tore his eyes away from him in disgust. He'd had enough and was eager to finish the whole sorry episode as quickly as he could. He waved his hand in front of him to shut him up.

"Does it ever occur to you to actually wash your hair?" Glen snarled.

Drew looked back in incomprehension before Glen's fist smashed into his face. His body buckled as he was thrown against the door frame. A second blow landed on the side of his jaw. There was a loud crack of bones breaking as Drew's head collided with the hardwood door. His long scrawny legs gave way, but before he reached the floor, Glen grabbed him by his shoulders and hoisted him to his feet to continue the onslaught. Blood oozed from a swollen mouth. The punches kept coming as Drew slumped to his knees and the assault ended.

Glen crouched down to inspect the knuckles of his bloodied hands with a meticulous eye as he hovered over Drew's writhing body. "You are disgusting," he said. "Don't ever touch her again."

Glen turned to leave. "Clean yourself up. And for God's sake, wash your filthy hair."

One foot had just reached the pavement when Glen heard his daughter's screamed warning. He swung back around, but it was too late. The hard metal of Drew's baseball bat connected with the side of his head. He almost lost his footing as he lifted up his arm in time to block the next shaky blow. He snatched the weapon from Drew's grasp and swung it with all his strength at Drew's knees. The man fell to the pavement with a thud, and threw up his arms to ward off further blows, but Glen threw the bat aside and stormed off as Drew lost consciousness.

Millie was unable to tear her eyes away from the savagery she had just witnessed from her father. Her eyes widened in a strange combination of horror and pride when he brushed past her without a word and disappeared into the house. This was a side to her father she had never known, despite being aware of his violent tendencies. He was like a stranger to her now, and she knew she could never forget the sight of the devastating rage she had just witnessed, and it was all *her* doing. She ushered Emily back in the house and into her room and went after her father. She did not know what to expect. All she knew was that she had to see him and find out for herself. For now, the balance was redressed.

In her haste, Millie failed to notice her younger brother slip into the house behind her and Emily. If she had, she would have seen his pallid face, trembling lips, and the grey that crept into his eyes.

CHAPTER EIGHTEEN

November 8, 1991

M illie cried out as Emily's elbow whacked into her face as she slept. She shoved the offending elbow aside and rolled over with a groan. Emily had been staying with them since the night Drew had assaulted her. It had been a month now, and as much as Millie adored her friend's company, she hated sharing her double bed with her every night. However, she saw no end in sight for the near future, as Emily was still only part way through her hairdressing apprenticeship, and with her meagre wages, there was no way she could afford a place of her own. And returning to her home with her recuperating stepfather and her judgemental mother was out of the question.

She gazed around the room from her position in the bed. *Perhaps we could just squeeze another bed in here somehow,* Millie wondered, as she knew her room was too small for another bed. She felt Emily stir again, and dodged another flying arm. In a single smooth motion, she rolled out of bed and landed on her feet.

"Sorry," Emily's muffled voice said from beneath the sheets, while she stretched to enjoy the extra room that was suddenly granted her.

"Yeah, sure," Millie responded dryly.

She started towards the bathroom when she was forced to pause as nausea and dizziness hindered her progress. She sat back down on the edge of the bed as her mind went into overdrive, as this wasn't the first morning that she had felt like this recently. She knew she would have to face the sneaking suspicion that had plagued her over the last couple of days. Her period had not yet arrived, and coupled with the worsening nausea spelled one thing. *Great, just what I need now, and with Damon gone!* She had been trying to contact Damon using the information he had left for her but to no avail. The overseas phone number was not yet connected, and her letters had gone unanswered. Her thoughts became frantic at facing an unplanned pregnancy without Damon at her side. Then, unable to contain the nausea a second longer, she bolted to the bathroom.

She vowed to visit her doctor later that day to find out exactly why she had been feeling so sick. *It's probably just a little bug I've caught*, she told herself as she dry retched into the bowl of the toilet for the third time.

After washing up and dressing, Millie forced herself to nibble on a slice of vegemite smeared toast, knowing her persistence would eventually pay off and quell the nausea for a while. She could hear the beginnings of the household morning stirrings as she passed through the hallway and heard Emily showering, preparing herself for work.

"Good morning, Millie!" Ace called out from

behind her on his way to the kitchen to have his morning Weetbix before the school day began.

"Morning," she replied without enthusiasm.

She passed through the front door to attend to her daily ritual of checking the mailbox for a letter from Damon. She had recently finished her final year of school, and decided to look for a job to fill in her summer break, as she wasn't going to art school until the following year. *Perhaps I should try the little art gallery store in Rockton for a job*, she thought idly, while making her way down the porch steps to the pavement that led to the mailbox.

As she leaned to check for any sign of letters, Millie caught sight of Dawn Kent. The woman wore a floral shift dress that fell to her ankles and swished over and around the fleshy rolls beneath as she waddled past Millie. Faded blue-grey eyes were fixed ahead beneath a dark blonde perm that frizzled under the sweat inducing morning sun.

"Good Morning, Mrs Kent." Millie laced her greeting with mock friendliness.

Mrs Kent barely glanced at Millie as she grunted past as fast as her legs were able.

"Well, that was nice," Millie grumbled to herself as she watched Mrs Kent duck waddle past the front gate and towards her house, noticing the cloudy dark blue haze that had fallen over her fumbling figure as she had passed her by the front gate.

Millie's eyes paused on the now disappearing form of the woman, and wondered at the meaning behind the misty cloud of colours she often saw lingering around others. *It is easy to see why Emily has so much trouble communicating with her mother*, she thought as her hands came across a lone envelope laying at the bottom of the box, along with some dry leaves that had flown astray in the wind, only to find themselves captive with one envelope addressed to Millie from the United States of America. Her mood instantly brightened as she recognised Damon's bold handwriting, and she hurried back to the house.

Once inside her room, she realised it would be at least an hour before she had the privacy she wanted, as Emily was buzzing about to prepare for work. So, bidding her farewell, Millie got in her car and drove south to the willow tree at the water's edge.

Once there, she hastened down the pathway to the clearing under the willow tree where she and Damon had made love. Her breath caught as she recalled the sacred moments they had shared the day before he had left for New York. Entangled in the throes of an inescapable web of bittersweet nostalgia, she laid herself down on the soft grass, her mind filling with the memory of their love-making. She closed her eyes and relived the ecstasy of their passion, and as she wandered deeper into those moments she had experienced only a handful of weeks before, her body stirred with the passion she had yearned for since he had left. As the desire grew within her, she felt the lustful surge arouse her, and she allowed herself to succumb to the desire as she moved her body in harmony to his imagined presence until her breath became short and she moaned and quivered with orgasm.

She opened her eyes slowly as she regained her senses. Sitting up, she curled her legs beneath her while the euphoria gradually dissolved. She flicked her eyes around the clearing, feeling suddenly foolish, conscious that somebody might have seen her lose herself in that moment of self-pleasuring. She sighed with relief to see that she was totally alone. She peered up at the languid leaves of the willow and whispered a "thank you" to the only witness of her sexually new beginnings. She smiled a secret smile to the tree. "Okay, you know my secrets; how about yours? I bet you have many living here by the bank of the bay."

The warm skin on the back of her neck pricked with a whisper of tingles when, as if on cue, a fluffy white dandelion thistle drifted down from within the cluster of branches. Eyes widened when another thistle joined the first and she watched as they danced before her in the slight breeze that blew around her like a gentle kiss. The thistles glided closer until they landed in the palms of her upturned hands.

Millie's mouth fell open. "Ohhh," she said as she beheld them. They were so light that she could not feel them on her skin. She knew the action of the two little dandelion seedlings was no accident. She reasoned that if only people took the time to listen, the universe would always talk to you. *If only we would be awake to it!*

She raised up her palms and gave the little thistles a blow with a warm breath, sending them on their way. Then finally, she picked up Damon's letter, and opening it as carefully as she could, settled in to reading the message in its folded page.

Dear Millie,

I have only just received your letters, and all three arrived on the same day, causing me to have little faith in the international postage system! But at least they finally found me, and when I saw them and held them in my hands, I was overcome with the most heartbreaking emotion, Millie.

You see, I miss you so very much. I have found our separation unbearable to say the least. Then I see a part of you arriving on my doorstep in your letters. I hold the letters against my heart in some small hope that this will allow me to feel your fingers upon my skin, the beating of your heart next to mine. I bring your handwriting under my nose so that I may better remember the sweet scent that lingers with you. My eyes close so that I may lose myself in the brightest of emeralds, and I smile so that I may better be captive to your charm. I cannot help but recall the last of our moments together under the willow tree. Oh how I had waited so long to make love to you! And oh, how sweet and fleeting were so precious those moments between us!

My eyes can only close for so long, and my heart can only shatter to so many pieces, Millie. So they open reluctantly, and I am no longer holding your beauty under the willow. The pain becomes even more consuming, and I know in the deepest recesses of my aching heart, I cannot continue in this way.

I have discovered the traineeship I have started will continue for a period of six years. I'll also be studying along with the job. I have also discovered I have quite a knack for this line of work, and I am enjoying it very much. It helps to keep my mind occupied from thinking of you. It doesn't pay much, but as soon as I can save up enough I plan to come back to visit you. Perhaps I can smuggle you back to New York? I just know you would love this city. It is nothing like I have ever seen! I know also, it would not be fair to ask to you wait for my return. For we are both young, and the future awaits. Although it is hard to imagine a future without you, I am uncertain how it will unfold between us under these circumstances. I have tried to call you, but to no avail. I long to hear your voice, and I shall try again soon.

I will forever be the guy that loves you endlessly; of that, please do not doubt. But Millie, while my flesh is not by yours, we need to live it so.

Find your dreams and relish every moment of the beautiful life that I know is yours for the taking. You are special Amelia Anderson, never forget that.

And I shall never forget you.

Love, Damon

The final lines of his letter blurred under the tears that fell from her eyes. She watched in an odd moment of fascination as the salty liquid smudged the ink of his handwriting against the white of the paper. She didn't mind that the words he had printed were ruined between quivering fingers. Desperate fingers began to twist the paper between them, scrunching and twisting. They began to tear and shred at those damning words until each line resembled the shattered heart he had described upon them, and they lay all around her a torn and crumbled mess. All energy left her, and Millie fell back against the grass, pulling herself into a tight ball as she grieved for the boy that had swept into her heart with a vengeance years before, and had kept it captivated within the sweetest moments she had ever known. Images of his blue lagoon eyes flashed through her, and her body shook with the knowledge that he might be forever lost to her. *My beautiful blue lagoon. Oh, how could he let our love go?* She fought to understand his reasoning, unwilling to accept that he was prepared to accept a future without her.

She shut her eyes and lay there feeling helpless. The longing she had been feeling for him heightened, and Millie felt the bitter loneliness. Short breaths caught in her throat while she struggled to regain herself. *Breathe,* she instructed her body. Focusing strictly on her breathing now, she found relief for a few moments. Her contemplation was then drawn to the distinct caress that grazed over her left cheek. A familiar tingle prickled its way through the nape of her neck, running down the ridge of her spine, confirming that she was not as alone as she had felt.

Words filtered into her mind. *"Millie, we are here with you. We love you."*

She gasped and opened her eyes to see numerous dandelion thistle seedlings falling down all around her. She watched as they fell about her in an endless stream, like a translucent mantle of softly falling snow.

"Wow!" Her eyes again filled with tears, only now they were tears of joy, because she knew she bore witness to a divine phenomenon, and she felt the presence of God in every little thistle that fell around her.

After her doctor's appointment that day, no sooner had she walked through the door to her house than the phone rang. She threw the black leather bag at her bed as she passed her room, and ran for the phone in the lounge room. She chimed with a "Hello" as she hoped it was Damon.

She sighed when it became apparent that it wasn't Damon. Instead, it was a stern voice demanding that someone collect Ace from school, as he had been involved in a fight.

"A fight?" She was nonplussed.

"He beat up another boy because the boy refused to

share his lunch money. The boy didn't know how to defend himself against the attack."

"Oh! That doesn't sound like something my brother would do."

"Well he did. Please come and collect him; he has been suspended from school and needs to leave the grounds immediately."

"Yes, of course," she stammered.

She retrieved her bag and keys and hurried out to her car. Her mind swirled with confusion as she drove to the school. She had noticed his behaviour had been different over the past few weeks. He was not the happy, joking boy he usually was. She had figured this was due to Damon's sudden departure, because she knew how much Ace adored Damon. But surely this attack on another boy could not be the result of Damon leaving? Her instincts told her that this was something else and she needed resolve. She steeled herself against the disapproving attitudes she knew awaited her at the school office.

Ace remained silent for most of the drive home as his sister plied him with questions about his behaviour. He glared back at her while she spoke about how wrong it was that he beat that boy up.

"Just leave me alone," he scowled.

"No way, mister. This is not like you at all. Why did you hurt that kid, Ace?"

Ace glowered at her.

"Ace! Answer me!" Millie shouted as the car pulled up outside their house. "Why would you hurt someone so badly?" Her voice softened, and he caught the plea in her eyes as she searched him for a satisfactory explanation.

Ace gazed around the quiet street. He was surprised to see his father's car parked in the driveway. "Did they call dad too?" he asked.

Millie's stare was relentless. "Ace, please …"

He gestured at his father's Holden. "I just did what he does, that's all," he shrugged.

He unbuckled himself and casually strolled away from the car, leaving Millie open-mouthed. She noticed the menacing dark blaze in his eyes and sat for a few moments while watching him bound up the porch steps and disappear through the front door of the house. Her stomach tightened into a knot. Millie felt the weight of dread as she made her way to the house, while a whisper within her sounded off like a siren. One word formed as it pounded her mind like an unstoppable freight train. The bitter taste of bile rose in her throat – *Terror!*

SIX YEARS LATER…

"And though thy knees were never bent

To heaven thy hourly prayers are sent

And whether formed for good or ill

Are registered and answered still."

Ralph Waldo Emerson

CHAPTER NINETEEN

November 17, 1997

Dark brown eyes sparkled as they rested on the familiar features of an old friend. The two men exchanged an awkward embrace. It had been at least seven years since they had last met. He gave a hearty laugh from the depth of his belly and grinned at his old friend.

"Jack, you are a sight for sore eyes."

With a hand still gripped in a firm handshake, Jack's grin matched those of Scott's. "As are you, Scott … as are you."

They were both standing alongside the pool at the hotel bar where they had arranged to meet. Jack was older than Scott, and feeling every bit of his 63 years as he dumped himself into his chair with a relieved sigh. He gestured at Scott's hair while Scott slid in a chair beside him under a large umbrella to avoid the burning midday sun.

"Look at you!" Jack chuckled. "You've finally lost the battle of the grey! Too many to pluck out now."

"At least I still have hair, old man," Scott said, indicating Jack's receding hairline. "Besides, would you believe I actually don't mind?"

"Oh yeah?" Jack teased.

"Yeah."

"So how about all those extra wrinkles I see road mapping your face then, you mind those?"

Scott laughed. "How else would I find my way around?" he said with a shrug.

Two attractive women wearing bikini tops and Balinese sarongs neared their table, catching Jack's eye as they sauntered past.

"It appears others don't mind your road maps either," he said, inclining his head at the passing women.

Jack sigh miserably as he watched the women. He hadn't managed to score a piece of arse like that since his early forties. Jack had lived on the Gold Coast his whole life, and enjoyed every moment, until he had lost his self-made fortune to an overzealous gambling habit about ten years before, along with his much younger ex-wife. It had been a classic case of "Goodbye money; Sayonara wife". Since then his life and his health had taken a definite downslide, and he had found himself hustling for a quick dime in any way he could. Only these days the natural magic touch that used to be his when it came to busting a nickel, appeared to evade him.

Scott chuckled at the nostalgic look of longing that etched itself across Jack's wrinkled features. "You really wouldn't want to try and keep up with it, Jack" he teased. "Too high maintenance."

"Oh, I would give it my best shot!" he bellowed.

The two men spent the afternoon catching up and reminiscing about the wild days of old when both owned the two most popular clubs on the Coast. Scott was relieved to be in the company of a familiar trusted friend and confided this much to Jack, along with the last years of his life on the road with Kate. He was tired of the travelling and wanted to settle in some place quiet with her, but Kate would not allow it.

"I think you can stop running now," he had pleaded.

"I can *never* stop running!' she cried through a drunken stupor. Her face was contorted as she attempted to focus her eyes on him. "Why don't you just leave me if that's what you want?"

But Scott could not let her slip from his life again. Not his beautiful Lilly Pad. So, he had resigned himself to the constant life on the road. He watched her succumb to the gripping claws of alcohol with an aching heart. He lost himself in a world churning with desolation and havoc, hangovers and hair of the dog mornings, and felt helpless to give her the help that he knew she needed. Years had passed, and throughout them all he remained at her side until finally he could lead her back to the Gold Coast – the town she had avoided since her parents' deaths some years before. He could no longer endure the burden of the life she had chosen. The decision had not come easily. He had made the critical phone call to the most prestigious rehabilitation clinic on the Gold Coast a few days ago, a clinic that would become Lilly's new home for some time – at his own cost, of course. He just had to convince her to stay there.

And then I will be free, he thought with regret as

he half listened to Jack talking about old times. *And then she will be free*.

"He was a really big, stocky bloke, and he seemed more interested in Kate." Jack's booming voice cut through his thoughts.

"Huh? Who was?" Scott said, puzzled.

"The man that come into your old club about a month or so ago." Jack shot him a perplexed glance. "Where are you, anyway?"

"Sorry," Scott mumbled. He was all ears now.

"I had just stopped by the club for a quick drink; you know how it is." Jack mopped the sweat from his wiry brow with a handkerchief he pulled from his shirt pocket. "I heard him asking about you and Kate. He mentioned he was a friend of Kate's." His eyes went up as he racked his memory. "Oh yeah, that's right, he mumbled something about having news of Kate's daughter."

The hackles on Scott's neck rose as he listened to Jack's description of the man looking for them. Jack had no way of knowing that the woman Scott had been spending his life with had been using a name not really belonging to her, nor that any person on this planet should know that Kate did indeed have a daughter. But how could Glen have connected Lilly, aka Kate, to him? Scott wondered. His mind began to scan back over the last few years, and finally his thoughts hovered over a lone incident that may have revealed *their* connection to Glen – Cindy Churchill.

They had bumped into her two years previously while they were travelling through Cairns by road.

They had stopped there for a few days to take a break from the road. They had not been in town for sightseeing or socialising of any kind, and yet Lilly insisted one morning that they visit the Daintree rainforest. Scott had reluctantly agreed, as they had already made the visit numerous times in the past and the rainforest was one of her favourites. *Anything to see her smile* again, he had thought. They had been relaxing on some boulders by the river after hiking through the rainforest when they had heard the voice of a woman call out to them.

"Oh my God!" The voice called as she came rushing to them, "Lilly Winston and Scott Perry!" It was Cindy Churchill.

She had always been an athletic student at school, Scott recalled, remembering that her forte had been swimming, and she had retained the physique of a trained swimmer. She had solid shoulder muscles which flexed as she opened her arms to hug Lilly. Scott had done his best to ward off the unwelcome school reunion, quickly ushering Lilly away from the questioning intrusion with promises of meeting her for a drink later that evening. Cindy thrived on gossip, and Scott knew that that meeting would be too much for her to keep to herself once she returned to the Gold Coast.

Scott gathered all the information he could from his friend, who described the man inquiring after them as tall and solid with short, clipped spiky hair.

"Like a beefcake!" Jack chuckled, then his expression became serious. "But it was really his eyes that stood out to me the most. They were like the flames of hell," he said, lowering his voice and frowning.

A streak of laughter shot through Kate's numbed mind, shocking her into a hazy awareness. "Damned people," she grumbled, as she fumbled to sit up on her beach towel. Dull bloodshot eyes regarded the shadowy beach while she struggled for a few clouded moments on her whereabouts. *Ah yes*, she thought as she frowned up at the laughing couple strolling along the sand, *I'm at the beach*. She vaguely remembered stumbling down the short pathway across from Scott's old apartment. She had been surprised when she had learned that he had kept the Gold Coast apartment after their years on the road together. This had only caused her to wonder what other secrets he had kept from her. She hadn't voiced this much to him – yet. However, his disappearance that afternoon spiked her suspicions, and she had grown impatient with waiting around for him to return. *Where did he go again?* Her mind wrenched as she attempted to recall that information. *Ouch!* She reached for the half-full bottle of vodka she had brought along for company. Dreary lifeless blonde hair fell back off narrow bony shoulders as she took a generous gulp from the glass bottle. *That's better*, she thought, as her mind began to whip into a more coherent line of action. "Probably screwing another woman," she muttered out loud. *Yes! That's*

what he's doing. Sneaky, cheating arsehole! Another generous swig of alcohol coursed its way down her throat. The fog in her mind cleared as she grappled around with twitchy fingers for her cigarettes. She lit one and inhaled the thick toxins before allowing the white curl of smoke to drift from her lungs.

The looked down at her body. The once vibrantly taut skin now fell loose and grey around a gangly, ossified body. Nails and hair had lost all youthful appearance, leaving a brittle dull shadow of what once had flourished. *No wonder he wants me no more!* she thought, as tears of despair welled within her. The whisper within her, although constantly buried deep amid a murky alcohol-induced haze, mourned at the person she had allowed herself to become. The strong determined woman who had left a monster with great plans to create the life she had always wanted, had faded from her vision completely. *This was not how it was suppose be!* she cursed herself. And yet, as she lifted the bottle to her lips another time, she felt powerless to be otherwise.

She surveyed the almost deserted beach, and for the first time in the ten years, Kate admitted to herself that she needed help. Tears coursed from hollow eyes and toppled down the sunken pockets of flesh under her cheekbones. The salty warm liquid blended with the lingering salty air that drifted above the cooling sand in an opaque, misty haze and stung the graze of her lips. She shuddered as she came face to face with the reality *she* had created for herself. Every dream she had ever aspired to had fallen through her fingers and evaporated away. Every thought that went unwatched; every discordant feeling that was pondered over and over; every twisted emotion of guilt and spite haunted her as her body shook at the life she created for herself. *The grudging alcoholic I have become!* She sat there feeling every sober moment of her self-created life. She allowed the emotions to permeate through every part of her being, as she knew she had to feel it in order to make a positive change. She was so engrossed in her new realisations that she failed to hear the thud of sand-muffled footsteps as they neared her from behind.

Scott took in the scene before him with a broad glance. He noticed the tremble of her slight body, the almost empty vodka bottle cast aside in the sand next to her, and limp golden hair hanging bleakly around her shoulders as he drew closer. He looked to the only woman he could ever love with a sense of despair. He brought his arms around her and kissed her forehead. She turned and reached for him, nuzzling dry lips against his. He was surprised that his presence evoked a response in her that he hadn't seen in years.

He brushed the tears from her face and gazed down at her. "Shhhh," he soothed, "What's going on, baby?"

Vulnerable blue eyes looked into his with the innocence of a small child. "I need help," she whispered. She fell against him as she abandoned herself to the confession that had escaped through cracked lips.

It didn't require much strength to hold her

quaking body. Scott saw a flicker of hope as she wept in his arms. Relief flooded through him as his own tears joined hers as he realised how deep hers words scorched through him. All thoughts of the man he suspected might be her estranged husband faded from his mind as Scott lost himself to the joy this moment gave to him. All that consumed his mind now was Lilly and her willingness to sober up. He took a long breath and tentatively began to explain to her his plan for the rehabilitation clinic.

Nestled in a reclusive little niche amid the lush rainforest and hinterland of the Numinbah Valley on the Gold Coast was the white homestead style mansion of The Rosebud Retreat. Kate found on this bright morning that it was abstinence treatment that brought her here. The willingness to change the boozy life that she had acknowledged while sitting at the beach a few days ago, stuck with her. But it wasn't enough to stop the emotions that bubbled unchecked beneath the surface of her delicate demeanour. She knew the detoxifying days that lay before her would be difficult and lonely and she already felt like she was entering a barren stretch of no-man's land.

The car finally pulled to a stop in front of a broad grand verandah that wrapped around the whole of the building. Pale yellow window panes dotted with colourful flowers among their sills, along with the vast growth of hanging baskets that hung cheerfully from its eves, gave the homestead the comforting feel the owners set out to achieve. Kate could see there were other smaller cottages scattered among big trees behind the manor. A stable with horses stood beside a paddock. She sighed and swallowed hard to shift the lump taking refuge in her throat as she regarded a well-loved garden. In the garden were a sprinkling of people perched quietly, each before an easel and engrossed in their painting. She looked to Scott, unable to conceal her anguish that increased with every beat of her heart. She was to stay here for three months. *Three whole long months! Oh my goodness!* She could barely breathe.

He smiled down at her and caressed her cheek. "It's okay," Scott assured her. "It's all going to be okay, I promise."

She gave him the bravest smile she could manage to summon before they both alighted from the car and walked hesitantly towards the house.

Kate removed her large sunglasses as they stepped into the foyer. She gazed around the house with foreboding, while clinging to Scott's arm with the skittish manner of a wild, frightened animal. *Do I really have the strength to do this?* she wondered. She looked back at Scott and found herself consumed with the love she found there. It was the boost of courage she needed to keep going. She was well aware now that her abstinence hinged on much more than just her own personal interests. She knew the future of the relationship she shared with the man walking next to her rested on her cleaning up. *And maybe... just maybe,* she contemplated, *one day soon my children might allow me to visit with them.*

A woman called Deborah greeted them warmly. "You can call me Deb," she said. Her smile revealed a depth of kindness that glowed behind brown eyes.

She took them through the proper formalities in her office and showed them to the quarters that Kate would call home for the next three months. Deb sat down with them in the living area of the casually decorated suite and explained the twelve-step program that Kate was about to embark on. She emphasised the self-determination that Kate would need to sustain, as well as the support she would need from her partner. She arose to leave Kate and Scott to their goodbyes, and turned to them with a gentle smile. "It gets easier. You are in good hands."

Her body twisted beneath him while she purred like the engine of a finely tuned sports car. *Yeah, sports car.* For a moment the idea enticed him as he toyed with images of a sleek red Lamborghini while he pushed himself into her. *Many of those sports cars are named after Spanish legends.* He opened his eyes a little and caught a glimpse of the bubbly blonde squirming under him. *This one is far from an exotic Spanish beauty,* he thought, while the purrs escalated to an irritating screech as he reached the height of the mediocre sexual rendezvous he had managed to squeeze in between lectures. A slight groan involuntarily released itself, and without another thought to the young woman who had shared her bed with him that afternoon, he rolled off in one swift, athletic movement.

"Hey! Come back here. I wasn't done!" she protested

The bulge in her grey eyes protruded to the point that he wondered if they might pop out of her plain face. He grinned at the thought. "Oh, I'm sorry sugar-puss." Dirty blonde hair fell over one eye seductively while he turned on the charm. "I'm late for class."

He pulled on his jeans and strolled casually up as he perused her naked body. *She does have a great body*, he thought. *Pity about the face though*.

"How about we finish this later?" He swept her lips in a brief kiss. "Can I have your number?"

Her expression relaxed under the alluring magnetism that oozed from him. She grinned back and scribbled her name and number on a yellow Post-it note and handed it over to him with as much seduction in her movements as she could possibly conjure. Cathy had been chasing this guy for months and it had only been yesterday that he finally realised she was, in fact, alive. She wasn't about to let him go *that* easily.

She looked up at him hopefully. "Promise you'll call me?" Cathy giggled nervously.

He suppressed a rising sigh. *Way too overeager*. "Sure," he replied. His smile held her mesmerised.

He swung the black leather biker jacket over broad shoulders and pushed his sunglasses on his nose before straddling his prized Harley-Davidson Softail Heritage. The bike roared to life and a smile played on his lips as he felt the usual arousing sensations that spiked their way deliciously through him when the engine purred beneath him. Placing it into gear, he thundered his way off campus towards home. *If only a woman could evoke such feelings in me as this cherished Harley easily accomplished, I might actually keep one around for more than a few days*, he pondered. He hardly understood why he had so little respect for the girls that paraded through his life in quick succession. All he knew was that they came too easily, and with it, too willingly. He found no challenge in finding an eager woman. They were all the same. They were all like *her*. Perhaps one day someone might surprise him. However, he was highly doubtful. They were all "bitches" as far as he was concerned; bitches that could not be trusted, just like her.

Some 30 minutes later he pulled up out the front of the house he shared with his father, and breezed through the empty house, relieved to have it all to himself for a while. Taking full advantage of his time alone, he played the tunes of Third Eye Blind at full volume. To the strains of a *Semi Charmed Life*, he pulled out a boxed package of black hair dye from his backpack, stripped down and made his way to the bathroom. There, he spent a few minutes of admiration while he scrutinised every inch of skin that appeared in the mirror before him. Only after he was completely satisfied with the image, did he pull the bottle from its packaging and begin to apply the tint to conceal his natural dark blonde mane.

His blue eyes became transfixed by the thick

liquid that clung to the strands of his hair, almost as if he were in a trance. And like the dye in his hair, he felt as if he was victim to a black trance he could not escape. He had learned long ago that it was useless to fight it, and in doing so, had completely succumbed to its dark will, allowing the dense fog to dim the light he used to be. He didn't possess the strength to fight its grim force, as he had spent more and more time alone over the last few years in his growing manhood. It was all the time needed for the demonic thoughts to ensnare him in its roots until it became a part of him. He had become an expert at concealing the demon to those he knew, even to his own father, who he was sure still thought of him as his little boy. His father was quite proud of the strong ambition his son had in his studies towards a Bachelor of Science, majoring in Astronomy. His lips curled into a twisted smile. He knew his father was "clueless" as he put it. The set of his high cheek bones distinguished a handsome face, which contorted as his thoughts turned to her. *Soon,* the dark force whispered through the recesses of his soul, *you will know her whereabouts.*

He watched with a slight twist of the head as black droplets fell like the tears of a weeping devil from his hair. Another slight twist sent the dye dripping down the pale skin of his face in a cavort between light and dark. *Oh!* He gazed at the gruesome reflection, *How beautiful! And Oh, how I have longed to see her!*

CHAPTER TWENTY

T he sounds of laughter interrupted the brush stroke on the canvas before her. She turned to peer towards the giggles of the child, and her expression softened with the warmth of her own giggle.

"Mummy! Mummy! Look!" the child shrieked. "I *am* a butterfly!"

Little arms flapped about while tiny feet skipped along in the wake of the two white butterflies that fluttered through the sunshine at Rockton town park. Russet coloured hair tumbled in waves to the bottom of Arella's tiny waist, and bounced in a veil as she ran about in circles after the butterflies.

"I always said you were," laughed the five-year-old's mother. "You're *my* little butterfly."

Millie drew in a deep breath as she watched Arella play make-believe butterflies, until finally the tiny insects fluttered out of sight.

Arella fell panting against the open arms that awaited her. The blue-greens of her almond eyes gazed up towards her mother dubiously. "Mummy, why do you call me butterfly all the time?"

Millie planted a tiny kiss on the tip of Arella's nose. "Because butterflies are a symbol of transformation," she explained, smoothing out the furrow on her daughter's brows. "They remind us to keep our faith. *You* remind me of that every day, my little butterfly."

Arella contemplated her mother's explanation for a moment. "I love butterflies," she declared.

The child's eyes squinted at the canvas, skimming every detail of the almost completed painting. She examined the layers of pigments that had been applied, revealing a glimmering scene of the bay. The lights in the background of the painting reflected against the water, frozen in gentle swirls that gave the surface of the water its magical shimmer. And when her eyes beheld the image of angel wings suspended in the cloud drifting over the bay, she gasped.

"Oh! I love this too!" she said, flashing a smile at her mother.

Millie laughed. "I'm so glad you like this painting, baby," she said, sweeping Arella onto her lap. "It means a lot to me." Her voice became wistful while a glimmer of a teardrop stung the corners of her eyes safely concealed under her sunglasses.

From the moment she could walk and talk, Arella had been an exceptionally bright child, impressing those around her with the fast progress she had made with meeting all the childhood milestones unusually early. She was stringing together full comprehensible sentences with ease by the time she had reached eighteen months old. At three, her little fingers were able to grasp and direct a pencil with the competency of a child more than twice her age. Writing out the alphabet and her name became normal. Millie had found her daughter to be extremely sensitive to the world around her, and particularly receptive to other people. Arella would often tell her mother who they might bump into when they left the small apartment they had shared since she was born. She could also foretell who might call them on the phone that day. When she began to accurately predict events, Millie knew her daughter's gifts went beyond an academic level. Strangely, Millie found comfort in her daughter's clairvoyance, as it gave her own metaphysical experiences validation. However, it was becoming a challenge when she wished to conceal something personal from her daughter, because as Arella grew older, so too did her receptive attributes.

When she knew for certain that she was pregnant, despite her planned enrolment to attend art school the following year, Millie knew there was no choice to be made. After adjusting to the enormity of the news, she welcomed her impending motherhood and she wrote to Damon excitedly to tell him the news. She waited anxiously for his reply and when none came, she accepted his silence with a stony heart. Although she knew her life would never be the same, she ignored the cries of protests from her father, but took her mother's departing advice and listened to the whisper within her.

During the early days of her pregnancy, Millie had managed to secure a job at the art gallery in Rockton. The small gallery, along with displaying and selling local Australian art, supported budding artists by holding their own workshops twice a month. There, she learned to explore basic elements of design, to recognise and identify the timeless qualities of great art, as well as developing and improving upon her own artwork. After recognising the natural talent of Millie's art, her employer, Mrs Bartlett, welcomed her talent, and soon they had formed a special bond.

The two women worked together tirelessly on improving and renovating the gallery's interior design during the months before Millie gave birth. Mrs Bartlett had been especially impressed with the elegant modern touches Millie had added to her small shopfront, promising Millie not only the security of returning to her position after some time off with her new baby when she arrived, but also offering Millie a small corner of the gallery for displaying her artwork. Mrs Bartlett had gained a reputation over the years for her sharp eye in the art world, and despite her flamboyant and eccentric clothes, she had earned her acclaimed reputation among even the most articulated of art connoisseurs.

"Every piece of art is an expression of God," Mrs Bartlett often told Millie over the course of their liaison. "We are but clothed in different skins; but do not forget my young friend, we are all but one."

Mrs Bartlett had become a close dependable figure in Millie's world over the years, and an aunt to Arella who often accompanied her mother into work before the start of her schooling.

Arella's birth was followed with a few months spent at home in the unit Millie shared with Emily. Her father had begged for their return home, offering to help with the costs of raising his granddaughter, and although Millie considered his offer, she could not bring herself to return to her father again. She had confused emotions about her father, who could mete out such brutal abuse yet had such a love for his children. Glen seemed to dangle on the thinnest string of light, and if she were to exile him from her and Arella's life, she knew it might be just enough to sever that shiny thread.

Millie came back to the present as her daughter looked at her with a perceptive eye.

"Are you okay, Mummy?" Arella said.

"I'm fine baby girl," she replied, chastising herself silently for revealing the slight hint of sentiment that the painting had evoked in her. "Now, let's go home. It's getting late and we are meeting Craig for dinner tonight."

"Yippee!" Arella hurriedly helped her mother to gather their belongings.

Millie was glad her daughter had taken a shine to Craig, as he was the first man since Damon had left that had really captivated her own interest. She regarded the diamond solitaire that ornamented her left hand, and she smiled at her daughter. It was the first time in years that she had allowed someone in close enough to touch the heart that had waited for the return of first love. The softest of caresses was all it had taken for Craig to shatter the past she had clung to with a stubborn hope. *Or perhaps the past still clung to me*, Millie wondered while fingers twisted at the half-heart that hung around her neck. Arella reminded her of Damon with every storm in those aquamarine eyes, and every shrug of the dark veil that cascaded down her back. Nevertheless, her heart had been freed to love another again. Craig was a good man, and soon would be her husband.

Spirits soared as mother and daughter pulled up outside the tan-brick block of apartments which housed their own two-bedroom condo. Arella caught the colourful whirl of her new wind-spinner that was embedded in one of the many pot plants that filled up almost every bit of spare space on the tiny balcony that spilled out from their lounge room.

"Look Mummy! My wind-spinner is going crazy!" Arella laughed.

Millie peered up at their balcony and the recent gift Craig had bought for her daughter when picnicking the weekend before.

"It sure is! I think we are going to go wind-crazy too if we don't get inside."

Millie shut the car door behind her and carefully juggled the canvas against the growing gale. She hugged the creation against her chest before setting off after Arella who had already raced ahead and disappeared into the entrance of the building.

"Millie!" Emily called out over the wind that gusted across the bay.

Millie was surprised to see Emily pushing the

double stroller that carried her twin boys towards her.

"Emily! What are you doing out in this weather with the babies?" Millie nodded towards the building. "Hurry, let's get inside."

Once the six-month-old twins were settled among the toys and pillows on the floor of Millie's small lounge room with Arella watching over them, the two women talked in the kitchen while making tea.

"I'm sorry for just turning up like this, Pussy-cat. I just had to see you," Emily said.

Millie placed two mugs on the bench-top and aimed a subtle frown at Emily. "Such nonsense you talk, Em. You know you are always welcome here."

She rested her eyes on her friend. "What's going on sweetie?"

She knew Emily had come here to seek her out for more than just a friendly hello, and she knew her friend's life with the twin's father, Chad, had been recently plagued with torment.

"He's getting worse." Emily squeezed her eyes shut for a moment, trying to shake off her tears. "He is sleeping with someone else. He didn't even bother coming home last weekend. When I asked him where he had been, do you know what he told me?"

Millie hated seeing Emily being treated this way, and especially with the twins in her care. She knew since the arrival of her twins, Emily had been struggling with postnatal depression, and the extra stress Chad imposed on her friend would only add to it.

"He said he spent the weekend with a *real*

woman," Emily said, bursting into tears.

She covered her face with her hands and sniffled, and appeared so frail that Millie was scared that she might fall from the wooden stool she was sitting on. Chrome bangles clanked against the bench-top as Emily slumped over. Mascara streaks streamed down her chalky skin.

Millie stood behind her and cradled her in her arms. "Shhh … it's okay sweetie. It's okay."

"I don't know what to do," Emily cried.

She lifted her head and turned her tear-stained face towards Millie, grave blues narrowed while the lines of her brows furrowed for a moment in serious contemplation. "There is no way I can raise those two boys on my own."

Taking the stool next to Emily, Millie focused on her friend and the extent of the words that she had just divulged. "Em, listen. You are not alone! I can help you with the twins. You don't have to accept Chad's treatment of you and the boys. There *are* solutions, and I can help you work it out."

Emily shook her head. "There is nothing you can do, Millie," she murmured.

"Sure there is. You and the twins can move back here with us for awhile."

"There is no room for me plus two."

"We can make room!" Millie said, grasping at her hair. "We'll just be like sardines for a bit," she said, trying to lighten the mood.

When she had discovered her pregnancy, it hadn't taken long for Millie to decide that she wanted to move away from her father. Besides, not envisaging Emily's departure from her bed any time soon, spurred the idea into realisation. Millie had figured that if she could find a full-time job, Emily would make the perfect housemate instead of bed mate. Emily jumped at the idea, and within weeks the two girls had secured the beachside apartment that Millie now still occupied with her daughter. Emily was with them for the next three years and became a second mum to Arella as she assisted with the care of the baby. Emily took turns during the night feeds so Millie could get some rest; she changed soiled nappies and gave Arella baths. And on Saturday mornings, they would walk to the park together.

It had been on one of those Saturday morning strolls that Emily met Chad Turner – the love of her life, or so she had thought. She had been pushing twelve-month-old Arella on the swing when he had offered them each a lollipop. His jet black hair coupled with his brooding chocolate brown eyes had been enough to send her into shivers of excitement all that morning. It was a thrill that grew and matured over the next weeks of dating Chad into something far deeper. And to her surprise, Emily realised late one night that for the first time she was in love.

Love, Emily found, knew no time nor limitations. It wasn't long before Emily said goodbye to the apartment she had shared with Millie and Arella, and moved in with Chad. Life had been good when lived in love. She would go into work every day drifting on a silver-lined cloud, a smile never far from her lips. She would hurry home each afternoon to fix Chad his dinner, and afterwards they would sometimes watch some television together, while at other times they would go for a walk if the weather and mood fancied them. And at the end of every evening, their bedroom blazed with the fire of passion.

Life had been good when lived in love, and for the very first time, Emily thrived with every embrace, kiss, and awakening beside him. Never had she known such an intensity of passion, and never had she felt so protected. She dismissed his tendency to be possessive and domineering, and when he proposed one evening over a candlelit dinner for two, she accepted without hesitation.

Emily contemplated Millie's offer. "I'll give it some thought. Thanks Pussy-cat." She forced a smile to ease Millie's concern.

Life had been good when lived in love.

Emily stared at the hot milky broth in front of her as though it revealed the answers she sought. She sighed as the cries of her twin boys in the living room taunted her. Emily didn't bother to look to Millie when she left to tend to her children. *How could I have been so wrong about him?* she thought as a fresh flood of tears streamed down her face. Dreary, muddled thoughts clouded the space in her mind like a dense fog, and she remembered the good years. A brief smile played on her lips as Emily remembered the love on *his* lips that had struck her heart like cupid's arrow.

They were married a year later. Millie had been her bridesmaid in pale pink chiffon, and Arella her flower girl. Adorned in a simple black tailored suit, Chad had awaited her arrival under a garden arch festooned in lilac flowers, and when she approached dressed in an ivory silk gown, she felt profoundly contented. He was flawless. Her love knew no limits despite his growing paranoia every time she left the house. It only proved his love for her, she told herself. His nightly love-making had earned him the label of her sexy vampire.

When she discovered that she was pregnant with the twins, she jumped into Chad's arms to share the news. They were to be a family! But to her dismay, he did not share her spirited sentiment. To the contrary, the news appeared to heighten his paranoia, and as each month passed, so too did Chad's delusions of her deceitfulness. He disbelieved that the twins were his bloodline, and had convinced himself that she had been unfaithful. Emily's cries of protest landed on deaf ears, until she had resorted to consoling herself that her husband would have a change of heart once he saw his sons, as they would most certainly reflect their father's physical traits and he would forget this nonsense. As Chad's animosity continued, Emily lost her joy in the pregnancy and started to resent it. Days grew grey and lonely and most nights were filled with tears and restlessness. When the time for the twin's births had arrived, her husband was nowhere to be found. Her only support was in Millie, as she had avoided her family since Drew's brutal beating for which her mother blamed her. Her brothers also sided with her parents.

Six months had passed since her boys were born, and the change of heart she had hoped to find in her husband did not come. The distance between them had grown to the point that Chad seemed to be disgusted with her presence, and that of their children. She found no joy in her new role as a mother, and had become a lost soul trapped in a numb body that barely made it through each day.

Life had been good when lived in love.

Craig listened to Millie's worried banter about her friend. His cheeks dimpled with his gentle smile. "It must be hard for you to see her in such a state." He murmured while clasping his hand over hers.

She took a breath as if she were about to say something, then fell silent as she appeared to look right through him. "I … just feel helpless," she finally uttered. "Thank you for listening, Craig."

Millie's fingers squeezed his big knuckles. Her smile was apologetic as she decided to steer the conversation to lighter subjects. But the background noise in her mind continued to hover over her concern for Emily and her babies, because try as she might, she was unable to convince her friend to stay over during her visit that afternoon. Instead, all she could do was drive Emily and her babies' home through the windstorm.

Millie could not shake off the troubling feelings that plagued her. She knew Emily had been dealing with Chad's horrible attitude for some time now, and that she had been depressed after the birth of the twins, but there was something else she could not pin down. Something had shifted in her friend that afternoon; a certain compliance seemed to shadow her. It was as if all her hopes and happiness had been dashed and thrown astray. *Maybe I could try and talk with Chad*, she thought while Craig spoke to her about planning their wedding. *Perhaps, if he realised how depressed she was.*

"Country elopement perhaps then?" Craig's dark brows lifted as they awaited her response.

"I'm sorry." Millie cast a guilty grin towards him.

The sound of the telephone disrupted their disjointed conversation as they sat drinking some red wine in the comfort of the small lounge room.

"Hold that thought." She moved to quell the strident noise before it awoke her sleeping daughter. "Hello?" she said into the phone.

Craig sprawled on the small two-seater lounge, almost consuming the whole of the plump couch while he watched her every elegant movement. He was sure it was a pastime he would never tire of. He appreciated the generous, shapely curve of her denim clad buttocks that extended into long slender legs tucked into knee-high boots. His gaze lingered on her ample breasts that swelled under the thin fabric of her bra. Her swan-like neck arched beneath her mahogany hair that tumbled loosely over slender shoulders, almost reaching the small of her back. Craig sat upright when he noticed her stiffen. His brow knitted with concern as he watched her almost lose her footing while she visibly reeled back in shock.

He stood and went to her side just in time to hear the muffled whisper that passed through her trembling lips.

"Mum? Where are you?"

CHAPTER TWENTY-ONE

A freight train, balancing precariously on flimsy railroad tracks charged through her head at an alarming speed. The relentless wailing pierced through Emily's ears. She squeezed her eyes shut. *Just stop for God's sake!* She gritted her teeth and plunged her face under the feather down pillow, and turned her back on the cries issuing out of the nursery next to her room. *Why won't they stop? Just let me be ...* "Just let me be!" she shouted.

She knew Chad had already left for his job as a plumber. Most mornings he was gone long before she or the twins had woken, and most evenings he arrived home late when he knew she would already be in bed sleeping. Her mind drifted to the only relief she knew. If she could manage it, she would spend all her life asleep, because her only escape was when she was asleep. All she wanted to do now was go back to sleep, but *they* wouldn't allow her. Her mind shifted back to the twins' cries, which had reached a frenzy. It took every ounce of energy she could gather to leave the warmth of her bed.

"I'm coming ... I'm coming," she called to them. After all, she *did* love her baby boys. She just wished she could feel the same way about her life.

Emily paused to look at Lachie and Kaleb as they balanced on chubby legs, grasping the wooden posts of their cots for support. Identical chocolate eyes stared back at their mother as they both paused in their hysterics. Emily scuffled near them with her hair unkempt and a pink night dress that hadn't seen the washing machine for five nights. Emily figured they could get a few weeks wear out of all their clothes before they ran out. She sighed heavily as she dragged her feet to tend to her children. *I guess someone might have to wash something eventually.* But that someone was not going to be her, because a few weeks ago she had a new idea. It had started as just the tiniest fantasy, but the more she thought on it, the more it had become a real option for her and the boys – a way out of this nightmare. Emily knew her plan was right for her and her little boys because even thinking about it gave her great relief. But first, before she could execute her plan, she had to give her husband one last chance to turn his hard-hearted actions around. It would be one last chance to claim and love their family before they would slip away from him forever.

She bent forward to pluck up one of the boys. Kaleb smiled and gurgled while clinging tightly to her nightdress. Emily drew nearer to Lachie who had bounced back to the soft mattress beneath him. Butterball fists climbed their way up the railings to stand proudly again as she closed in on him. Kaleb gave a happy squeal as they approached his twin, and his little pudgy fingers reached out for Lachie's. Their eyes locked and they gurgled and giggled at each other as they became aware that a new day for them had begun and they would be taken out of their nursery.

The babbling banter of the twins penetrated through the haze that smothered her. Emily glanced down at Lachie teetering before her, and reached out to stroke the soft jet hair that crowned his small round face.

She allowed the faintest of smiles to soften her haggard face. "And what are you two talking about, eh?" she said.

The diversion was fleeting, as troubled thoughts of Chad filled her mind again. She set about changing the twins and preparing their breakfast in a pre-programmed and automated way. Every breath she drew almost felt like an objection, for life no longer shone without the love once known to her. *Tonight I shall try and talk to Chad. Perhaps he will see before it's too late. Perhaps.*

Chad slowly steered his ute into the driveway of his home. Killing the engine, he continued to sit and finish off the joint he had lit a few blocks back. He closed his eyes and sank into the car seat, willing away the strain from a busy work day. He took a sip from a freshly cracked can of beer and crooned along with Gwen Stefani on the radio before casting his eyes up at his house. It hadn't felt much like *his* house over the last year. Now it was filled with the family he had never wanted, and he felt like a stranger to them and to the house he had worked so hard to pay for. He had tried to dissuade Emily from keeping the pregnancy. He had been so happy when it was just the two of them. However, his pleas had fallen on deaf ears. For a little while he had toyed with the idea of being a father. He had seriously contemplated what life might be like once they arrived into the world, but no matter how much he attempted to adapt, he just couldn't bring himself to want them. He knew that with every loathing glance and snide comment he made, that her heart was shattering. And yet, he could not stop because he felt her betrayal with each passing month. So, instead of telling her the truth about how he detested her pregnancy, he had turned the blame on her. He accused her of being unfaithful, ignoring her tearful pleas, until the pleading stopped. And when the twins arrived, his heart remained cold, and so too did his resentment for the woman responsible for ruining his life with the burden he didn't want.

Six long and loud months had passed in which his home was transformed into a never-ending cycle of crying babies and a wife that he thought looked like a puffy-faced hag. This was exactly why he had never wanted children in the first place. Although, after all this time, those little mirror images of him might actually be growing on him. Just a smidgen, because when Emily wasn't looking, he had taken to communicating with the twins, and to his surprise, discovered that he enjoyed it. But he would not dare tell his wife; not yet. He had not forgiven her betrayal of placing this burden on him against his will. He wanted her to suffer some more before he might consider playing family man with her. *Let her stay a pawn in my game just a little longer before I play hers,* Chad thought. After all, she had to learn her lesson.

"Bloody hell!" he muttered when he noticed the dim light of the bedroom still lit. *She's still awake.* He slammed the car door and stalked towards the front door. He was in no mood to see his wife tonight. It would be when *he* was ready and not before.

He crept into the house, removed his greasy work boots and placed them neatly, as he did every night, at the tiled entrance. He made his way to the bathroom, undressed and stepped into the shower. He took his time showering with the hope that the house would be in darkness when he was done.

Chad peeked out from within the cloud of steam that wafted over him. A glance through the bathroom door met with disappointment. Not only was the light still on in the bedroom, but a flood of light also issued out of the lounge room. After some hesitation deliberating over facing his estranged wife, he acquiesced.

Emily was standing in the corner under the light of the free-standing lamp when he entered the lounge room. She held a crystal framed photo of the two of them taken on their wedding day, and still hadn't noticed his presence. Separated only by a lounge suite, a coffee table and several toys, she was startled when she became aware of him watching her.

She turned to face him, and drew in a deep breath. A tiny nervous laugh escaped her lips as she motioned to the frame she held before replacing the photo back to the side table.

"Better days." Her smile wavered.

She summoned up the confidence she had once known well, and faced him again, lifting the dainty point of her chiselled chin. "Chad, I would like to have a quick chat."

"What about?" His voice was gruff as he perched on a lounge chair. "And don't start crying again, for God's sake."

Emily came to sit opposite him, giving her enough time to gather up the tiny scraps of courage that remained in her aching heart. "I am not doing so well, Chad," she said.

Her stare pleaded with him.

Chad held her gaze, not offering a word in return. She fidgeted and bit at her already ravaged fingernails.

She drew a short, uneasy breath. "I … I mean we can't keep living like this. It's no good for any of us."

"What is no good for any of us, Emily?"

Emily knew her husband would not make this easy for her, although she hoped he might finally be ready to cast aside the dominating ego he thrived on.

"Hope is a funny concept," she said and gave a whimsical laugh.

The hope she held onto for the survival of their marriage seemed to be just a faint flicker at the end of a long dark tunnel. Hope paled in comparison to the power of faith she had heard Millie speak of a million times over the years. She vaguely recalled her friend attempting to convince her of the importance of faith over the years they had lived together in that little apartment. However, back then she had been way too busy living and enjoying her life, and dating new men between the wild partying at night clubs. She had brushed aside Millie's talk of faith and thoughts, and creating our own experiences.

"I have given our marriage a whole lot of hope over this past year; for instance, I hoped that you would be happy when we fell pregnant. I hoped that you would realise the gift those two little boys are to you. I hoped you would forgive my 'betrayal', and I hoped that tonight you might be ready to finally put all this bullshit behind us."

Her hope was no more than a futile wish made through the tarnished mirror in which she viewed her life. And the only faith she could manage to conjure up now, appeared in the back-up plan she had been making for her and the twins. Emily pulled a bleeding nail bed from her mouth to inspect the damage for a moment.

"I know now it really wasn't hope that I should have been practising. It was faith. Faith in myself." She looked at Chad with an eerie calmness.

"You're losing your mind, woman!" Chad rolled his eyes. "I can't do this now Emily, I need some sleep."

"Fine. I am done with hoping for us," she said quietly. "If you can't forgive me, Chad, then I will do it for you."

Chad made no effort to conceal the aggravation

that afflicted him. "Now I'm sure you've lost your mind! Just who do you think you are? Nothing but a disloyal bitch that betrayed her husband, that's who! You ruined our life, and now *you* have the audacity to forgive *me*?" His voice rose and white droplets of spittle foamed in the corners of his mouth as he tumbled over his words. "Oh, how I should thank you for your kindness in forgiving me. Ha! You just went ahead and did as you pleased. Never did I tell you that I wanted a family. Never! And now look at the dirty hag you have become … Get out of here, Emily, I want to go to my bed you have parked your arse on." He stormed out of the room, leaving her to contemplate the venom of his words.

She watched the door where he had exited with a trace of indifference. She willed herself to adopt the detached attitude she felt sprinkling through her mind like a relieving mantle of golden fairy dust. She acknowledged the fate of her future that now spread out before her with a certain ring of clarity. She knew she could no longer endure a loveless life with the man she had given her heart to so completely.

As she rose with a wince, her thoughts turned to the happiest days of her childhood. She recalled holidays she had spent as a child down on the south coast of New South Wales with her parents. Treasured visions of the days spent with her real father appeared in her mind as she made her way to her bedroom. She remembered how she had loved the south coast and its rocky cliffs that overlooked the roaring sea, and as she lay her head down on her pillow, Emily knew it was those cliffs along the ocean that called out to her now. Closing weary eyes, she fell into the deepest, most settled sleep she had enjoyed in a long time. She had finally found the respite she sought, or rather, it had found her.

The Softail Heritage thundered along the expressway with a rumbling roar. He grinned with satisfaction as he gave his attention to the sound of the engine beneath him. The arousal the Harley induced in him did not fail. Stimulating thoughts permeated his mind as he weaved through the traffic. He felt a deepening urge as Cathy tightened her grip around his waist as he accelerated.

"Slow down!" she shouted into his ear through the cutting wind that circulated around them.

He laughed, then shifting the throttle, gunned the engine even harder down the expressway. Thin long fingers dug into his abdomen as her screams competed with the rush of cool air, lending to the thirst of his desire. He sped on towards her dorm quarters with the urgency of the excitement that grew within him. *Wow! What a combo!* His mind raced between the combination of his beloved bike and the panic of a screaming girl as his passenger. As he neared their destination, he could feel the growing bulge that strained against his jeans, and pulled the bike to a halt. *I need her now, damn it!*

He dismounted hastily and turned to hustle her

off to her room. "C'mon," he urged, pulling on her slender arm towards the dorm.

Cathy yanked her arm away and glared at him. "Why did you do that to me?" She smoothed back the wisps of ashen-blonde hair that clung around her face.

"Do what, sugar-puss?" he crooned.

"You know what!" She punched his arm before swivelling on her heels and sashaying towards the small rooms she would call home for the next three years.

"Ouch!" The lust in his eyes intensified as his eyes swept over the smooth curves of her denim-covered buttocks.

He followed at a leisurely pace, eyeing her body with sexual anticipation.

He picked up the pace as she neared her door and, with the turn of the key, swung a black leather-clad arm over her head to slam the door behind them. She gasped and turned to face him, and just as the thin line of her lips opened to express her disapproval, she found herself being pushed roughly into the room.

He groped feverishly at the black leather that separated the two of them, and casting both their jackets aside, moved onto the next item of clothing. He ripped and clawed at her blouse. The material split easily between his fingers to expose perky breasts. She struggled in vain against his strength, finally letting her arms fall as he became more excited.

He tore at her tight blue denim jeans, avoiding her protesting kicks as he grappled with her bony ankles, pinning them under him with the ease of a slick hunter. This was a new game to him; had he realised just how exciting this could be, he would have worked on his hunting skills sooner. *Perhaps women could uphold my interest after all,* he thought, with a flick of the black hair that fell over his eyes. Pressing the full weight of his body against her, he hushed the muted whimpering that came from terrified lips, with the soothing tone of his deep voice and a large, sweaty palm over her mouth. Then savouring throbbing rush between his thighs, he moved into her smooth parted legs, and like the most deadly of black snakes, entered the sweet secret place that had opened just for him.

He lost himself to the hedonistic cloud that had engulfed him. This was *his* made-up scene, and *he* was the star. The filth beneath him was merely a pawn to be moved and manipulated at his will, as this was *his* creation. His heart raced as he picked up his pace, slamming against his prey with the full force of his weight. She squirmed beneath him in vain, then the hand he had over her mouth slipped for a moment. Teeth bit down in desperation to deliver the potency of a bite that instantly drew blood.

Pain sliced through the fantasy of his gruelling madness. He withdrew his hand and examined the torn flesh of his finger. Cathy took the opportunity to bring her knee up with force into his scrotum. He screamed out and rolled off her, doubling up on the floor near her, and nursing the wounds she had inflicted upon him.

He glimpsed her still lying next to him before moving away. He snatched out at her ankle and flipped her to the floor with a loud thud, winding her. *This isn't over yet, bitch! This is MY scene!* Arms and legs thrashed as he mounted her with a renewed sense of determination. He could feel the eerie darkness of the familiar dark cloud rise through him and seep into the deepest pits of his mind. He wrapped her neck in his large hands and pressed his thumbs into the soft flesh over her airway with just enough pressure to give her a scare. *Teach her not to fuck with my game.* And as he watched her eyes widen in terror beneath his fingers, the college girl transformed into someone else. She was now the woman who had taunted his fantasies since he was twelve. It was *her!* The dark force within him arched to new heights as the quickening of his heart thumped beneath the concave of his ribcage with sheer excitement. He snarled as he savoured the increased pressure of his thumbs as they bore their way deeper into her flesh. He squeezed harder and harder as he looked on at the weakening body he straddled like a conquering warrior. Finally, the movement slowed and stopped and the gurgling choking sounds that were her last had ceased forever.

He watched the pale body of a woman he had barely known with deranged fascination. He watched her until the light of the afternoon faded. *Where had she gone?* Trance-like thoughts ran through his confused mind as he pondered the finality of death for the first time in his life. He found the vulnerability which the breath of life hinged on to be captivating. He watched as the formidable cloud that had shrouded him shifted to reveal the smallest part of him that still loved, still felt and still yearned for the light to bask over him.

He moved to cradle the weight of her head in his lap, and began to rock back and forth. "I'm sorry … I'm sorry," he whimpered, as memories of the loss of his mother bubbled to the surface and trembled through him. Tears fell freely and he moaned as he struggled to come to terms with taking a life. He wept for Cathy and for the boy he used to be; and most of all, the mother he had loved so much. "Mummy … Mummy …" His body shook with choking sobs while he gently stroked the blonde hair he cradled tenderly. *Where did she go?* "Why did she have to leave me?" he cried.

Hours passed while he fought to regain control, until finally he gave in to the depraved beast responsible for murder. He knew it would be the only way for him to cope with the gravity of his actions. And as the first glimmer of dawn began to radiate through the room where he had sat unmoving all night long, he leaped into action. He scrubbed and cleaned every part of the room and Cathy's body with methodical precision, down to carefully scraping under each of her manicured nails. When he was satisfied that there was no evidence left at the scene, he left discreetly.

CHAPTER TWENTY-TWO

Glen inspected the freshly shaven image that reflected back at him in the mirror. His hands skimmed across his shortly clipped hair before he headed off to fetch his car keys. Today was his favourite day of the week – Saturday. And that meant it was *his* day to spend time with his granddaughter.

Millie worked at the gallery on Saturday mornings, usually until noon. It hadn't taken Glen long to jump at the opportunity to offer his babysitting skills when his daughter had found herself in need of someone to look after Arella when Emily had moved out of their apartment years before. Glen had not missed a Saturday with his granddaughter since. He and Arella enjoyed each other's company, and a strong bond had grown between them over the years. He would do anything for his grandchild, the apple of his eye, and found himself often caving in to her every whim. Arella knew this of him, and being a child of her age, took full advantage of his devotion on more than one occasion. However, Glen didn't mind as she reminded him so much of his own little Millie-pie when she had been a little girl. And now, he was able to experience a touch of Millie's sweet childhood again through Arella. Today he had plans to take his little Rella-Bella on a train ride into the city to watch a movie, followed with some ice-cream in Circular Quay where they could stroll around the harbour and catch all the city weekend hurly-burly, as he liked to call it.

Glen paused to take a quick peek in at Ace who was sleeping. He poked his head through the door to Ace's room, and waited until his eyes adjusted to the dimness of the room. He smiled when he sighted the lumpy figure of his son slumbering soundly beneath a tangle of sweaty bed sheets. He seldom saw his 18-year-old son at home as Glen worked late through the week and Ace was busy with his studies and a casual job at the weekends. He sighed momentarily as he thought about the stranger Ace was becoming to him. Their relationship was marked only by brief exchanges of greetings within a dim hallway. He decided he would try and make it home in time with Arella that afternoon to catch his son before he had to leave for his job as a bartender at the local club.

He frowned as he recognised some blood smeared over a small patch of the bedsheets where Ace lay. *Probably just a shaving cut,* he concluded. He thought no more of it and turned to leave to collect his granddaughter.

Glen arrived at Millie's apartment to hear her calling him from her bedroom. He had helped himself to some coffee in the kitchen, sucking in the aroma through his nostrils with a sigh of pleasure. He loved the coffee at his daughter's unit. The whiff of freshly ground coffee beans beat the instant coffee he had settled for at home. He vowed that one day he would buy a real coffee maker for himself, but he knew he never would, as he liked it just fine that this was a treat he knew only at his daughter's place. It made coming here all the more special.

"I'll be out in a second, Dad! Have some coffee," Millie called out again from the muffled walls of her wardrobe.

Millie appeared flashing a smile as he and Arella prepared for their day together. She was dressed from head to toe in black. Her slender tanned legs stepped on the pile carpet with black kitten heels. Her emerald eyes danced about like fireworks and she wore a smile that she couldn't conceal even if she tried.

Glen surveyed his daughter with a curious eye, as it was obvious to him that she was itching to give him some good news. The animated expression on her face enchanted him, and he found himself lost in a flood of memories of her childhood days.

He recalled Millie's wonderment when they had released a full bunch of rainbow coloured balloons into the air at the bayside. She had watched those balloons until they had disappeared from sight, and all the while he had watched her until her eyes widened and glistened with tears, and had turned to him with the devastation of a five year old – "But who will love them now, Daddy?"

The sound of Millie clearing her throat broke through his daydream as she watched her father with puzzlement. He recovered swiftly. "Funeral?" he teased with a grin. It was rare for his daughter to relax enough in his presence to evoke such joy, such excitement; their relationship had remained strained since she had dug up that box from under the avocado tree all those years ago.

Her russet hair cascaded over the black chiffon blouse she wore, falling almost to her waist when she threw her head back in laughter. "Very funny Dad, but much more exciting," she said.

"Oh, what could be more exciting, I wonder?" He jested with Arella beside him. "Do *you* know Rella-Bella?" he said, pulling a face.

"Nope," Arella replied.

Both sets of eyes turned towards Millie as they awaited the promised exciting news. Millie took a deep breath and began to spill the news she was bursting to share. "A man from New York came into the gallery a few days ago on my day off; apparently he has very influential connections in the art world all over the globe." The pitch of her voice grew, while arms gestured widely to encircle the world in her announcement. Coffee spilled from the mug in her hand. "He fell in love with my dusky bay painting; you know the one with the lights reflecting over the water?"

"Oh, I love that one mummy!" Arella's little bottom squirmed as she knew instantly how it would finish.

"He has offered a lot of money for my painting, but he is insisting on meeting the artist – *moi* – before he buys." Her eyes brightened. "He is coming in today!"

"Oh Millie-pie!" Glen hugged her. "I am so very happy for you."

"Thank you, Dad," she replied.

Glen's eyes clouded over for a moment as he watched Millie gather her handbag to leave for the gallery. He recalled his answer on bent knees to a five-year-old Millie who had watched those balloons disappear. "Love never fades, Millie-pie. They will carry your love with them just as you carry my love with you." He rested the palm of his hand on her heart. "Right here."

The mid-afternoon sun burned fiercely when Glen and Arella strolled into the house. They had gone to see *Home Alone 3*, and by the time they reached the porch, both agreed the movie had not been as good as the first two in the series that had starred a different main character.

"Macaulay Culkin was just that bit smarter," Glen remarked. "Too smart for his own good I think," he chuckled.

Arella raced into the house in search of the uncle she hadn't seen for some time. "Uncle Ace!" she called as she skipped towards the kitchen, helium inflated balloons trailing behind her. "Uncle Ace, there you are!" she said as she spotted him eating an afternoon breakfast.

Ace swivelled around and grinned as she flew into his outstretched arms and snuggled into the envelope of his scent.

Arella gazed up at him and frowned. "Uncle Ace, you've changed. And you haven't come to see me for ages and ages!" she scoffed.

"I know, buttercup. I'm sorry." Lips swept against the tip of her pudgy nose. "Will you forgive me?"

She nodded. "Yes!"

Arella began to tell him about her day out with her grandfather. She talked so fast that she hardly seemed to draw breath. Ace and Glen listened intently and spoke only when she paused long enough for them to get a word in. Ace made her a honey sandwich and finally told her that he needed to prepare for work.

Arella's face drooped as she looked down into the plate Ace had just placed before her. "Will you come and see me soon, Uncle Ace?"

"Sure." His smile was forced.

He reached out to stroke her dark curls as he attempted to change the subject. "Did you know that girls have more tastebuds than boys?"

Arella shook her head and looked at him wide eyed.

"So, that means this honey sandwich would taste so much better for you than it would for me." Ace smiled down at her with raised eyebrows. "Better eat up, buttercup."

Ace made for the door but stopped short when he heard his niece talking to him.

"I know you are not feeling well," she said. "I know you are not well at all, Uncle Ace."

The words did not match the girlish tone in which they were delivered. Her eyes glazed over as they met his. "I wish it wasn't so. It's not your fault. It's the dark cloud that hovers over you sometimes." She turned her eyes towards her grandfather who sat across the table from her. "And you too, Grandpa."

"Arella? Are you okay, buttercup?" Ace laughed nervously. She appeared to see right into his soul.

Arella's face contorted as she struggled to process the information that dripped into her consciousness from the outer recesses of her soul. Her eyes turned murky as disturbing images flashed before her in a tale that served only to make her more puzzled. Her tiny body began to tremble against the old chair she sat on, as her hands flew up to conceal her face from their prying eyes. She curled up her knees under her chin as she started to cry.

"Mummy," she whimpered as her hands became wet with her tears.

Glen and Ace watched bewildered.

"She wouldn't leave us! Mum!" she screamed. "Mum! Mummy … please … please don't leave me." She wept as if she were a prisoner to a trance that had captured her. "Mummy! Mummy... No!" she cried.

"Arella? Arella?" Glen shook her shoulders gently. "Baby girl. What's wrong?" He glanced back at Ace for support as he felt his tongue lose all moisture and cling to the roof of his mouth. *What is she doing? What is wrong with her?* He noticed all colour drained from his son's face and the wiry blonde hairs on his arms were standing up as if he had put his finger into an electrical socket. *What is going on here?* All he could do was to be the observer of a phenomenon to which he had no control. Nevertheless, he knew that whatever was playing out before him, it was very significant.

Silence hung like a heavy blanket over the room after Arella had stopped sobbing and crying out. She stared at Ace with a startled expression as she had no recollection of the stirring that had overwhelmed her. She was only aware that something powerfully symbolic had transpired. The smallest of smiles crept across her face as she recognised her uncle's astonishment.

It was at that precise moment that the loud bangs of coloured balloons bursting broke the silence. Neither Arella nor Ace reacted as their eyes remained fixed on one another while bits of latex fell to the surface of the table.

Arella broke the stare and examined the shrivelled bunch of fallen balloons before addressing Ace. "Your inner peace awaits you, uncle. And so does *she*. You will find her up north in a Rosebud Retreat."

After her tongue uttered those profound words, it had taken a moment for Glen to catch on. One by one, each word spoken in his granddaughter's whispered tone hit him like lightning. And as the last piece of the puzzle fell into place, his stare hardened.

Lilly? Glen was seized with a sinister elation. His

relentless search for his missing wife had got him so far, that at times he could almost smell her musky perfume. He had thought his search had finally come to an end a couple of years earlier when he had tracked Lilly and Scott down to Cairns. Thanks to the loose lips of an old school friend of theirs, Cindy Churchill, a few glasses of Chardonnay and a few shots of charm, she had been very accommodating to his needs. He had systematically contacted as many of Lilly's old school colleagues that he could find, and Cindy had been most helpful. He was so chuffed when she recalled her brief brush with Lilly and Scott in Cairns that he had taken her back to his hotel room and given her a night she wouldn't forget easily. How his veins had throbbed that night with the taste of vengeance so close. However, his victory was short lived. When he flew up to Cairns shortly afterwards, he found no sign of his wife nor that of the alias he knew she had assumed since she had left him, despite combing through every inch of that town with meticulous precision. He had returned home empty-handed but he wasn't about to give up. After all, he had waited this long; what difference did it make in the end? He had enjoyed playing the game of the hunter. It gave him the perfect antidote for filling the spare time he found as Millie and Ace grew older. He had devoted a whole room in his home solely for the investigation. The room was kept locked, and when anyone asked, he told them it was full of his boring old work gear. He never wavered from his search, and he knew that one day all his efforts spent tracking her down and imagining her slender neck beneath his hands would eventually arrive.

He had no doubt about that happening as he had paid attention when Millie told him about her beliefs one day. "We are what we think," she told him when he complained to her about working at the milk factory. "Our lives reflect our thoughts and beliefs … and that's that." Then her green eyes sparkled at him. "Knowing that kinda makes you feel good, doesn't it?" she laughed. "The keys to the kingdom of heaven really is within our reach … if only we will grasp and hold firmly to our desires."

Glen had considered his daughter's words about the kingdom of heaven being within our reach. He knew his daughter had been speaking in terms of a divine, higher nature, but what if the same principles could be used for a darker good? Images in his mind ran rampant when he was alone, allowing him to cultivate his fantasies until he knew it was only a matter of time that they would manifest into his experience.

Finally, here she was, Mrs Lilly Anderson, handed to him on the shiniest silver platter he could have ever imagined. His heart pumped hard against his ribs as he felt the familiar black serpent uncoil its ugly head and hiss with satisfaction. He gripped the prickly whiskers of his face as a twinge of pain shot through his mind with the release of the serpent. The monstrous presence seethed within him as he felt euphoric as this newest revelation.

"Grandpa?"

Arella's voice interrupted Glen's private thoughts while he used all the strength he could summon to tame down the beast within him. *Not around my grandbaby ... not around my Rella-Bella*, he remonstrated.

"Let's get you home, shall we?" Glen rose to his feet and reached for the car keys, ushering Arella out of the kitchen.

Forgotten in the rush, Ace continued to stare in shock as his insides twisted with the little boy's cries for his lost mother, and the realisation that now he could finally go to her.

Arella glanced up at her uncle while Glen led her away, and for a second, she shuddered.

"Have I done something wrong, uncle Ace?" she said, as she noticed the dark haze brewing around him.

His eyes pierced down to her like daggers. "Not at all, buttercup," he grinned.

CHAPTER TWENTY-THREE

The crisp morning air evaporated into the warming breeze of the dawning day as Millie bounced down the street towards the gallery. After leaving Arella with Glen, she decided the morning was too glorious to drive her car the short distance to the gallery. Besides, a stroll might help her sort out her mixed emotions. There seemed to be so much going on lately that she could barely organise her thoughts, and that was something she hated, especially since she was well aware of the power of thought. Thank goodness for her daily meditation! The habitual practice over the last few months had trained her to enter a deeper centre of her own consciousness and make contact with her infinite self. *How deliciously exhilarating is the spiritual centre of gravity!* She knew she had discovered the portal through which an ascension could be achieved. The key to the kingdom of heaven dwelled within *her,* as she believed it did in every person.

It was only recently that Millie completely understood the words of Mrs Bartlett when she had told Millie that "every piece of art is an expression of God". Millie finally comprehended the truth in those words – it was *she* who was an expression of God. And it *was* God who held her paint brushes. *He* manipulated every stroke against the canvas. She had determined that the mighty current of God flowed within us all, but it was how we chose to colour that pure spark of divine energy that determined the way we saw and created our lives – as individuals, and together as a collective consciousness.

Sometimes Millie found it difficult to grasp the enormity of the revelations that drifted into her awareness. She was also aware that she stood only at the threshold of all to be revealed on her ascending path.

All those years spent trying to understand the power of thought-faith and creating had culminated in this simple truth that can only be learned through experiencing it. The vital fact that the consciousness that lingered within her was the same consciousness as the creator therefore made her a creator. If she nurtured and aligned herself with this divine consciousness, and anchored deep within this knowledge, she was certain anything is possible.

She knew it would take some practice, discipline and self-correction, and she recognised that there would be times when outer conditions would penetrate through her resolve. However, she was aware that the path had chosen her, and it would be worth every effort she made to stay true to her inner divine presence. If she were to hold steadfast to these convictions, together with an unwavering belief, eventually she was sure to hold dominion over her life and create exactly what she desired.

Oh, the love and the tranquil peace I perceive beyond the physical world here on earth! The hallowed meetings she had experienced with Samantha in the past and still to this day was all she could compare with the absolute serenity she found within the pure light of God. Her thoughts trailed back to her surprise at the previous week's phone call from Lilly, the woman she still thought of as her mother.

When she had casually answered the telephone that evening, the familiar notes of the voice that greeted her had delivered an overwhelming jolt to the core of her being.

"Millie? Is that you?" Lilly said.

It took all her effort to steady herself from the shock. She became aware of Craig's comforting presence at her side as she attempted to process the reality of her caller. She rested her head into Craig's downy chest. "Mum? It's you."

"Yes Millie, it's me," came the hesitant reply.

They spent more than an hour on the phone that night. Their conversation was guarded and stiff at first as they caught up on a decade of silence. Millie could hear the nervous banter that her mother tried to conceal between bouts of rushed questions. And she had many questions, as did Millie. After a while, the talk between them became more relaxed and easy, giving Craig the cue to leave them to their privacy.

Lilly told her of the years she had spent travelling and running on a never-ending road. She also confided her love for a man she had known since she was a teenager in school. "You will adore Scott,"

Lilly assured her. Then Lilly revealed her addiction to alcohol – "Can you imagine," she whispered, "Me? An alcoholic." Lilly gave a bittersweet laugh. "I never did what I told you I would do in the letter I left. I didn't create my life purposely! Just the opposite, in fact! I've made so many mistakes. Can you ever forgive me, Millie? Can Ace ever forgive me?"

"Oh mum," she cried, "there really is nothing to forgive. I know you did what you thought best to survive." The relief was overwhelming. "I love you mum," she said, her voice breaking.

The strain of 10 years of guilt and self-punishment in her mother's speech was obvious. How could she prolong the suffering this woman had created for herself? However, she wasn't so sure Ace would feel the same way, as the distance that had grown between them over recent years had reached a new pinnacle recently, and she had no idea why or how their relationship had become so estranged. She knew he harboured a deep resentment towards their mother. Thank goodness Arella could talk to him as she was the only family member he had shown any kind of affection or interest towards for a long time.

Lilly told her that she had been living at a rehabilitation clinic in the Numinbah Valley called The Rosebud Retreat. She described the beauty of the rainforest and mountains that surrounded the retreat and how lovely the support she had found in the people there. Then her tone became sombre. "The last few weeks have been tough but well worth it. It is time to reclaim my life again, Millie, and I would love for you, Arella and Ace to be part of it." She uttered the last words with a mixture of apprehension and hope. Lilly did not have to wait long for Millie's reply. Millie agreed to fly up the following fortnight to visit her at the retreat, eager to see her mother in person. She had many questions for her mother concerning Samantha and her father; questions that had needed answers for the longest time.

Millie decided not to mention to Arella her impending trip to Queensland, as she could not take the chance of her father and Ace discovering her plans to visit Lilly just yet. However, she did share her news with Craig who had fallen asleep by the time the phone call ended.

Craig stumbled out of bed and made them tea while he listened to Millie's banter. Two hours later, he gazed at her with a sly smile. "Come here my pussy-pie," he teased and pulled her gently into his arms and kissed her.

Millie's kitten heels turned the corner to the main road where the gallery sat amid other shopfronts. Clear windows displayed strings of glittering fairy lights highlighting the paintings on the walls. Canvases stood on black iron-cast easels, their frames curled in smooth spirals against handcrafted sculptures, encrusted jewels and wood-carved pieces of contemporary furniture. All this was displayed against a backdrop of rustic, dusk-pink walls and a ceiling dappled with white sheer fabric that weaved throughout the candle-scented gallery. It was Millie's pride, her joy, and a whole lot of her heart. It was a place where she easily found tranquillity and peace in her life; a home away from home, and as she reached the glass door that read "Holly's Art Studio" in bold black lettering, her smile affirmed as much.

Today the New York art buyer would be coming in to meet with her and, she hoped, purchase the canvas she had recently finished and put up in her little corner of the gallery. She had sold many of her paintings over the years, and was steadily carving out a name for herself amid the art world here in Australia, but this guy from New York could take her paintings to new international heights. The excitement that danced around in her tummy confirmed that something good was making its way into her life. It had been a very long time since she had felt the soft wings of her little butterfly friends. She had not felt their tiny tickles since she had first started dating Damon. She frowned. *Why on earth am I thinking of him now?* It had taken her many years to push Damon from her mind, and she wasn't about to backtrack now.

The long rope of tiny brassed bells tingled in announcement as Mrs Bartlett breezed through the entrance, relieving Millie of further struggle with the haunting reflections that had been drifting through her mind. She threw her handbag behind the counter, and broke into a wide smile as Mrs Bartlett came towards her.

"Good morning, Amelia," Mrs Bartlett said.

"Good morning, Mrs Bartlett."

Mrs Bartlett stopped and looked at Millie. "For goodness sake child, how many times do we have to discuss this?"

Green and pink feathers swayed with the tilt of her head in an elaborately decorative fascinator, while the thin lines of her pencilled-in eyebrows lifted as she awaited Millie's reply.

"Oh, but I am in gallery mode," Millie grinned. "Surely *you* remember?"

"Hmmf. Gallery mode is Holly mode Amelia, it's about time *you* remember that, surely." She didn't understand Millie's insistence on maintaining formalities between them at the gallery, as their relationship had grown beyond the need for formal courtesies.

Her silk blouse swirled around her gaunt ageing body gracefully as she moved to place her handbag behind the counter. Millie pecked her on the cheek, and her eyes gleamed at her young protégé.

"So, is my little angel excited about our sleepover Monday night?"

Holly was looking forward to babysitting Arella who was unlike any other child she had known. She felt calm in Arella's company; the usual background noise that raced around her mind always graduated to a serene, welcoming halt. There was just something about that child.

Millie's eyes fogged over for a moment as she began to busy herself around the gallery. "Well, I haven't exactly told her just yet. I can't tell her the truth, yet I can't lie either. You know Rella, she always spots a lie."

Her voice trailed off as she fiddled absently with

a shelf that displayed a small collection of sleek crested swirled glass supported on tapered steel arcs. "I'm really unsure how to handle this actually. Any suggestions?"

Holly sat on a stool behind the counter. "Hmmmm." Faded freckles crinkled under the face powder as she consulted an A4 business diary and flicked through a few pages before looking back at Millie. "You know dear, I do have some business for you to take care of at an art gallery on the Gold Coast. Those people are driving me nuts. All these negotiations over the phone just don't work for me. Please be a dear and fly up there and take care of it for me?"

"Thank you, Holly," Millie said, relieved. She did want her daughter to eventually meet and know her grandmother, but it would be for another time. Millie had plans to explain to her daughter everything she needed to know after she went to see her mother. First, she had to see Lilly and find out for herself, as she had to be sure of Lilly's intentions.

"You're welcome, sweetness." Holly's husky tone betrayed her affection. "All set for your buyer this morning?"

"Yes."

"He should be here soon. Did I mention how darkly handsome he was?"

"I don't think I heard you mention that between all the gushing," Millie teased.

"Oh, if only I were thirty years younger," Holly said.

The tingle of brass bells jangled, interrupting the hearty laughter. Both heads turned towards the door to catch sight of Emily struggling to push the pram carrying her twins through the door.

"Emily! Hi." Millie rushed to the door and held it open for the pram to wheel through easily. The two women embraced, and Millie surveyed her friend. *Emily appears much more settled … and perhaps even happy?* Millie thought, knowing that Emily's sudden happiness now would be odd. *What's going on?* she mulled as she leaned towards the babies to coo them a greeting.

"Hello Mrs Bartlett." Emily smiled at Holly, who returned the greeting from behind the marbled counter with a quirky grin and a waving hand at the twins.

Emily's expression grew sombre as she faced Millie. "I have come to say goodbye, Pussy-cat."

"What? Where are you going? What do mean, Em?"

Blonde hair swung over her shoulders while her head jerked in an exaggerated laugh. "Relax! I'm taking the boys down to the south coast for a few weeks. We are going to stay with some old friends. I need to get away from Chad. Need some time to figure out our next move, that's all," she shrugged.

Millie's face relaxed. "That sounds like a good plan; I mean, it would be good for you to get some breathing space." She stroked Emily's arm as she scanned Emily's face. "Are you okay? I didn't know you had friends down south."

"Yeah, childhood friends," Emily mumbled

before she broke into a big smile. "You once told me that I couldn't find love from external forces. I wasn't really sure what those words meant at the time, and I used to think about it a lot." She chuckled as she pushed a thin lock of hair back behind her ear. "I thought you must be wrong because everyone is looking for love. They even write songs about it." She clasped Millie's hands in her own and gave them a short squeeze. "But I understand now, Pussy-cat. I loved. I did! I gave all my love to another person, and I hinged my happiness upon him … and that love …" She drew in a deep breath as her eyes became moist. "The thing is, I'm not like you, Millie. I don't even know where to begin to find the love inside me. Where do I find that spark of God within me?" Her voice dropped to almost a whisper. "I don't think I'm worthy of that love." A tear escaped down her cheek. Emily turned away and brushed her face with her fist as she looked down at the twins sucking on bottles with sleepy eyes.

Millie watched her friend's intentional distraction over the twins as Emily bent over them, and began to notice a hazy dark blue hue tinged with a hint of lemon-yellow surrounding her slim form. She had cultivated this unusual gift enough to recognise the colours around her friend signified fear.

"Em, you *are* just like me. Don't you see? The spark is the same in all of us; the key lies in how we choose to use that pure energy."

She pulled Emily up and gently squeezed her arm in an attempt to stress her point. "You *are* more than worthy of that love! We all are. The Source wouldn't have made us had he not loved us. You are thinking too much, time away from Chad is just what you need to get to know yourself again, and what it is you want."

"I know, Millie. That's why I decided to do this. To sort this all out in my silly head!" Emily moved to grasp the handles of the pram to steer her children out through the door. "I'll let you know when we get back."

She stopped next to Millie and hugged her. "You are the star of my life, Amelia Anderson. You always were … I love you."

Millie gulped back tears. "I love you too, Emily Turner. Be safe, yeah. Call me as soon as you return!" she murmured.

Two hours later Millie was engrossed in conversation with a middle-aged man who had come into the gallery searching for the right piece to give his young wife for their third wedding anniversary.

"To tell you the truth, I'm really not sure she'd like this one," the man said, as he referred to a bold abstract work.

The piece was one of Millie's favourites. She loved the bold opaque splashes of colour combined with the textured swirls, and it emanated a certain daring character that she admired.

"Well, perhaps one in the back corner might be

more to her taste?" She gestured to the corner where her own work hung.

The man paused in front of a portrait of Millie's angelic dark mother, which she had completed months before with a blend of bleeding watercolours.

"Tell me about this one."

Millie's smile broadened as she began to talk about her creation. She was so completely absorbed in her explanation, that she did not hear the soft chimes of the brass bells that signified the arrival of the New York buyer.

The man with Millie was swooped up in her enthusiasm. "Such passion … and devotion," he remarked, stroking the ends of his wiry beard. "I'll take this one. I'm quite sure." His face resumed its business-like expression.

"That's great, Mr Barton!" Millie said, noticing his gaze diverted to someone behind her.

She swivelled around to inspect the man who had stood discreetly to the left behind her, and let out a startled gasp. Her breasts heaved under black chiffon with the sharp intake of breath as her emerald eyes lost themselves within the clear depths of a blue lagoon.

CHAPTER TWENTY-FOUR

Emily parked her car in a small parking lot alongside what she considered to be the most beautifully positioned graveyard she thought might exist in the world. The tombstones that littered the tidy graveyard spread over the green pastures that sloped drowsily down towards cliffs overlooking the Tasman Sea.

A fleeting smile drifted across her face, as she knew that this was perfect. She glanced behind her at the boys sleeping in the back seat of the car. *They are good boys. Too good for their father. Too good for me.* Their lips were smudged with the chocolate ice-cream she had stopped to buy them along the way on their drive to the south coast. *But what a treat it has been!* It had been their first taste of ice-cream. She figured they had deserved that. She soaked up the details of their sleeping bodies. Their black hair fluffed in soft spikes on top of round pudgy faces. *My angels ... my sleeping angels.* Her thoughts were vaguely whimsical.

She removed a cigarette from its pack with unsteady fingers as she left the car and took in the view. The inhale of smoke calmed her nerves. The balmy ocean breeze tickled the fair hairs of her arms and danced over her pale skin, and she smiled again.

White fluffs of cloud hung above the ocean, lazily drifting along the horizon with the spark of a silver lining ringing radiantly around the wisps of their bouncy edges. Emily beheld it all and knew that it was perfect. She observed the wafting smoke of the cigarette that curled between her fingers, and threw the butt on the ground where she crushed it under her sandals. She took a deep breath, closed her eyes, and stood still for a moment to allow the calm to permeate through her. There was no turning back. Life had been good when lived in love. And it shall be good again, she was convinced.

She walked back to fetch the double pram out of the boot of the car and collect the sleeping twins before any trace of doubt could change her mind. She covered each of her babies with kisses and embraced them, before placing both of them gently into the stroller. Once the boys were safely buckled in, she turned to push the stroller over the vast field of grass. The breeze that had gently swayed the long blades of grass that edged the clearing, suddenly picked up its momentum, and began to gust against her long unwashed hair. Emily steered the wheels of the pram over the rocky path to the cliff. Her ears pricked as they heard the stifling cries of Lachie and Kaleb as the wind gusts unsettled them. Still she pushed on as every step she took increased her feeling of calm as the promise of freedom loomed close. And she knew that this was perfect.

As they neared the edge of the cliff and the coastline that stretched out before them, her steps hastened and her smile broadened. She felt all limitations loosen, all torment fade, and all blame disappear for the first time in her life. The constant despair began to lift and the torment of the past flew away with the cleansing surge of the wind. Emily walked on against the flurry of air whirling in short gusts from the ocean, against the elements that sought to bring her down again and again. She walked until there was no solid ground beneath her. She walked until she was free from the dark clutches of the black dog that had plagued her for so long. She was free, and in her freedom, she would spend an eternity with her two dark-haired angels that she had freed from a life of straining to survive in a life without love.

Life had been good when lived in love.

CHAPTER TWENTY-FIVE

H*mmmm, what to pack?* he thought while he eyed the black duffle bag that would hold very few of his belongings. He really didn't need all that much, because how many items could one need for an expedition such as this? He shut his eyes against the dizzy spin of his mind. He sat on the edge of the double bed and clutched at his hair. A shooting pain cut through the deepest part of his mind while he groaned at the dominance of the coiling black snake, as the beast anchored itself deep within him. *We must go to her and make her pay,* it hissed.

"Yes," he replied in a hushed tone. Maybe then he would be free of the beast that overtook him. It was all *her* fault! Cathy was dead because of *her*. The whole campus had gone crazy since the discovery of Cathy's body in her dorm room. He had spotted dozens of police officers scouring the university grounds and questioning the students. He knew it was only a matter of time until they sniffed their way around to questioning him. Nobody knew of his private liaisons with Cathy, unless she had spoken of him to her friends, despite him urging her against doing that.

"Let's keep this on the low, sugar-puss," he had told her the second time he had called on her. "Word spreads like fire around here. Let's just wait and see how it goes."

She had agreed to his request in the hopes of snagging him for herself. Had she not known he saw right through her? And now she was dead. And it was all *her* fault. The only difference now was that he knew where to find *her*. And as it happened, it was a good time to leave town for a while.

He began to throw a few of his belongings in the duffle bag he would carry on his back during the length of his trip. As he packed, the train of his thoughts lingered over the sweet lips that revealed where to find *her*. *Oh the pure innocence of my darling little niece. How ignorant Arella was to the wheels she had set in motion that afternoon!* She was the only soft spot he had left in this world. But as the dark force within him reared up stronger through the years, he had deliberately tried to steer clear of his young niece, as he didn't want her touched by the evil that lurked inside him. He had always known she was special, but what had transpired the week before almost blew his mind – reliving the heartbreak he had felt when he had discovered his mother had left them at the tender age of eight.

It hadn't taken a lot of research to discover that there was a retreat called The Rosebud Retreat, and it happened to be in the Numinbah Valley. He wondered if Arella had told his sister the same information, but it didn't really matter as he intended to arrive to their mother's side before Millie, if she knew at all. *Silly Millie*, he thought, as he gazed absently into the ineffective fan. He recalled the vibration of his speech when he had called those same words into the fan when they were children. *Oh, how I loved my sister!* He loved her so much that this was the reason he needed to allow her to drift out of his life. He knew instinctively that Millie's path lay in direct opposition to the one that lay before him. *How could the light ever really love the dark?* he reasoned, before curbing the impulse to cry for the ache this caused in his heart. Ace had struggled with the battle of these emotions since he was twelve years old, deliberately isolating himself from his family until finally he became cold in the face of them.

Ace shrugged off thoughts of Millie and Arella. He reached into a drawer and grasped at something furry stuffed at the back behind some T-shirts he was seeking. His coldness melted for the briefest of moments when they rested upon the treasure of his old bed friend.

"Benny Boy." Ace chuckled as he remembered hugging Benny Boy close to his boyish heart. Then his chest tightened when he recalled the morning he had crouched in fear, clutching Benny Boy while listening to his father and Millie as they battled about that wooden box. That was *her* fault too ... it was all *her* fault.

The sound of heavy footsteps down the hallway brought him back to the present. He looked up as his father knocked before opening his door. "Hey Dad, what's up?"

"I'm just letting you know that I will be going

away for a few days," Glen said.

"Sure. A work thing again?" It took every bit of willpower to control the brooding cloud that permeated him. Taming the wickedness proved to be more difficult with the passing of time. This bothered him as he knew he had to keep some control over the evil force within him or it would eventually control him completely.

Glen's eyes settled on the half-filled duffle bag that lay on Ace's bed. "Yes. Are you off somewhere too?" he said, puzzled.

Just fuck off, old man! the black snake screamed inside him. "Huh? Yeah."

"Where are you off to?" Glen looked at him with a critical eye as it had begun to dawn on him that something was seriously different about his son.

Oh for fuck's sake! "Just drifting around on my bike for a few days, that's all," Ace shrugged. "Things have been crazy on campus lately. I need to get away." Ace began to fiddle around with the clothes that lay scattered over the bed.

"Yes, I heard about that girl that was found murdered recently. Did you know her?"

Glen watched for the slightest reaction. His son's stiffening back did not go unnoticed, and that was all it took for him to realise that Ace had fallen victim to the poisonous fangs of the black serpent, the same dark force that had tormented him for all these years. After all, like finally recognised like.

Ace gasped at his father's words. It was that moment he knew that his father had finally acknowledged the beast that dwelled within him.

"Not really," Ace said casually, turning to face his father.

"Poor girl," Glen said without emotion.

The air between father and son tensed with the raging current of the unspoken knowledge that brewed between them. Ace stared back in defiance, daring his father to call him out. *Just try it old man for I am the new improved version of you.* His smile confirmed this when his father broke their silent confrontation and left the room.

"Drive safe," Glen called over his shoulder. He knew, with a pang that struck his heart, that he had recognised the malicious serpent that occupied Ace too late.

CHAPTER TWENTY-SIX

Millie recovered quickly after the unforeseen brisk dive she had taken into his blue lagoon. Well, at least outwardly in the way she had presented herself to those around her. She turned her attention back to the art buyer and summoned the most magical of smiles. However, judging by the instant frown that appeared on the man's face, it was perhaps a little too magical.

"Mr Barton, shall we take care of the business end of the matter?" Millie gestured for him to follow her towards the counter.

Mr Barton looked slightly amused at the distinct sudden change in his art dealer's manner. "Certainly," he said, stroking his beard as he followed Millie towards the counter. "Good day," he said, bowing at Damon as he passed.

Millie ignored Damon as she breezed on past him, not flinching as she marched up to the counter. She sashayed ahead with as much poise and sophistication as she could manage. Inside however, the track of her thoughts twirled in circles. *What is he doing here? He can't just walk in like this. Oh my goodness!* Butterflies flocked in her stomach. *And where is this New York art buyer?* Her stomach started doing flips.

Oh, he looks soooo good. Anger surged through her. *Stop that Millie! He has no right to come here! Fuck!* She felt his eyes following her, smothering her. She stole a glance back to the tall figure still lingering at the corner where she had left him. She caught his smile, and snatched her eyes away from him as she finalised the deal with Mr Barton and bid him goodbye.

"Come Amelia," Holly cooed. "Allow me to introduce you to Mr Richards; he is visiting from New York and is very interested in your art."

"I'm sure," she muttered as she allowed Holly to lead her back to him.

He did look good, much to Millie's annoyance. She cursed his good looks as they approached him together. She took a deep breath while feline eyes prowled over him. He stood with a slight tilt to his head of hair that licked the black collar of the suit he wore. He showed a brilliant set of teeth as he greeted Mrs Bartlett.

"Mr Richards," Holly gestured towards Millie. "Meet Amelia Anderson. She is responsible for the beautiful piece of art you are interested in."

Damon's blue eyes swallowed her entirely within the deep caress of his gaze. "Hello Millie."

The mellow nature of his demeanour infuriated her. Despite the cultivated pleasantness he portrayed, Millie recognised the return of Damon's ego-driven old self.

"What are you doing here, Damon?" *Let's see how Mr Confidence handles this now,* she thought.

"Oh my! Amelia!" Mrs Bartlett was baffled at

Millie's reaction to such an important art buyer.

"It's okay, Mrs Bartlett. Millie and ..."

"It's okay, Mrs Bartlett," Millie interjected loudly. "If you will please give us a few minutes. Mr Richards will be soon leaving."

"Oh! Yes, of course," Mrs Bartlett replied, taken aback.

However, it hadn't taken too long for her to catch on to what was transpiring. As she turned to leave them alone, she whispered in Millie's ear, "I won't be far away if you need me dear."

Millie thanked Mrs Bartlett then turned daggers at Damon.

"I had to see you," he said with a slight shake of his dark hair. "It's so good to finally see you, Millie."

Suddenly, she found herself reeling back in time in a flick of a second, and every moment of the love she had felt for him came rushing back to the surface. And with it she tasted that bitter edge presented in his silence after she had wrote to him about her pregnancy. Millie steeled herself as she relived that wrenching moment, and a teenage pregnancy he had left her to endure alone. *No! No!* Millie thought, digging her heels in, *He turned his back on me. How easy was it for him ... No! My life is just as I want it; I didn't ask for this!* Her stomach began to churn uncomfortably. *Or did I?*

She tried to clear the persistent tickle in her throat, and dragged her eyes away from his gaze. He had always been exceptional at deciphering her mood through her eyes, and she couldn't risk him seeing the remnants of feelings that remained within her for him.

"Well, I guess you've seen me. Now, you can leave," she said.

"Millie." Damon ran his fingers through his hair.

She held the palm of her hand up to him. "Damon, what did you expect? A warm welcome? A gushing rush into your arms? You dumped me. I wrote to you and told you about … you left me alone to …" Her voice faltered.

"To what Millie?"

"Never mind. It doesn't even matter anymore." She shook her head. "I have a different life now."

Damon's eyes grew wide. "You wrote to me? I never heard back from you, Millie. I must have called a thousand times before your number went dead … and so many letters."

"Yes I wrote you!" she snapped. "I gave the letter to my father to post with his mail."

His eyes taunted her. *Why has he come back now?* she thought. Yet somehow, she knew that he always would return, thanks to that trusty old whisper within her.

Damon regarded her closely before clearing the lump in his own throat. "It was your father I last spoke with on the phone. He told me that you had moved out. After that I couldn't get through anymore."

"What are you suggesting, Damon?" her eyes narrowed at him as she attempted to piece together this new information. *It can't be so …* she churned.

He smiled. "I have taken a fondness to this particular piece." He stared at the canvas that attracted his interest.

Millie looked into the painting with a blur. All she saw now was a colourful bleed of shaded blends of paint on a canvas. Nothing more. The cloud in her mind muddied all perception as she attempted to adjust to his presence next to her. Part of her wanted to yell and demand his departure while another part was terrified that when he did walk out of that gallery door, it would be the last time she would ever see him. Millie found herself tuning out to the words that fell out of Damon's mouth, while allowing her ears to just linger over the melody of his tranquil voice. And while his honey-smooth sentences filtered through and rebounded inside her ears, the heart that had longed for him for so long, leaped in a fleeting moment of joy.

"Your art possesses a creative, cutting-edge force, Millie."

"Let me help you lay the ground work, get the exposure you need."

"With my marketing experience and your gift, your art will be world famous."

"Maintain a public presence … articles … reviews … catalogues …"

Millie heard all but a snippet of what Damon was saying to her, but a sense of exhilaration seeped in through the nostalgia of her thoughts. She turned and looked at him with wide eyes as it finally dawned on her what he was suggesting. "You want to work with me, Damon? That's why you came here today?" she asked.

He appeared puzzled for a moment, and in all

his years working the rat-race of marketing in New York, Damon found himself speechless, and this was rare for him.

"Millie, I'm so sorry. I should have tried harder to contact you. My heart ached so much for you … when I heard nothing, I assumed you had decided to move on," Damon confessed. "But I have never stopped loving you."

Millie slowly shook her head. "It's too late, Damon. I'm getting married."

Damon's eyes glazed over as he processed the words that had just fallen on his ears like the sharp edge of a sword. "Okay … Okay..." He took a quiet breath, stunned, then turned to leave the gallery. "Think about my business proposal at least. I meant what I said, Millie."

"Sure Damon."

He took a few steps, then hesitating, swivelled around to face her. Long, thick fingers reached beneath his shirt and exposed a chain of gold upon which dangled the diamond encrusted half-heart of gold. "I have never once taken this off." A faltering chuckle escaped his lips while the yearning in his eyes stripped him naked. "You still take my breath away Amelia Anderson!" he declared with a slight quiver.

He turned and strode out through the glassed doors, leaving only the slightest scent of Yves Saint Laurent's Kouros in his wake.

Millie stumbled to the nearest French provincial chair and slumped into it. She thought she had it all figured out – the people that had played a pivotal role in her earlier life decided to return uninvited. She bent down and nursed the ache in her head as Holly came and placed comforting arms around her.

"Are you okay, Amelia? Who is Mr Richards?"

Millie squinted up at Holly. "He is Arella's father," she whispered.

CHAPTER TWENTY-SEVEN

K ate paced up and down the small living room of her suite, and stole glances at the clock that hung above the arched doorway that led through to the kitchenette. She realised that only two minutes had passed since she last checked. She was awaiting the arrival of Millie. She couldn't bring herself to eat lunch with the impending arrival of a daughter she hadn't seen in ten years. *What if she hates me? What if she really can never forgive me? What if she doesn't understand?* Kate was aware of the pounding that hammered her temples, just as she became conscious of the light pound on the door. Electric jitters pulsed through her body at the sound of the rapping noise on the other side of her door. Kate momentarily wished she hadn't agreed with Scott that she should do this alone, as she yearned for his comforting presence. However, she knew it was something she had to do on her own.

Pushing all the "What ifs" to the edge of her mind, Kate took a deep breath as she approached the door. This was her moment of truth. She could no longer endure the consequences of her past actions, nor the guilt that plagued her until it had consumed her in the bitter stench of alcohol. After the hollow days of craving and stress that she endured within the walls of The Rosebud Retreat, this was to be her reward. Kate steadied her quivering fingers and reached for the brass door knob.

As soon as her gaze met her daughter's, Kate knew that her anguish had ended, because the affection she recognised in Millie's face revealed her sincere intentions. Kate sighed with a smile.

"Hello Millie-pie." Her eyes took in the image of her grown daughter.

"Hi Mum," Millie said with a smile, as her own gaze absorbed the image of her frail mother.

The two women embraced, and as Kate held her daughter close, she shut her eyes in a brief moment of respite. She relaxed against her, as gratitude overcame her nerves.

"Come in Millie, we have many things to discuss." She led Millie into the small suite she had called home for the last three weeks.

Mother and daughter spent the next hour together on the little lounge setting in the corner of Kate's suite. "I really didn't think there could exist a smaller lounge room than mine," Millie remarked with a grin. "Turns out, I was wrong!"

After an awkward start, they both relaxed enough to chat easily. Kate thought her daughter appeared quite elated when she spoke about her life with Arella and Craig. And when Millie spoke of her artwork with a glint in her eyes, Kate knew that her daughter had found the calling of her heart's desire. Their conversation became sombre when Kate had asked her about Ace and how she was eager to contact him too. Noticing the smoggy cloud that crossed Millie's eyes, Kate ventured to ask if there remained a chance that Ace would allow her back into his life.

"I don't know, Mum," Millie said with a sad shake of her head. "I just don't know him anymore."

Kate knew enough not to press the subject for the moment; there would be time enough for everything, before a chilling thought gripped her. "Does Glen know where I am?"

"He knows nothing, Mum," Millie assured her, and she rested her hands on her mother's. "You are safe."

Millie then steered the conversation over to Samantha. Kate discerned the undertones of Millie's voice when she ventured onto the subject of her birth mother. She stilled the constant tremble of her fingers – a side-effect of abstinence – and suggested they go for a walk in the garden to continue their discussion.

They stepped out the French doors that fringed Kate's tiny lounge room onto a terracotta-tiled patio. Large terracotta pots planted with ferns and miniature trees sat behind smaller pots full of roses in full bloom, adding a cosy seclusion to the small patio. The two women strolled over the manicured grounds of the retreat, pausing at the stable to look at the horses.

Millie admired the lengthy mane of a Belgian draught horse while she stroked his broad nose. "Oh …" she laughed, "You are just lovely!"

A wet nostril nudged at her hand as the big horse sniffed her out for a snack.

"I'm sorry, buddy. I don't have anything to eat for you," she said.

They continued on to find a park bench overlooking a clear stream that bubbled and splashed over rocks and stones and down through the valley. Birds flew and circled the meandering curve of the stream as they dived and hovered for fish and insects.

"It's beautiful here," Millie said, surveying the serenity around her. "I shall paint this when I return home."

Her expression became sombre as her eyes searched her mother for an explanation of the past.

Kate rested her hand over her daughter's. "When I met your father, you were only weeks old." She chuckled at the memory of the baby girl with a shock of dark hair that had stolen her heart. "So tiny you were. And so helpless! Your father, God help him, did his best to care for you, but you needed your mother, you see?" Kate stared towards Millie. "You needed me... and I needed you."

"What happened to my mother? I know she is no longer alive here on earth, for she visits me with the colourful wings of an angel behind her... What happened to Samantha?" Millie asked.

Kate's ponytail swayed as she nodded. A fleeting smile swept across her face while her gaze continued to linger on Millie. "I always knew you were special, Millie. I knew you were gifted. I just knew ..." Her voice trailed off as her smile faded. "There lives a demon within your father, Millie. A dark, evil serpent that shows itself to the world every now and then.

Your mother knew of his dangerous side, yet she loved him enough to try and flush it from him with the radiance of her love."

A wistful smile appeared on Millie's lips when Kate spoke of her mother's enduring love for her father.

"What happened to her? Did he …?" Millie faltered as the words were too much for her to utter. Her face contorted as she contemplated the unthinkable. But she had to know the truth.

"It's a funny thing: love," Kate chuckled. "The things we do." Her eyes glossed over for a moment as visions and memories of a past she longed to forget flooded back. "He confessed everything to me one night during an emotional breakdown; it was the guilt you see … he had to tell someone. He had to find his solace. His justification."

"What did he tell you?" Millie pressed.

"He knew she had had enough of his demons. He knew he would lose her, and you." Kate shook her head as her eyes brimmed with tears. "He came home from work one night, and Samantha had been taking a bath while you were sleeping." Thin fingers tightened over Millie's hand. "He crept in the bathroom behind her … and he pushed her head under the water until the very last breath of life had slipped out of her. Glen told me that what had irked him the most was not that he had murdered the woman that he loved, but that when he had pushed her head under the bath water, she looked up at him without a scrap of struggle or fright within her eyes. All he saw there was love."

Tears rolled down her cheeks while Millie grimaced at hearing the raw truth.

"Samantha," she whispered. "He took her from me, from the world." Millie shook her head slowly and looked out at the stream.

The ache that had wedged deep within Kate's heart throbbed as she looked at her daughter. "Millie, he couldn't bear to lose you. His mind is not always his own," she stammered. "I helped your father conceal the truth from you all those years. I am so, so sorry." Kate leaned closer and embraced Millie in silence for a few minutes.

"She forgave him as soon as he had pushed her beneath the water," Millie's ruffled whisper broke the silence between them.

Kate noticed the whimsical expression on Millie's face as she gazed through the lances of sunlight that pierced the canopy of trees around them, glistening in short bursts of rainbows against the spray of the stream.

"How do you know that?" Kate asked.

Millie turned to Kate. "Because she is frolicking with the butterflies among the rainbows before us. She smiles at us, and she wants us to know that she exists in glory."

Kate felt a contented wave of happiness flush through her as she briefly discovered the pure tickle of joy that bounced through her spine. She had not felt this comfortable for the longest of time, and she knew its effect was one of healing – curing the mind, mending the heart, and healing the soul. She perceived every atom of the divine power surrounding her, and somehow knew that the source of the angelic energy belonged not to Samantha but Millie. *Samantha was waiting for Millie to recognise her power!* Kate suddenly became aware that her daughter was unaware of the crucial path that lay before her, and the role she was to play in shifting human consciousness so the light may flood the earth once more. The divine nature of the revelation was so fleeting that Kate's stillness almost betrayed the disappointment that now briefly engulfed her.

Kate found a delicate smile playing across her lips, and turning to Millie, directed its warmth towards her daughter. "Glory," she murmured with bright eyes. She tilted her head up at the lush green canopy hanging over them and began to laugh. Small cackling bursts grew into giggles until her laughter echoed against the trees. She laughed with the abandonment of freedom clasping at her heaving chest. She laughed with the impulsive liberty of a child, as years-long hindrances fell away from around her heart. Kate felt free for the first time in years of the guilt that had shadowed her since she had left her children; free from the crippling constraints of the uncertainty that had plagued her life for as long as she could remember; and free from the exhausting wheel of emotional pain that had brought her down.

She turned to Millie. "Can you hear them, Millie?" Kate asked.

"Hear who, Mum." Millie watched her mother with gentle amusement.

"The birds," Kate said, as she gestured towards the trees above. "Listen … They sing for you. What do you hear?"

Millie looked up into the radiant shine of the green canopy. Her lips widened into a grin when she heard their song, as it was a song she had heard them sing ten years before when she had been laying broken and trembling upon a bed of cool tiles on a gritty bathroom floor. She looked back at her mother with eyes wide and glistening, and smiled. "I hear all the people of the world," she said.

Kate nodded in agreement. "You can help change their world, Millie."

"How?" Brows knitted in confusion.

"Use your imagination, sweetheart."

Millie had stayed with Kate until the sun had almost faded from view over the horizon. It was then that they ambled back to Kate's ground floor rooms in the big manor, taking their time in each other's company while both of them purposefully strung out their last moments together. When it was time for Millie to leave her, Kate hugged her daughter close and breathed in the sweet scent of perfume that drifted from the nape of her neckline.

"Thank you for coming to see me today, Millie."

Millie returned Kate's embrace. "I have a meeting tomorrow for the gallery, then a late flight booked home. I would like to come by before my flight, if that's okay with you?"

"I would like that very much," Kate said.

"Great!" Millie turned towards the hire car she had driven out to the valley. "I'll see you around six tomorrow night."

Kate wrapped her arms around herself as she watched the white sedan trek its way down the long winding dirt road back to the city. She sighed with contentment as the afternoon she had spent with Millie had brought with it much more than she had ever dreamed possible. Those few precious hours had somehow alleviated the weight in her heart and had given her a renewed determination to complete the abstinence program at Rosebud. For now, she knew she had found a family again – *her family*. She skipped up the stairs of the big white house and hurried towards her rooms where she could dwell in the loveliness of her thoughts and await Scott's arrival.

CHAPTER TWENTY-EIGHT

Bringing the maroon Softail Heritage to a rumbling stop, Ace paused to peer along the road that led to the prize he had been seeking. The blue glint of his eyes concealed themselves behind the dark tint of his sunglasses while they scanned and plotted the final moves in the game in which he had found himself. *I wonder how quickly she will recognise her baby boy.*

He couldn't wait to see the expression on her face when he revealed himself to her. How intoxicating the anticipation felt within him. He sneered with pleasure at the projected images of what was to come. Ace gave the powerful engine a shot of fuel, and gazed around to find cover for his bike between the nearby thick foliage. There he would find the perfect hideaway for his bike, and the privacy to indulge in the sensual urges that seduced him. *And why not?* Ace thought, as he reached for his pulsing member, deliberately enticing a further bulge under his jeans.

The last two days had been a long trek, and he needed to unwind a little. He reasoned that he couldn't risk any silly urges fogging up his mind when he performed the task ahead of him. He needed clarity on his side.

Ace smiled to himself while he savoured the final throbs that raced through his body. His long fingers dug deep inside the hidden chest pocket of his leather jacket, and he grinned when he touched the object he sought. He studied the cold steel edges of the chrome switchblade with fascination. He shut his eyes and allowed the serpent to encompass him totally. It quashed every inch of light within him, every laughter and joy that remained, and every bit of love that still traced through his veins.

Ace granted the rancour of the black serpent to flourish through every part of his being while allowing the demon unlimited admittance to seek and destroy any relics of affection for his mother that might still be lurking within him. He knew there would be no room for error during the visit he was about to pay his dear, dear mother, and no room for doubt.

As the last scraps of love succumbed to the drowning darkness that engulfed it, Ace had the dreaded sense that when these hours came to an end, so too would the love in him end. Yet he knew he was powerless to stop it – the black serpent was too strong for him to fight – even if he wanted. *And hey, who wanted to?* This was all he knew. He found a strange comfort in the painful writhing movement of the black snake when it ventured through his mind.

Ace replaced the switchblade to the confines of his leather jacket before springing to his feet. The afternoon sun flickered down through the rainforest around him as he strode in under the cool cover of a lush green canopy. He had a long-awaited date with the woman who had starred within his warped fantasies for the last six years, and ready or not, she was about to meet the grim reaper of the guilt he knew must have plagued her since she had abandoned him. *Pay back is a bitch!* A bizarre giggle escaped through his lips. *What a fitting cliché for this fine day.*

The light within him dimmed as his eyes surveyed the big white manor from the mask of trees beyond the clearing. The light in him flickered to a smoky-grey before extinguishing from his heart entirely.

The late afternoon sun flared in his green eyes as Glen peered towards the mountain ridges. He brought the Holden Premiere to a halt at the start of the dirt road that stretched out in front of him while he rustled around for the road map. He scanned the map before his mouth widened in a triumphant sneer as he confirmed that he had arrived.

A cold rush of exhilaration converted the ache of a long drive into a renewed surge of vitality, as the black serpent uncoiled through his mind. *At last! I shall have my day of reckoning!* All the hard, unrelenting years he had spent searching, hunting and planning were finally about to come to an end. *Pay day has arrived!* he thought, yielding to the sinister force of the black snake that rampaged through him. His cold eyes glanced around for a suitable camouflage for the car. He would leg it from here; he wasn't about to take any unnecessary risks of being discovered, not at this crucially vital stage. Thoughts of her pale slender neck being strangled under his hands tempted him.

Glen spied a perfect spot for his car a little further down the road within the dense vegetation of the rainforest, and hid it under the lush canopy. He alighted from the vehicle and set off towards the white manor that awaited him at the end of the winding dirt road.

Glen couldn't wait to savour the surprised look of terror that would inevitably wash over her pretty expression when he revealed his venom to his dear, dear wife. *Oh! The sweet anticipation!* Glen mused while stealthy steps drew nearer to their destination. *Pay back is a bitch! And today, the bitch will know pay back!* His eyes danced feverishly as they scanned the big manor, seeking his little mouse to catch.

"Mousy, mousy," Glen whispered through the trees that concealed him. "Come out, come out wherever you are." A warm chuckle emanated from his lips as he readied himself for the detailed search of the property.

Millie threw the last of the few belongings she had brought with her into the overnight bag, then skimmed the hotel room one last time before she left. Satisfied there would be nothing left behind, she grabbed the hire car keys.

Twilight was fast approaching, and the city

glistened crimson in the dying sunlight, giving the dazzling city a flaming, surreal appearance. Millie grinned at the beauty of the view as she thought about the visit with her mother the day before. It had been a good trip, and she was glad that she had finally had the chance to rekindle her relationship with her mother. Millie recalled the words her mother had spoken at the stream, and as her mind lingered over Kate's words for a moment, an excited shimmer passed through her and nestled deeply within her consciousness.

"Use your imagination sweetheart," her mother had said, and her grin broadened, as her imagination *was* her painting – and her painting *was* her imagination. Somehow, Millie sensed that the path her mother had spoken of rested in the brush strokes of her artwork. Everything seemed to makes sense to her now – Damon's unexpected arrival at the gallery and his plans to expose her artwork to the world; the melody she heard in the birds at the stream; her mother's words – all appeared to be lighting a path before her. She gave a contented sigh and swivelled around to collect her overnight bag, then she set off to visit Kate one last time before her flight home later that evening.

The phone rang just as she was about to close the hotel room door, stopping her dead in her tracks. "Shit," Millie mumbled, as she turned about and made for the phone.

"Millie?" Craig's voice spoke before she could even manage a greeting.

"Craig! What's wrong? Is Arella okay?" Millie

said.

"Arella is fine, sweetheart," Craig soothed. "It's Emily ..." He hesitated before revealing the news of the death of Emily and her twins.

Millie collapsed onto the bed. *No! No! Not my Em.* Millie struggled with the news of physical death. She had the inner knowledge that death was but a transitory state of affairs because her own birth mother was alive and well in another realm, yet an aching sadness overcame her, pulling her down into a profound grief and denial for the loss of her dearest friend and her little boys.

Millie attempted to comprehend the horror of Emily's actions. "Why? Why?" She sobbed a river of tears. She wept for the lives lost to the sweet experiences ahead of them, the beautiful exposure to life that would have enlivened their senses, and the humbling lessons of love they would no longer learn in this embodiment. But most of all, Millie sobbed for the utter hopelessness and loneliness she knew must have tormented Emily to drive her to carry out such a final act of departure. She wished that she had paid more attention to Emily over the last days that she had seen her. *Perhaps I could have prevented this,* she thought, as a great feeling of guilt tormented her. "This is my fault!" she shrieked. "My fault."

Millie fought hard to regain control over the hysterics she felt gaining momentum over her emotions. *Breathe ... just breathe*, she told herself, taking big gulps of air. *Breathe ...* A slight sense of calm began to unknot her stomach as her ears pricked at the gentle tones of a familiar voice.

"*Millie,*" it whispered. "*Millie.*"

Millie opened her eyes to the empty hotel room and looked around for the source of the voice. A dusky stream of sunlight gleamed through the uncurtained window, filling the space around her with tinges of rosy gold.

"*Millie,*" the voice called again.

She turned towards the source of the voice and caught her breath when she glimpsed the angel wings that spread against the sunset blaze of the window. A wave of peace overcame her, turning tears of sadness into ones of joy and love. Opaque hues of red, purple, green and blue filled the feathers of the vast wings as they presented themselves to her in a display of mystical transcendence. Her eyes widened at the sight of the being with the brightest radiance washing over and through her in a white beam. Millie's face softened in adoration.

"Hello Mummy," she whispered, recognising Samantha.

The celestial image smiled down at her, and emerald eyes flickered with unconditional love. "*My daughter.*" Her voice was a hallowed whisper. "*It is time for you to better understand the path you have chosen in this embodiment. Do not waste your time with emotions that will not serve you, it is not your fault.*"

Samantha spread the palms of her hands out towards her. "*Freewill is given to each of us, and so is the wonderful stream of God's energy. Each of us decides either consciously or unconsciously how to direct the energy given to them."*

Millie contemplated Samantha's words. "But …" she hesitated, mesmerised. "But … I should have known. I could have prevented this."

"It was not for you to intervene, Millie. It was done by works of her freewill. No longer could Emily see who she really was; no longer could she realise the cause of her own life."

"Her own conscious creation?" Millie ventured.

"Yes," Samantha smiled. *"You have been gifted with many past lives of accumulated light. In this life, you carry the light much brighter than ever before."*

Millie stood in silent awe as she waited for Samantha to continue.

"You will learn to consciously charge your paintings with a great light stream of energy filled with love, faith, charity and healing. You shall choose which divine energy is required for each canvas you mark. Do not concern yourself with who the recipients of your work shall be, for that will be arranged by higher dwelling beings."

"But, but how will I do this?" Millie asked.

"You will learn, Millie. It is your destiny to help shift the collective consciousness of the world." A gentle laugh escaped Samantha's lips as she gazed at her daughter. *"You must go to your mother now; she needs you!"*

The image faded, leaving her thoughts in disarray. Millie leaped into action with an inexplicable urge to get to her mother. She collected the hire car keys, scooped up her belongings and dashed down the corridor towards the elevator. *Hurry up! Hurry up! Damn it!* She willed the elevator's arrival with an impatient tap of her white sneakered foot. The compulsion to go to The Rosebud Retreat totally consumed her now.

CHAPTER TWENTY-NINE

Kate gave a contented yawn as she sat out on the sun chair on the patio of her suite. She smiled towards the mountains as she eagerly awaited Millie's arrival before her flight back to Sydney. She marvelled at the rich crimson-pink hues that struck the feathery clouds that stretched out over the mountain range as the sun melted into the horizon.

It had been a very long time since she could recognise the humbling enormity of the small gifts of the earth. The sound of footsteps through the garden that edged the patio startled her, and she was surprised to see a dark-haired young man making his way over to the sun chair adjacent to her.

Thick lips grinned broadly beneath a prominent nose that supported darkly tinted sunglasses.

"It is you indeed; for a moment I wasn't quite sure," he declared with widespread hands declaring his pleasure.

Kate's hands became clammy, and instinctively her nerves were on end. Something was horribly wrong. Kate wondered if she knew this young man at all as it appeared he knew her.

"I think you have the wrong person; who are you looking for?" she forced a smile.

"Oh! I'm sorry," he apologised. "You don't recognise me." He removed his sunglasses to reveal piercing sapphire-blue eyes. "Mum." His grin widened as he saw the shock etch over her gaunt face.

"Ace?" Kate asked, grateful that she was already sitting down as she would have collapsed otherwise. The heart in her chest quickened as she processed this sudden turn of events. *How did he find me here? Millie must have told him.*

"Ace! Oh my goodness, you have grown!" she tittered nervously. "I hardly recognise you."

No, Millie assured me she told no-one. Why is he looking at me like that? she mulled. *His eyes are different. I know this look.* It gradually dawned on her with a frightful realisation of the crazed shadow that dwelled in her son's eyes. She had seen the same lunacy reveal itself in the eyes of the man she had married years before.

Ace chuckled softly while relishing the obvious edge his presence had evoked in his mother's nerves. "Ten years of growing, Mum. I am a man now," he declared. "Funny … you are not as nearly pretty as I remembered you to be. You have aged," he said, emphasising the impersonal nature of his tone. "But then again, I can imagine guilt to be quite the ager." He chuckled again before looking at her with such intensity that it made her squirm uncomfortably.

"Ace," Kate started, her voice trembling, "I wanted to take you with me. I knew that you would be hurt and I'm sorry but I was frightened … so frightened."

"Uh, Uh, Uh!" Ace shook his head and put up his hand to silence her. "I didn't come here to hear your excuses, Mother. The morning after you left me, I ran and ran through the house searching for you. I couldn't believe that you would just leave me like that." He cocked his head as he leaned closer to her. "And then do you know what happened, Mother?"

Kate slowly shook her head as the breath within her froze. "No," she whispered.

"My heart shattered into a thousand pieces. I thought I was going to die."

"Ace ... I," she stammered as he held a hand up to silence her.

"No excuses, remember," he chuckled. "It took a long time for me to adjust with no mother around. Millie took good care of me though. I would have almost forgiven your betrayal, but then one day you tore our family apart with a small wooden box."

He leaned closer still. Kate could smell the trace of peppermint that circled under his breath.

Ace grinned. "Do you think I could forgive you now, Mother?" he whispered.

Kate attempted to rein in the screams that echoed through her mind as she concealed the involuntary shudder that swept over her. "Then why did you come here, Ace?"

She lifted herself up to peer through the high plants that edged the patio in the hope to catch somebody walking through the grounds, but there was no-one.

Ace's eyes darkened as he attempted to control

the serpent that hungered to sink its fangs in her neck. "Interesting question, Mum."

"No, it's a simple question, Ace," Kate said with an air of resignation in her voice.

"I'm not your baby boy anymore, Mother." Ace stood up, purposely menacing her with his large frame. "As far as I see it, you revoked your questioning privileges the moment you revoked me," he hissed as clenched knuckles tightened.

Kate sprang up on her bare feet, and stretched up in a vain effort to level with the sting of his stare. A cold shiver speared through her spine as she realised that she was in grave danger. *Yet, he is still my son.* Surely she could persuade the demon within him to yield under her grace. Besides, she was also aware that Millie would arrive at any given minute. She was convinced that she could handle Ace until then. She must.

"Ace, why don't we go inside and I'll make us a cup of tea?" Her smile was forced as she turned away from him. "Millie will be here any minute; we can all have tea together," she said over her shoulder while heading through the open French doors.

She heard the fall of his steps behind her, and became acutely aware of his every move as he tracked carefully into the small sitting room. She did not miss his intentional action as he reached in his pocket and produced a white handkerchief. Kate's eyes skimmed over Ace in trepidation when he used the cloth to grasp at the brass handles of the doors as he closed them together securely. And when he faced her in a deliberately calculated move, a fidgety smile crossed her lips as her senses went into overdrive, as now there was no mistaking the unspoken communication between them. All the reasoning in the world could not find error in his ultimate motive.

He replaced the handkerchief into his biker jacket, and twisted his head in such a way to stare at her with eyes blazing with hate. "I'm afraid I don't have time for tea, Mother," he said, his hand lingering still beneath his jacket. "Nor to wait for Millie."

"Oh …" Kate could barely breathe now as Ace drew nearer. Her heart pounded and throbbed through her ears. It was all she heard as he began to mutter in a bizarre mumble of distorted sentences, and the haze that brewed in his eyes seemed to put him in a trance while his fingers drew out a switch blade. She regarded the sneer on his lips with resignation as he closed in on her.

Prowling among the shrubs and trees with the practised manoeuvres of a stalker, the black snake slithered through the grounds of the retreat unseen and unheard as he searched for his prey. Already he had carefully scoured every cottage window, and peered with the patience of a stealthy huntsman through every unattended doorway. Crouching at the rear of the property, he scanned the widely spaced rows of patios from a line of elegantly placed French doors. Glen knew he would comb through this place over and over if required. His spiky head jerked in alert at the sight of blonde hair as she stood beyond the potted ferns that bordered one of the patios. The beat of his heart leaped as he froze within the dense cover amid the trunks of thick trees. He licked his lips eagerly and grinned as he realised the hunt was over.

But wait. He frowned in annoyance. *She is not alone.* His lantern-green eyes narrowed as they honed in on her unexpected guest. "Fuck!" he cursed under his breath when he saw his son following Lilly through the French doors.

He glanced around to ensure there was nobody else around, then with a quick breath, he made a dash for the patio. Lingering cautiously between some large prickly ferns, Glen paused to find Kate and his troublesome son.

He found them in an instant and trained his eyes on them just as he saw the flash of a switchblade lunge deeply into her stomach. He cursed at the loss of his prey and watched stunned and helpless as the switchblade jabbed over and over into the flesh of its victim.

Regaining his senses, Glen lurched through the rose bushes and burst through the French doors with a harrowing gurgle escaping his throat. "Nooooo!" he shrieked, rushing at Ace who was now crouching over his mother.

Glen stopped beside the bent knees of his son and assessed the eerie scene before him. His eyes regarded the bloody gashes spread over Kate's body. Thick blood seeped into the carpet, coagulating between the nylon fibres on which Ace kneeled. Glen reached towards Ace, who gazed sobbing and dismayed back up at his father.

"Ace, get up now," Glen said, grasping his son's armpit and pulling up. "We have to go."

Ace rose shaking to his feet and stood helpless. "I'm sorry," he coughed, before falling into the outstretched arms of his father. "I didn't mean to … It was all her fault."

Glen caught him and embraced him, feeling every tattered emotion that coursed through the struggling heart of his son. His own heart shattered at Ace's distress at his own actions, and Glen knew that his son had little control over the menacing force the black serpent imposed upon him. He knew that the vindictive nature of the beast would eventually destroy his son if Ace could not learn to tame the demon within him.

"I know, I know. You are okay, Ace," Glen said gently between Ace's sobs. "Shhhh," he soothed, recalling how he used to comfort him when he was a little boy seeking the shelter of his daddy's embrace.

They stood in their embrace for a few long minutes while the violent quivers of Ace's choking sobs diminished.

Ace was startled at a light knock on the door, and broke away from Glen's embrace to spy Millie through the peep-hole in the door.

"Millie," he whispered urgently.

Millie called out to her mother from beyond the entrance to the suite. Glen's heart skipped a beat as his mind whirled. "What is she doing here? What is it with you two?" he hissed at Ace. *Could this get any worse?*

"Mum?" Millie's voice rose in volume, as the next raps rang louder.

Glen glanced towards the door then back at Ace. "Go!" he ordered. "Get out of here, quickly!"

"But," Ace said.

"Go Ace. Now!" Glen gave him a little shove as he heard the door swing open and his daughter's insistent call echoing into the room.

Glen turned to face Millie's impending arrival as she barged into the room just in time to catch her brother's stolen glance at her before dissolving through the French doors and disappearing into the shrubbery. She paused stunned as her eyes beheld the bloody scene strewn before her. Glen watched with heavy heart as her face paled faint and her eyes widened at seeing her mother lying in a bloody mess on the floor.

"Mum!" Millie stumbled frantically to kneel beside Kate and scoop her head up into her lap. "No … no. Nooooo!" Her dark hair shook against her mother's motionless body, while tears poured down her face. Millie stroked Kate's blonde fizzled hair from her face. "Mum?" Millie's voice trembled when she felt her mother shift slightly within her arms. "Mum?"

Watching with awkward discomfort, Glen's concern for his perturbed daughter reeled wildly off-track when he realised Kate was still alive. He edged closer to peer towards the shallow gurgles of the woman that had deserted him ten years earlier – the woman who had captured the keen attention of the black snake since her disappearance from his life; the woman who he had once loved before she compelled that love to hate. He watched her shallow breaths coldly.

"M … Millie." Kate's whisper was barely audible.

"Oh Mum!" Millie turned her face towards Glen. Her expression darkened. "Call for an ambulance, Dad – now!"

He sprang into action at Millie's insistence and made for the kitchenette.

"Millie," Kate said. "Ace …"

"Ace?" Millie repeated numbly.

Holding her mother close, Millie cried as the words of her mother echoed through her consciousness, and she realised who was her mother's aggressor.

Kate rasped shallow breaths and smiled through moist eyes at Millie. "M … Millie." Her voice was a hollow whisper as she reached with her fingers to brush Millie's cheek. "Remember, your imagination will take you everywhere." Kate's arm fell and her head drooped to the side as her eyes fluttered closed.

Clutching desperately at the lifeless form of her mother, Millie wept for the undeserving horror of Kate's death. She wept for the years that had been lost to them, and for the promising future that been taken from them.

She wept for the loss of not only the mother that had just found her, but also for the friend in Emily she would never again find. And with the choking sobs that engulfed her inconsolable emotions, Millie cried for the love of the brother she knew had been changed forever.

As Glen returned, he stopped short of the scene in front of him. His mouth gaped open and his eyes widened as a beam of light extended down from the ceiling to encompass Millie and Kate. He gasped as a large pair of coloured angel wings appeared as if from his daughter's back while she cradled Kate's body. The wings spread wide and in one graceful movement encircled over Kate to envelope her entirely under the bright beam.

"Millie?" he uttered and moved closer.

Millie's eyes were closed. Her chest heaved with her breath and her head was lowered towards Kate.

"Millie-pie? Are you okay?" He dared not touch her as he struggled to comprehend the phenomenon taking place before him.

The hues of the wings sparkled brighter while their streaks flashed in dazzling beams all through the room in a final burst of colour before fading entirely from Glen's shaded view.

Closing in behind her, the light touch of his arms penetrated through her awareness. And as Millie turned to bury her shattered face against his chest, the blaze within his eyes diminished as a shard of light surged with love through his flesh.

"Millie …"

Both of them looked down to Kate as she fluttered her eyes to focus on her daughter.

"Oh mum!" Millie cried through a smile. "I

thought you were gone."

Kate nodded slightly. "Yes, but you came for me," she rasped as her eyes welled and she reached for her daughter.

EPILOGUE

December 20, 1997

Dear Journal,
I found you this morning among the contents
of an old wooden box that I had buried far
back beneath the rummage under my bed. And as I
flicked through pages of written entries from a teenage
girl, between the tears and smiles the scribed paper
provoked within me, I thought it fitting to fill the last
blank page with one last entry – this time with the pen
of a 24-year-old woman.

I am undecided where I stand with my father,
and I know the future will involve further pondering
until I straighten the jumble in my mind that
surrounds my relationship with him. As it is, I am all
that he has at the moment, for Ace has vanished and I
suspect that we won't be seeing him for a very long
time – if ever at all. I cannot shake his fleeing image
when I saw him at my mother's. It was not my brother
I saw at all. When he turned to look at me, I saw the
image of a black serpent with deep blue eyes looking
straight into me. I still shudder at the thought, and I
fear for my brother's safety.

When I was a girl, I would cast my vision in the
mirror and wonder who it was that really peered

behind the green stare that reflected back at me. Still, I do not have all the answers that I seek. And still, I do not pretend to understand the great mystery of life and death. I have, however, learned to accept the miraculous presence of the creative source, and attempt to stay as closely aligned to it as much as possible. I know now that the being that watched my reflection all those years ago and continues to do so, is my real self; the self that has embodied many bodies before this one and knows the secrets of life; the self that judges, condemns or criticises no-one in thought or word; the self that dwells within me with the burning flame of a spark, and is always available to me; the self that loves unconditionally and is by no means ego-dominated; the self that has the power to create my life as I choose – *my God-realised self.*

My only wish is that I could live wholly from my true self at all times. And while I know this attainment is possible, it is one of great discipline. I realise that it will require time, sincerity and expansion. But hey, we all have plenty of time to choose to evolve – right?

And with the wings of an angel firmly placed behind me, I shall go on painting, and I shall spread the light.

In Love, Faith, Charity and Healing,
Millie xo

CONNECT WITH KIM:

Website: kimpetersen.com.au

Facebook: facebook.com/kimpetersen11

Twitter: twitter.com/kimpeace11

Visit http://www.kimpetersen.com.au/ and sign up to receive a free ebook!

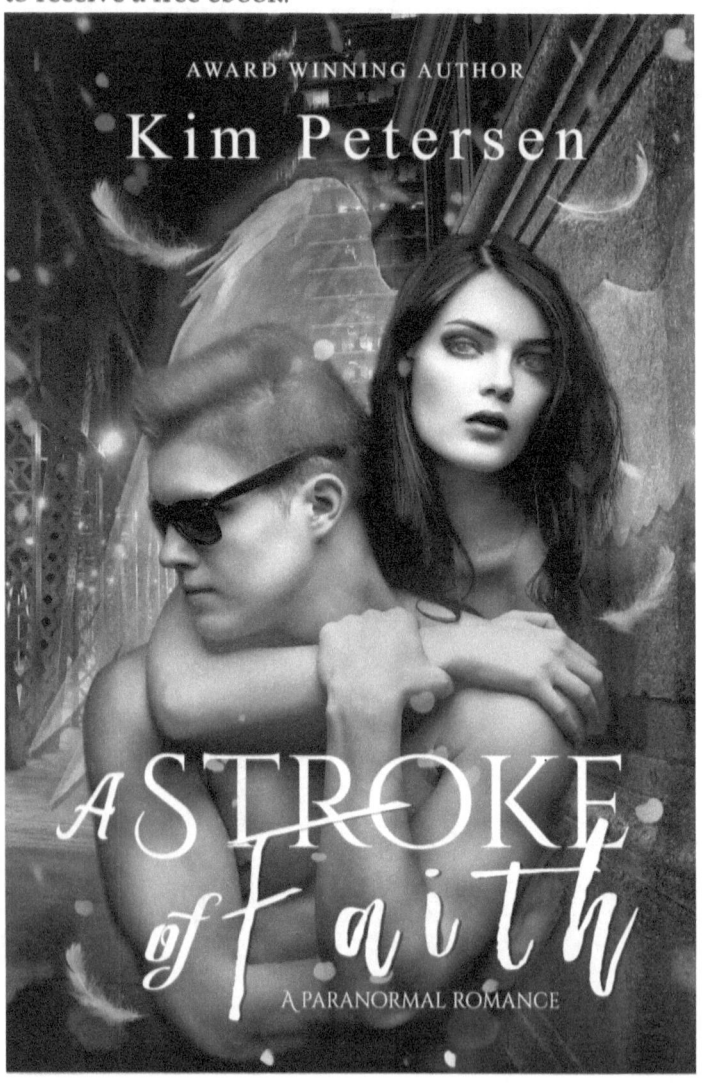